MURDER ON THE ORIENT ESPRESSO

Maggy Thorsen and her beau Jake Pavlik find themselves plunged into a real-life mystery as baffling as any Agatha Christie classic.

It's November and Maggy Thorsen, co-owner of the Wisconsin gourmet coffeehouse, *Uncommon Grounds*, is in South Florida at an annual crime-writers' conference with her beau, local sheriff Jake Pavlik, who is due to speak as a 'forensics expert'. Maggy's pledge to behave solely as a tourist becomes trickier than she anticipated when the conference's opening night event turns out to be a re-enactment of Agatha Christie's classic, *Murder on the Orient Express*. As Maggy and Jake reluctantly set off on the night train to the Everglades to solve the 'crime', it's clear that, as in the original novel, nothing is quite what it seems. And amidst rumours of careers taken, manuscripts stolen and vows broken, it seems that in the Everglades – as in life – the predator all too often becomes the prey.

Further Titles from Sandra Balzo
The Maggy Thorsen Mysteries

UNCOMMON GROUNDS
GROUNDS FOR MURDER *
BEAN THERE, DONE THAT *
BREWED, CRUDE AND TATTOOED *
FROM THE GROUNDS UP *
A CUP OF JO *
TRIPLE SHOT *
MURDER ON THE ORIENT ESPRESSO *

The Main Street Mystery Series

RUNNING ON EMPTY *
DEAD ENDS *

* *available from Severn House*

MURDER ON THE ORIENT ESPRESSO

Sandra Balzo

Severn House Large Print
London & New York

This first large print edition published 2014
in Great Britain and the USA by
SEVERN HOUSE PUBLISHERS LTD of
19 Cedar Road, Sutton, Surrey, England, SM2 5DA.
First world regular print edition published 2013 by
Severn House Publishers Ltd., London and New York.

British Library Cataloguing in Publication Data

Balzo, Sandra author.
    Murder on the Orient espresso. -- Large print edition. --
(A Maggy Thorsen mystery ; 8)
    1. Thorsen, Maggy (Fictitious character)--Fiction.
    2. Detective and mystery stories. 3. Large type books.
    I. Title II. Series
    813.6-dc23

ISBN-13: 9780727896841

Printed digitally in the USA

MURDER ON THE ORIENT ESPRESSO
Narrated by Maggy Thorsen

Cast of Characters – in order of appearance

Jake Pavlik, Brookhills county sheriff, as our victim, Ratchett

Zoe Scarlett, conference organizer, as the Woman in the Red Kimono

Missy Hudson, assistant conference organizer, as Mrs Hubbard

Laurence (Larry) Potter, reviewer and guest of honor, as Hercule Poirot

Rosemary Darlington, author and guest of honor, as Mary Debenham

Markus, nonfiction writer and librarian, as MacQueen

Prudence, aspiring writer, as Princess Dragomiroff

Grace, aspiring writer, as Greta Ohlsson

Carson, germaphobic literary agent, as Count Andrenyi

Danny, young writer and 'sycophant,' as Colonel Arbuthnot

Boyce, coffee cart owner, as M Bouc
Pete, bartender, as Pierre Michel
Big Fred, aspiring writer, as Foscarelli
Harvey, aspiring writer and actor, as
Hardman
Audra Edmonds, wife of Laurence Potter,
as the second Mrs Hubbard

ONE

'They *look* normal. In fact,' I swiveled my head to survey the people in the South Florida hotel lobby with us, 'if it was July instead of November, we could be in Uncommon Grounds.'

Tennis togs, check. Golf shirts, check. Business suits, check. People with time on their hands and too much money in their wallets. Check, check.

Even the smells reminded me of my upscale coffeehouse back home in Brookhills, Wisconsin, though these were emanating from a small cart near the elevators. To one side of it, a stylishly dressed, fashionably slim, unnaturally endowed redhead (check, check, check) seemed to be holding some sort of planning meeting, the group around her listening attentively.

All of them were ... extraordinarily ordinary. 'Where are the Edgar Allan Poes with their ravens? The Sherlock Holmeses wearing their deerstalkers?'

Brookhills County Sheriff Jake Pavlik, my

7

main squeeze – hell, my only squeeze, since my ex-hubby Ted ran off with his dental hygienist – looked down at me, blue eyes amused. 'You were expecting costumes?'

I shrugged. 'I worked on GenCon when the gaming convention was in Milwaukee and you wouldn't believe the outfits. Every kind of superhero imaginable. People wearing wings and not much else.' I sniffed. 'I don't even see a Miss Marple or Hercule Poirot and what would that take? Tweeds and knitting needles? Some hair wax and a fake mustache? How tough would any of that be?'

'Might depend on whether knitting needles or wings are allowed on airplanes,' Pavlik said, but he must have heard the disappointment in my voice. 'Sorry, Maggy, but Mystery 101 is a crime-writers' conference for people who want to write mysteries, not a fan convention for readers. However, even if it were, I doubt you'd find it resembled a gamers' event like GenCon.'

The sheriff lowered his voice as the desk clerk signaled for the next person in line. 'Though if *you're* game, I'd wouldn't mind giving the "wings and not much else" idea a whirl.'

His breath on my neck gave me goose bumps, and I couldn't stifle the moan that rose in my throat just as the dark-suited woman in front of us turned to gather up her wheelie. She glanced at Pavlik and me and then skyward, as if to say, *get a room.*

Which, in fact, we'd do posthaste just as soon as she moved her butt toward the registration desk.

While Pavlik had been engaged to speak at the writers' conference, the whole idea of my tagging along was for us to spend some time together away from the impending winter snows and the demands of both his job and mine. Yeah, I know – county sheriff and coffeehouse owner might seem miles apart stress-wise, but you'd be surprised.

I twisted around and tangled my fingers in Pavlik's thick dark hair. 'What happens in Fort Lauderdale, stays in Fort Lauderdale,' I murmured before bringing his lips down to meet mine.

'A noble sentiment,' Pavlik said when we finally broke. 'Though remember: the conference organizers are comping me for my travel and the hotel room you and I are sharing, and paying me a speaker's honorarium to boot. I, at least, have to maintain some semblance of professional dignity in the lobby.'

I grinned. '"Not I, said the little red hen." And speaking of birds, maybe instead of wings, we—'

'Jacob? Jacob Pavlik?'

I turned to see that the redhead had broken away from her dispersing planning group and was swooping down on us, her crimson wrap dress billowing as it waged a losing battle to contain her after-market breasts. Before I knew it, those puppies were pressed against my sheriff.

Pavlik looked appreciative, if startled. 'Yes, but...' His eyes narrowed and he pulled back to get a fuller perspective. 'Zoe?'

'Of course, silly.' The woman did a little pirouette. 'Didn't you recognize me?'

'Honestly? Not at first, and I'm supposed to be a trained observer.' His eyes were bugging out of his head. 'Wow. You look amazing.'

'Divorce.' She posed shoulders back, right hip cocked like an Angelina Jolie wannabe. 'It does a body good.'

As did a competent plastic surgeon, I'd wager.

'Well, that's great. Good for you.' Pavlik's eyes did a fly-by up the woman's leg to her waist and past her cleavage, before landing innocently on her face.

Like many people in law enforcement, Pavlik had the uncanny ability to enter a room and take in everything without seeming to. Though, in the current example, a pair of bodacious D-cups was admittedly hard for anybody to miss.

The clerk was signaling for us to approach the desk and since everyone appeared to have forgotten I was there, I cleared my throat. 'Umm, Pavlik?' I'd started calling the sheriff 'Pavlik' when he'd suspected me of murder – not as unusual a circumstance as that might sound – and had never gotten out of the habit.

It had become our little joke, but now, with this beautiful woman spidering all over him, my use of his last name seemed less ... cute. I mean, how was I supposed to mark my territory when I didn't even call said territory by its first name?

'I'm sorry?' Pavlik was still ogling Zoe.

'Jake, the desk clerk is ready for us.' I stuck my hand out to the other woman. 'Hi, I'm Maggy Thorsen.'

'Zoe Scarlett.' We shook professionally. Kind of.

'Zoe was with the Chicago Convention Bureau when I was the sheriff's office liaison to the bureau.' Pavlik, having put his eyes back in his head, seemed to realize an explanation was called for. 'We worked together a couple of times and when Zoe moved to Fort Lauderdale and became the conference organizer for Mystery 101 a couple of years back, she asked me here to speak.'

'And we're very glad to have you back.'

Zoe was bouncing up and down. Or parts of her were.

'How nice,' I said lamely, thinking, Scarlett? Like Miss Scarlett in *Clue*?

The woman in question turned to Pavlik. 'Are you two ... together?'

Apparently she'd missed our clinch, or maybe that sort of thing was common behavior between strangers in a Florida hotel line. Either way, the conference organizer recognized the way the question sounded and actually blushed. 'I mean, I'm not sure a double room was specified.'

I glanced at Pavlik. Hadn't he told her I was coming?

'I'm sorry,' the sheriff said, 'I—'

'Missy?' Zoe called to one of her minions in the milling mass near the elevators, the millers seeming to have regrouped. 'We'll check with my assistant, but I'm sure it's just a matter of making sure there are enough towels and the like. Missy Hudson!' Zoe Scarlett put a command edge in her voice this time. 'I swear that girl just pretends not to hear me when—'

'Excuse me, ma'am,' interrupted one of a foursome of golfers that had fallen into line behind us, toting bags of clubs that could have stocked a Cro-Magnon arsenal. 'If you aren't quite ready to check-in, would you mind if we play through?'

'Oh, no. Not at all.' Zoe waved for us to step out of the line. 'We may need to handle our situation with the hotel's event co-ordinator anyway. You just go ahead.'

The men hefted their golf bags as a young woman of about twenty-five with hair just on the blonde side of brown reached us. 'I'm sorry, Zoe. Did you need something?'

'Missy, this is the featured speaker for our forensic track, Sheriff Jacob Pavlik. I don't believe you were on the committee the last time he spoke at Mystery 101.'

'Good to meet you, Sheriff Pavlik. I'm Missy Hudson.'

'Jake, please, Missy,' he said, shaking the young woman's hand. 'And this is Maggy Thorsen.'

'Oh, of course.' Missy flashed a smile at me. 'I received your email saying Ms Thorsen was accompanying you, which was no trouble at all, given that Zoe had already requested a suite for you.'

Again, Zoe flushed. 'Well, good. Not to worry, then.'

It didn't take a mind-reader to realize that Zoe Scarlett – and could that be her *real* name? – had designs on something more than putting on a kick-ass conference this weekend.

'Is that Larry? Thank God.' Zoe was look-ing past her assistant and toward the front

13

entrance of the hotel.

I turned, following her gaze through the floor-to-ceiling windows to a lanky man who was stubbing out a cigarette as a curly-haired younger guy spoke to him. As we watched, Smoker held up a hand to Curly-top that seemed more stop-sign than farewell and stepped into the revolving door.

If 'Larry' was trying to get away from the kid, he didn't succeed. Curly-top followed him in.

'Missy, can you handle this?' Zoe asked, already moving away.

'This' presumably being Pavlik and me. 'Not to worry, we can just get back in line,' I said to Zoe's retreating back.

Then I noticed the dozen or so people who'd queued up since we'd moved aside. The way things were going, it would be hours before Pavlik and I were alone in his reserved suite.

'No need to do that,' Missy said. 'I have an inside track.'

Stepping to one side of the desk, she stuck her head through an archway. 'Excuse me, Louis, but we're getting backed up out here?'

A man came out, struggling into a red-and-gold uniform tunic. 'I'm so sorry, Missy. We'll bring out two more clerks immediately.'

14

'That would be wonderful. The people arriving now will be anxious to get checked in – and changed, of course – before tonight's event. And could you also give me the welcome packet for the Flagler Suite?'

'Of course.'

The young woman certainly got things done. And pleasantly. My oft-irascible if not downright cantankerous business partner, Sarah Kingston, could take lessons from the mouths of babes.

Age-wise, I mean.

Raised voices drew my attention back to the entrance. Curly-top was nowhere in sight, but Larry the Lanky Smoker was talking to Zoe. He had a shaved head and handlebar mustache above a dress shirt and sports jacket, dark slacks and a pair of mated wingtips below. I recognized the style of shoes because it was one many of my former colleagues in the financial industry had favored while conducting business in the office or – in a more colorful version – on the golf course.

None of those shoes, though, had quite the panache of this pair. With strategically-placed patches of soft tan, dark brown, pale yellow and forest green, these wingtips didn't look so much like golf shoes as what golf shoes aspire to be when they grow up. The man wearing them expected to be recognized. To the point of demanding to be.

But I'd be damned if I could place him.

'If I must, I must,' he was saying to Zoe as he fussed with his mustache. 'But prior notice would have been appreciated.'

'I'm certain you were sent—'

'Here we go.' Missy, apparently not noticing the dust-up involving her boss, handed Pavlik an envelope. 'Everything should be in here, including your tickets for tonight's event. Since it's just barely six, you'll have time to freshen up and change before we meet in the lobby at seven-fifteen.'

'The lobby?' Pavlik echoed, as I saw any hopes of an intimate evening in the hotel suite circle the drain. But then Pavlik had been invited as an honored guest and being on the conference's dime would mean that he also had to be on the conference's time, not my own.

Bright side, this was his show and maybe they were taking us out to dinner. A nice seafood restaurant on the well-tended waterfront would—

'Yes, here,' Missy confirmed. 'And, please, by seven-fifteen for the bus to the station. Oh, and you did bring costumes, I hope?'

I perked up. 'Costumes?'

Pavlik glanced at me.

Wings, I mouthed.

The sheriff suppressed a grin. 'Nobody

16

said anything about an event tonight, Missy, but you're paying me and comping us. The where and when are all we need to know.'

I admired the sentiment, if not the resulting postponement of nookie time.

'I'm so sorry.' Missy threw a concerned look at her boss, who was still deep in conversation with Larry the Smoker. 'Zoe didn't email you about our murder train?'

'No, but that's fine,' Pavlik said. 'By "murder train," do you mean like a mystery dinner theater, but on a railroad car?'

A similar train ran on weekends between downtown Milwaukee and Chicago's Union Station.

'Yes, though it's more "cars," plural, and we're just offering a mystery-themed cake and coffee. Not only is it cheaper and easier than full dinner service or even hors d'oeuvres on a train, but it gave me a great theme to build the event around.' Missy pointed to a sign.

'"Murder on the Orient Espresso,"' I read aloud, wondering why I, a public relations person turned coffeehouse owner – said coffeehouse even being in a historic train depot – had never thought of mounting an event based on Agatha Christie's classic 1934 mystery novel.

Though I wasn't above stealing the idea and smuggling it back to Wisconsin. 'What fun. Are you actually having espresso?'

'Yes. In addition to a full bar, of course.' She gestured toward the coffee cart. 'Boyce, the hotel's coffee vendor, will be onboard providing coffee and cake.'

I didn't point out that coffee – which could be easily brewed by the large pot – and espresso, brewed by the shot, were two entirely different efforts. Especially when dealing with a crowd. 'How many people will there be?'

'Fewer than twenty for tonight, which is a separate, ticketed event.' Missy frowned. 'I'd hoped for more, but then this is the first year we've done something on the eve of the conference.'

'That sounds like a very respectable turn-out, and it'll give you a chance to get the bugs out for next year.' One of the 'bugs,' perhaps, being espresso for twenty. 'I own a coffeehouse in Wisconsin, so let me know if your vendor needs help.'

'Oh, that is *so* nice of you.' Missy gave me an enthusiastic if unexpected hug. 'This train event was my idea and I really do want to make it a huge success.'

The girl seemed to be starving for approval, something she probably didn't get a lot of from her boss – especially if Missy was trying to spread her wings a bit. Zoe, as mother bird, seemed more like the type to

18

knock impertinent chicks out of the nest prematurely than to nurture them.

'Missy?' Zoe, as if she'd heard, came over with the lanky, bald man in tow. 'You and I discussed for weeks that Larry would play the role of our detective, Hercule Poirot, tonight. *Yet* he says you never even asked him to take part.'

Missy's eyes went wide. 'But Zoe, you said that *you'd* take care of...' Then, probably not wanting to argue the point publicly, 'I don't know what could have happened. Sheriff Pavl— I mean, Jake didn't receive an email, either.'

'Email!' Larry actually snorted. 'I don't respond to *e*mail.'

Even Zoe, trying as she was to calm the waters, seemed surprised by that. 'But your "PotShots" is an online book review site. How can you not—'

'Precisely,' the man interrupted. 'Which is why I don't open my email. Do you really think I want to hear all the belly-aching from authors – whether newbies or established franchises – who seem to think I *owe* them a good review?'

PotShots rang a bell. 'Why, you're Laurence Potter.'

I felt Pavlik's surprise as Potter turned toward me. 'I am, indeed. And you are?'

'Maggy Thorsen,' I said, holding out my

right hand. 'I enjoy your reviews.'

'Then you certainly can't be an author yourself.' Potter enveloped my fingers and drew their knuckles to his lips, a glint in his eye. 'How refreshing.'

'As refreshing as your critiques.' I took my hand back, willing myself not to reflexively wipe it on my pants. A rumored womanizer and sleazeball, Potter might be a nasty piece of work – as were his reviews – but he was also borderline charming and certainly entertaining. 'You sure don't pull any punches.'

A modest shrug, though I had a feeling that nothing Potter did was modest, and that what he did to appear modest was nothing like unrehearsed. 'Too many critics simply don't bother to review books that are dreadful. Personally, I don't subscribe to the old saw, "If you can't say something nice, don't say anything at all." In fact, I don't know why words uttered by some rabbit in a children's animated feature would be so revered in the first place.'

The words were 'uttered by' Thumper in *Bambi*. And it was 'say *nothing* at all,' not 'say anything at all.' Sheesh, if you can't trust a reviewer to get it right...

'What about the old saw, "those who can't do, teach"?' a voice from behind me contributed. 'Do you "subscribe" to that one, Larry?'

20

I turned to see a chic woman with short, choppy black hair. She wore a deceptively simple white blouse over designer jeans – and not the department store kind. I'm talking denims that command upwards of a thousand dollars. And have waiting lists.

'Laurence,' Potter snapped, his eyes narrowing.

The new addition to our group smiled icily. 'Oh, Larry, I've known you for years. Why so formal?'

'I've grown tired of correcting the hearing-impaired morons who insist on confusing my name with that of JK Rowling's detestable four-eyed wizard.'

Ah, Harry Potter.

'Be glad your name's not Dumbledore,' I said under my breath, winning me a warning look from Pavlik, who knew I liked to stir a cauldron myself now and then.

Meanwhile, the smile was etched on the chilly face of the elegant woman. 'So now you only need to inform them that Laurence is spelled with a "U" and not the more pedestrian "W."'

'As is the case with Olivier and Fishburne, so I'm in rather good company,' Potter said. 'And speaking of the company we keep, how nice it is to see you again, Rosemary.'

'And me, you,' the woman said. They air-kissed, each of them careful not to engage in any actual flesh-to-flesh contact.

It was obvious both of them were lying respectively through their tightly clenched teeth and suddenly I realized why. 'Rosemary Darlington. I've been reading about your new book, *Breaking and Entering.*'

And I had, on PotShots. The first book from the legendary lady of romantic suspense in years and Laurence Potter had absolutely eviscerated it. Called it smut, even. Apparently the 'Breaking' part referred to hearts. And the 'Entering' ... well, as Potter had written on PotShots, *Do I have to spell it out for you?*

Rosemary Darlington had reportedly done just that, explicitly and with quite a few redundant – and occasionally imaginative – variations over the four hundred pages of her erotic suspense novel.

I had the feeling that this *was* going to be a fun weekend – both in and out of the hotel's Flagler Suite.

TWO

'So, if you knew Rosemary's book would be a sore point,' Pavlik said as he squeezed shaving cream into his palm, 'why bring it up?'

'Potter's review was obviously the elephant in the room – or lobby,' I said, inspecting our digs. 'Best to trot the thing out and let it take a few laps – dissipate the sting.'

'Mixer of metaphors.' Pavlik's reflection in the mirror looked past me to the oversized numbers on the bedside radio alarm clock. 'We have to be downstairs in thirty minutes.'

'Don't worry, I'll be ready. What's this?' I pointed at a box that had been on the coffee table when we arrived. 'A welcome gift from your friend Zoe?'

'Afraid not,' he said. 'And Zoe and I *are* just friends, while we're trotting out the elephants in the room.'

'Hey,' I said, raising my hands in utter innocence. 'Did I ask?'

'Of course not. That would be admitting you cared.'

'But I do care,' I protested. 'You know that. I just don't get jealous.'

An outright lie, of course. But showing jealousy only gives the other person – or persons – power. And, besides, as my now defunct marriage proved, if two people are meant to be together they will be.

Or not.

'So what is this?' I asked again, tapping on the box.

'I shipped a few things ahead for my panel.'

I should have known. 'Welcome gifts' rarely arrive in hotel rooms via UPS. And this one was addressed to Pavlik care of the hotel in the sheriff's own handwriting. Though a forward-thinking man might have shipped a few romantic ... toys to surprise his lady friend. Perhaps flavored whipped cream or—

My stomach rumbled. 'Did Missy say they'll just have dessert on the train?'

'Cake, I think. Maybe we can grab a packaged sandwich or granola bar from the hotel's newsstand on the way out.'

Too much to hope the newsstand carried grilled snapper with lemon butter and capers to-go.

I picked up a glossy hardcover to the right of the UPS box. The cover of the book showed a steam train chugging over a narrow trestle, water on both sides of it.

'Flagler's Railroad,' I read aloud.

'Henry Flagler is a legend down here,' Pavlik said, apparently satisfied with the lathering of his face as he reached for his razor. 'Flagler's dream was to build an "Overseas Railroad" extending out from Miami over more than a hundred miles of mostly open water to Key West. And he lived to see it realized, too, but in nineteen thirty-five a hurricane destroyed large parts of it and killed a lot of workers. You can still see long sections of his railbed – mostly elevated – as you drive down the Keys.'

'He never rebuilt it?' I was flipping through the book.

'By then Flagler was dead, the railroad hadn't paid for itself and people had taken to calling the project "Flagler's Folly."'

'That's sad.' A grainy black-and-white picture showed the wooden trestle topped with thick crossties. The metal rail on one side of the track was completely missing. The other was curled like bits of ribbon, I imagined from the hurricane or its aftermath. The photographer must have been standing on one of the ties, shooting down the length. In the distance the trestle just disappeared into the water.

Had a train been on that trestle when the storm hit it? And if so, would we know it or would all traces of it – of *them*, the poor

25

workers – simply have been swept away?

'Don't feel sorry for Flagler,' Pavlik said, nearly finished with his razor. 'The man was a highly successful industrialist and lived to see his dream come true. How many people do we know who can say that?'

'Very few.' I flipped to the title page of the book. Published by Florida History & Tourism and written by ... 'Zoe Scarlett,' I said aloud.

'Zoe?' Pavlik repeated. 'I'm not sure she has dreams.'

I wasn't going to touch that one. I put the tourist book down, thinking it explained what Zoe did for the remainder of the year.

The man of *my* dreams set down his razor and inspected the closeness of his shave in the mirror. 'Not bad.'

'Not bad at all,' I agreed, unzipping my jeans. It was a shame we wouldn't be staying in tonight.

Based on my inspection, the Flagler Suite was large and luxurious, featuring a king-sized bed, ocean-view whirlpool and granite-countered kitchenette, should one need to grab sustenance traversing between the two.

Still, I told myself, if the room had romance written all over it, tonight's event promised more in the way of melodrama. Apparently the plan for the evening's loose re-enactment of Agatha Christie's *Murder on the Orient Express* featured Rosemary Darlington and Laurence Potter in the lead roles.

'I think you'd make a much better Poirot than Potter,' I said. 'Except for the mustache, of course.'

'Laurence Potter – and Rosemary Darlington – are the guests of honor. I'm just the lead forensics guy. Sort of the...' Pavlik's eyes followed me as I stepped out of my pants, '...working stiff.'

Thankfully, more like stiffy. Thus encouraged, I started to take my time, doing a bit of a striptease, unbuttoning my blouse to expose what I thought of as my 'good' red bra. Though, truth to tell, I intended it for no-good. 'Appropriate, then, that you're playing Ratchett.'

I slipped off the shirt and tossed it onto the bed, which had been turned down to expose the gazillion thread-count linens. 'You know, the *stiff*. So to speak.'

'So to speak.' The eyes in the mirror caught mine. 'I'm hoping we can get back here early.'

It wasn't so much Pavlik's words as the way he said them. Experiencing a little thrill down my spine, I sidled up behind him and wrapped myself around his bare torso, resting the palms of my hands on his flat abs. I'd forgotten how good he felt. 'Early would be great for me, too.'

Pavlik's eyes, usually blue against his tanned face and dark, wavy hair, could change to slate gray – nearly black – when he was … well, let's say 'agitated.' We should also acknowledge that this color transformation could come from anger as well as lust, and I had unfortunately seen more of the former than the latter.

Not tonight, though.

His mood-ring eyes were deliciously dark as he turned and tipped my chin up so my mouth met his.

'We're going to be late,' I said in a 'convince-me' kind of voice, tasting the lovely combination of residual soap and current sheriff.

'They'll wait,' he said, edging me toward the bed. 'The Orient Espresso isn't going anywhere fast. At least not without a corpse.'

As it turned out, Jake Pavlik was right.

In – oh, so many ways.

THREE

Luckily for our breach of punctuality, it turned out that wrangling mystery writers was akin to herding the proverbial flock of cats. When we arrived outside the lobby door ten minutes late, people were still milling about on the sidewalk.

It was dark, landscape lights illuminating the hotel's palm trees and tropical plantings. A tiny, nearly transparent gecko scurried past my foot and up the trunk of a— 'Whoa, what's that?'

The tree I referred to was shaped like a gigantic bunch of asparagus, thick multiple stalks topped by a wide green canopy.

'Impressive, isn't it?' Pavlik said. 'I asked about it the last time I was here for Mystery 101.'

'Impressive' was an understatement. The thing looked like it had been there for decades, if not centuries, a hunch borne out by the fact the tree seemed to have earned a spotlight and plaque of its very own. 'Incredible. And very southern-looking. Is it a mangrove?' I asked, pulling out the only tree name I could remember from the Florida guidebook.

'No, this is a banyan,' Pavlik said. 'You'll see mangroves mostly in coastal areas like the Bay of Florida and also in the sawgrass marsh of the Everglades. Mangroves can grow in salt water – even form islands. They're amaz—'

'And the banyans?' I reminded my own personal Mr Wizard.

'Glad you asked,' Pavlik said, grinning. He took my arm and hooked it around his to stroll closer to the tree. 'Banyans, *too*, are amazing. A type of fig or ficus, they're actually epiphytes.'

'Gosh,' I said, running my hand up and down his bicep. 'That *is* amazing. What's an epiflight?'

'Epiphyte,' he corrected. 'And it's a plant that lives off another plant.'

'A parasite.' If so, this was the Tyrannosaurus Rex of parasites. The canopy looked to be able to fill a city block and the gnarled trunk had to be eight feet across at the base.

'Technically, yes. Birds drop the banyan seeds, which germinate and grow in the cracks and crevices of other trees. As the banyan grows, its limbs drop these supporting roots you see and they eventually become the multiple trunks that wind around and envelope the entire original host tree.'

We were under the wide branches now, and I squinted up, trying to differentiate the leaves. 'So you're saying there's another tree in there?'

'Most likely just a hollow core where it once was. A banyan this old probably strangled the poor host tree long ago.'

'So the "guest" repays the host by smothering it to death and then taking its place like the poor host was never there in the first place.' I stepped back. 'Nice.'

'Don't worry,' Pavlik said, slipping his arm around my waist. 'I'll protect you from the mean old—'

'Excuse me,' a voice called. 'Can we *please* get everybody on the bus?'

Zoe Scarlett was standing under the hotel's marquis with a clipboard. She was showing even more cleavage than earlier, which I judged to be her idea of transitioning the look from daytime to nighttime.

'Thank God I can depend on you at least, Jacob.' Her gaze passed right over me to Pavlik in his black dress shirt, open at the neck, and black pants. 'Perfect.'

'I was afraid it telegraphed bad guy,' Pavlik said, flashing her a smile.

'*Stiff* bad guy,' I reminded him. Pavlik's smile grew broader.

Zoe swiveled to survey the floral sundress

I'd chosen for its vintage feel. Besides, it was quick. Not a small consideration since Pavlik, bless him, was not. 'Megan, you're going to freeze in that.'

'It's "Maggy,"' I corrected. 'And as for freezing, the sun is down and the temperature still has to be close to eighty degrees.' I'd heard Floridians' bodily thermostats were set a bit differently, but Zoe's prediction was borderline crazy.

'Only for now.' Missy Hudson had come up behind us. 'A cold front is coming through tonight bringing storms, wouldn't you know it? An unfortunate last hurrah for our hurricane season.'

'Hurricane season?' I repeated, thinking of Flagler's ill-fated railroad.

Missy waved her hand. 'Hurricane season, wet season, rainy season – it's all pretty much the same. May through to October, typically, though, Mother Nature doesn't always observe the calendar. November first, and we'll be lucky to reach seventy-five tomorrow.'

Brr, seventy-five degrees Fahrenheit. Fifty-five was considered balmy in Brookhills this time of year.

'Besides, it will undoubtedly be cold on the train. Everything in South Florida is way over air-conditioned.' Missy was pawing through a bag of clothing. She pulled out a

32

black shawl. 'Here, take this.'

'Thanks,' I said, taking the lacy wrap, though I doubted the train could be air-conditioned to the point that this Wisconsinite would feel a chill. 'But won't you need it?'

'Oh, not to worry – I have my fur.' She struck a pose. 'Can you guess who I am?'

Not surprisingly, Missy had gotten into the spirit of her event and the role she was to play. A wide-brimmed hat sat on carefully finger-waved hair and a white fur coat partially covered a long silver dress that pulled a bit over surprisingly voluptuous hips before stopping just short of her glittery silver shoes.

'Well, I...'

'Mrs Hubbard,' Missy continued, sparing me the need to answer. 'Though I have to admit, I opted for Lauren Bacall's version from the movie rather than the plainer "American Lady" in the book. Such fun to get really dressed up, don't you think?'

'Well, you do look wonderf—'

I was interrupted by a wolf whistle as two men in suits – one double-breasted navy pinstripe, the other cream-colored – passed by to board the bus. 'Looking good, Missy,' Pinstripe called.

'Oh, thank you,' she nearly squealed in delight, and then lowered her voice to address me. 'When I saw this at Sally's – that's what my friends call the Salvation Army store here – I knew it would be perfect.'

The girl was glowing. I had a feeling Missy Hudson didn't get the opportunity to be the center of attention very often.

'Missy?' Zoe's voice. 'Did you find Larry and Rosemary?'

Missy nodded toward the bus standing ready at the curb, its headlights glowing in the dark. 'Laurence is already onboard, Zoe. But Rosemary isn't feeling well. She suffers from motion sickness and is afraid the bus—'

Zoe interrupted. 'Tell the diva she can lie down in the sleeping car once she plays her part. But, until then, Rosemary needs to be on that train and mingling with our paying customers.'

'Oh, she will,' Missy said quickly. 'But I ... well, I told her that if she prefers, I'd drive her to the station.'

Uh-oh, I thought. Our favorite little people-pleaser might have to clone herself to keep both her boss and guest of honor happy. But, to my surprise, Zoe relented.

'Fine. So long as the two of you are on the train and everything is ready when we leave. This event was your idea and I have no intention of saving it by dealing with the train people myself.'

Having won the battle, Missy now seemed

appalled at the idea of her boss dealing with the 'train people.' Or any people at all, especially ones Zoe might consider underlings. 'Oh, no, you needn't talk to anyone at the station. I've arranged it all.'

'I certainly hope so.'

Missy was going through a small stack of cards and pulled one out for Zoe. 'Here's your event name badge.'

Zoe looked at it. 'Why do I need that? We'll have everyone's conference tags at registration tomorrow.'

'Well, yes,' Missy said, still holding it out tentatively, 'but these are for tonight's Murder on the Orient Espresso. See? They have our train-ride roles on them.'

The badge read 'Zoe' in big letters and, below it in smaller type, 'Woman in the Red Kimono.'

Zoe still didn't take the thing. 'What – no last name?'

'Well, no.' Missy pulled back her hand like she thought Ms Scarlett was going to bite it off. 'There wasn't room for that and the roles, if we wanted them to be readable. Besides,' Missy appealed to Pavlik and me, 'first names are so much friendlier, don't you think?'

'Well, it's for certain the only thing that *I'll* remem—' I started.

Zoe cut me off. 'Friendly, schmiendly.

Without the full names, how can attendees know who's important?'

'You mean for sucking up?' I asked.

'Of course. Literary agents, publishing house editors, established authors. How's one supposed to know?' Zoe demanded.

'The name badges for tomorrow will have full names and be color-coded with all that information,' Missy gamely assured her. 'But for tonight I thought it would be fun—'

'Fine, fine.' Zoe Scarlett turned her eyes to the list she held, her hand trembling in excitement or anxiety, I wasn't sure which.

Missy Hudson – or 'Mrs Hubbard,' I suppose – tried to appear unfazed by the tsunami of criticism, but I could see her fighting the tears in her eyes as she handed Pavlik and me our own badges for the night.

'"Maggy/Narrator,"' I read from mine. 'But will I really be doing any narrating?'

'Oh, no. Not to worry.' Missy seemed more apologetic than defensive. 'I just didn't have a role for you and didn't want you to feel left out.'

'That's so nice. Thank you.' I peeled the backing off the badge and stuck it to my dress, then went to help Pavlik, who was having trouble with his.

'Jacob/Ratchett,' I said, affixing it to the shoulder of his shirt.

'I'm so sorry Jacob and Ratchett don't

alliterate,' Missy said. 'Zoe decided which roles the sheriff and the guests of honor were playing.'

More special treatment for Pavlik, courtesy of our buxom conference organizer. But, hey, I rationalized, it had scored us a suite so far. As long as the woman kept her hands to herself...

Missy was leafing through the short stack of badges in her hand again. 'I chose the players and their respective roles so people could put them together easily either through alliteration or word association.'

'Which is why Zoe *Scarlett* is the Woman in the *Red* Kimono? Very clever.'

'Thank you. And then there's the fact that Agatha Christie never properly reveals who's wearing the kimono. Zoe didn't want to play a role.'

That figured. Nothing could top 'Countess of the Conference.'

The girl was pulling out another badge. 'See? I'm Missy/Mrs Hubbard.'

'Huh,' I said, looking. 'Missy, Mrs. And even your last names, when you think of it, alliterate. "Hudson" and "Hubbard," very neatly done.'

'Says the woman who attempted to assign seats in her coffeehouse,' I heard Pavlik say under his breath.

'They don't all,' Missy was saying. 'The

last names, I mean. That's why,' she lowered her voice and snuck a glance toward Zoe, 'I didn't put them on.'

I knuckle-bumped with her. 'Good for you.'

Zoe, who'd been running her finger down the clipboard, suddenly looked up. 'Good for who?'

'You and Missy,' I said with a smile. 'Are we all here?'

'Looks like it.' Zoe swept her hand toward the door of the bus, inviting Pavlik and me to climb on.

I went first, happy to see that most of the people who'd already boarded were wearing outfits that fit the 1930s, when Dame Agatha had set her *Murder on the Orient Express*. I loved old movies and though it had been a while since I'd read Agatha Christie's book, I'd coincidentally seen the 1974 movie version just a few weeks prior. It would be fun seeing who was who. Or was it 'whom'?

'Looking for a seat?' a pleasant African-American man on the aisle about halfway back asked. He was wearing navy pinstripes and I recognized him and the man next to him as the pair who had complimented Missy. He finished slapping on his nametag and stuck out his hand. 'I'm Markus, playing MacQueen, the victim's secretary.'

Markus/MacQueen. I was finding Missy's

system helpful already. And the use of first names only simplified things even further for a newcomer like me. 'Nice to meet you, Markus, I'm Maggy. I'm actually looking for two se—'

'Larry'll always make room for a good-looking woman.' A slightly-built older lady diagonally across the aisle nodded toward Laurence Potter in the aisle seat behind her. Potter's face was buried behind a *Publishers Weekly* magazine, his briefcase on the window seat next to him.

Typical commuter ploy to discouraging sharing, but I was busy studying the elderly woman, who was wearing a dark dress with layers of pearls around her neck. Even without the nametag, I thought I had this one. 'Princess Dragomiroff, I presume?'

'Very good,' the princess said. 'And this is—'

'Greta Ohlsson, who gives evidence in part two, chapter six.' The bespectacled middle-aged woman seated next to the princess wore a plaid blouse and tweed skirt like the 'Swedish Lady' of the book she held in her hand. The part had been played by Ingrid Bergman in the movie.

'A pleasure.' I pointed to my nametag. 'I'm not really narrating. In fact, I'm not even sure there is a narrator in the book.'

'The book was written third-person, so

there would be a narrative voice,' Markus/ MacQueen said. 'Will you be speaking at the conference?'

'Heavens, no. My friend,' I nodded toward Pavlik, who was still at the front of the bus engaged in conversation with Zoe, 'is, though, and we didn't know—'

'Ooh, you're with that good-looking sheriff,' Greta piped up in a soft, mincing voice. Tucking the copy of *Murder on the Orient Express* into her handbag, she turned to her companion. 'You do remember him from our conference two years back, don't you, Prudence? Zoe's "friend" from Chicago?'

The quotation marks around 'friend' were about as subtle as sky-writing.

On cue, the slinky redhead in question trilled out in response to something Pavlik had said. The laughter sounded more siren song than genuine amusement. Let's just hope the 'good-looking sheriff' could resist the lure of her silicone-rocky shores.

As if Pavlik sensed us all looking, he waved to me. 'Did you find two seats back there?'

I shook my head. 'Only one.'

'Go ahead and take that. I'll sit here.' As Pavlik said it, he slid into the seat next to Zoe.

My reasonable self told my other self that I didn't mind. After all, wasn't 'Maggy the

Narrator' the one who had just gotten frisky with Pavlik in the very suite Zoe had booked for him?

Or ... *them?*

The conference organizer whispered something into Pavlik's ear and then put her hand on his shoulder, hitching herself up with a smile to do a headcount.

It was a very thorough count, her breasts bouncing up/down and swinging back/forth next to Pavlik.

Game on, baby. I amped up my smile and said loudly, 'Excuse me, Laurence. Is this seat taken?'

Did I imagine it or had Zoe's smile slipped a bit? I glanced down at Potter, bald head buried in his magazine. Maybe Zoe, greedy girl, had designs on the guest of honor as well as Pavlik.

I cleared my throat.

Potter looked up. 'Sorry?'

Though we'd met just over an hour ago, he seemed to already have forgotten me. So much for Maggy Thorsen, femme fatale.

But Zoe could still be watching, so I kept smiling. 'I said, is that seat taken?'

'What she's too polite to say, Larry,' the aging-to-aged princess snapped, 'is you need to move your crap onto the floor.'

'Oh, I was simply and totally immersed in this article.' As Potter spoke, he lifted his briefcase and slid over to the window. 'Please. Sit.'

'You weren't saving it for someone?' As I sat down, I saw Zoe swivel back around toward Pavlik.

'More likely saving it *from* someone,' the princess said. 'I'm Prudence, by the way, and my seatmate is Grace.'

Prudence/Princess Dragomiroff and Grace/Greta Ohlsson. Missy deserved a gold star in my alliteration/memory-trick book.

I shook the princess's ring-covered hand. 'Maggy,' I said, before turning to Grace. 'Are you both writers?'

'Aspiring writers,' Grace said.

'Some of us aspire more than others,' the princess said sourly. 'Grace hasn't written a word since the last Mystery 101.'

'I teach kindergarten in Detroit,' Grace explained, unruffled. 'I'm afraid the little ones take up all my—'

'A word of advice, Maggy?' Prudence interrupted. 'Watch out for Zoe.'

'Zoe? What do you mean?' I knew exactly what she meant, but I wanted to hear it from her.

'She means,' Laurence Potter said dryly, 'that the woman is a venal fly trap.'

Venal, not venus. 'As in—'

'*As in* a mercenary snare of male privates,' Potter provided. 'Or must I spell it out for

42

you?'

He pretty much had. But since 'innocent' had gotten me this far: 'I thought Zoe was married, at least until recently.'

A snort from Prudence/Princess, but it was Grace/Greta next to her who answered. 'Ignore these two, Maggy. We all owe Zoe – and Missy, too, as of last year – a debt of gratitude for spearheading this conference.'

'Ah, yes,' Potter said, lifting up his magazine to eye level again. 'Though the job does come with certain ... benefits.'

Grace spread her hands. 'I'd like to know who amongst us doesn't come to these events partly to meet legends like Rosemary Darlington.'

'Legends.' The word came from behind the magazine.

'Whatever you think of the new book, Larry,' Grace said, 'you must admit Rosemary has written nearly fifty novels over the years, most of them very good. And now she's reinvented herself for a new generation. That makes Rosemary Darlington a legend in my mind.'

'And her own, if nowhere else.' Potter lowered his copy of *Publishers Weekly* and shook his head sadly. 'There was a time I thought Rosemary Darlington had genuine talent, but that woman could never have written this current pile of excrement.'

'Just because you don't like the romance genre,' Prudence snapped again, 'doesn't make it "excrement."'

'Absolutely right.' The magazine came down and the gloves, apparently, off. 'I've been unfair to excrement.'

Whoa, boy. This was getting fun. 'You're so knowledgeable,' I said as naively as a be-dazzled fourth grader to Potter. 'Do you write, yourself? Novels, I mean.'

'Yes, Larry,' Prudence said, sticking out her neck like an elderly, but remarkably aristocratic, chicken. 'Do tell us what *you've* authored.'

'Happily,' Potter said as the bus lurched away from the curb. 'In fact, I have a book in the works right now.'

'Are you—' I started, but the bus driver slammed on his brakes, sending me flying forward. Potter put his arm out to keep my head from hitting the back of Markus's seat, managing to buff my breasts thoroughly with the back of his forearm in the process.

'Thank you,' I said automatically as I right-ed myself and slid the spaghetti strap of my dress back onto my shoulder.

'He should be thanking *you*,' I heard the princess mutter.

'What the bloody hell is this idiot driver doing?' Laurence Potter demanded as the door of the bus opened.

44

'Sorry, sorry.' The curly-haired young man I'd seen outside the hotel earlier that day climbed aboard.

'Oh, that's just swell,' I heard Potter mutter. 'The merely excruciating has managed to become the intolerable.'

FOUR

'Do you know him?' I asked Potter, ignoring the fact I'd seen the two of them together.

'Just another sycophant.'

'Better honey than vinegar,' the man next to Markus said. Sporting a small mustache, blonde hair slicked back, he looked a bit like the actor Michael York in his cream-colored three-piece suit. His hands nervously circled the brim of a matching hat in his lap.

'But they *said* at the registration desk that the event wasn't filled to capacity.' Potter's 'sycophant' was arguing his case to the bus driver.

Zoe stood up. 'Are you a conference attendee?'

'I just signed up.' He held up a nametag. The big letters read 'Danny' but I couldn't see the rest.

'The lady said I could be...' Danny turned the tag around so he could read it, 'Colonel Arbuthnot?'

Sean Connery played the role of the British Indian Army Officer in the movie. And this kid was no Sean Connery. Nor, I might add, did his real and assigned names alliterate.

But talk, he certainly could. '...so I was late. But I did pay for the conference.'

'And this event?' Zoe asked.

Danny nodded.

The conference organizer gestured toward the back. 'Well, then, welcome aboard. You'll have to stand for the time being, but there will be plenty of room on the train.'

'Great, thanks.' The kid made his way back as the bus began inching forward again.

'So, Larry,' Markus said from across the aisle. 'This book you're writing. Is it a novel?'

'Mr Potter – *you're* writing a novel, too?' Danny/Col. Arbuthnot had stopped next to us. A studious-looking kid, his eyes were the color of unwrapped Hershey's Kisses and about as readable. They were focused on Potter.

'Perhaps,' said the Great One, irritably. 'But you'd be better served by my book on writing from a few years back.'

Potter's tone was downright nasty, but you had to hand it to Danny, he seemed unfazed.

46

In fact, the young man hunkered down in the aisle to talk earnestly across me to Potter. 'I'd love to read your book. It would be tit-for-tat, since I already sent you mine.'

I could practically feel the steam coming off Potter. 'What you sent, Master Danny, is a "manuscript." Not a "novel." If and when you get it published by a reputable trade house, I will be overjoyed to peruse it and tell the world exactly what I think.'

'Gee, that would be really great,' said the young man, either not getting or, at least, not reacting to Potter's sarcasm. Danny straightened up and extended his hand past my face to Potter. 'I'm going to hold you to that, sir.'

The reviewer looked at the hand before reluctantly shaking it. Then, with a guttural sound of disgust, he returned to his magazine.

Having apparently secured what he'd come for, Danny turned to me. 'Are you an author, too?'

'Nope. Coffeehouse owner.'

Weighing that, he must have decided there was no advantage to chatting up someone who could not help him in his intended career. Mumbling, 'Good to meet you,' Danny rose and moved on to a man in a blue, yellow and red checkered sports jacket sitting behind me.

The boy introduced himself and the two

chatted in low tones. So quiet, in fact, that I couldn't hear them from just one row away, despite my best efforts. As I started to swivel back forward, I saw the seated man nod toward Potter's back.

'The kid's got balls, I'll give him that,' Prudence said as the boy stood up and continued on, working his way toward the back of the bus. Every few seats he stopped to introduce himself. 'And sending an unpublished manuscript to a reviewer? Talk about a death wish.'

'I assume that's not done?' I asked.

The princess shrugged. 'What's the point? Unless, of course, you're the type who gets a kick out of having your unborn child torn apart by jackals.' She turned and glanced at the magazine held by the jackal in question. 'No offense, Larry.'

'None taken,' Potter said mildly from behind it, seeming pleased by the comparison.

'Please leave the boy – is it Danny? – alone.' Grace, kindergarten teacher and apparent defender of the young, spoke up. 'Who amongst us hasn't deluded ourselves into thinking we're the next Hemingway or Christie, just waiting to be discovered?'

A collective sigh – or maybe it was a whimper – came from the assorted aspiring writers seated around me.

I repressed a grin. 'I suppose it would be

logical to think that someone like Mr Potter would be just the person – in fact, that he could feel honored – to do just that.'

'Not if you knew him,' a voice behind us muttered.

'So is the kid's stuff any good, Larry?' Prudence asked.

I saw Potter roll his eyes behind the magazine before he finally lowered it to address the question. 'And how would I know that?'

'This Danny sent you a manuscript, or so he said.'

'And perhaps he truly did, but you can't honestly begin to believe that I open and read what the vast unwashed mail me *un*-solicited, do you?'

In these days of electronic bills and bill paying, I barely got any postal mail. What I did get were obvious solicitations which I had no trouble discarding. I couldn't imagine, though, not opening something that was obviously personally addressed to me from one human being to another.

'Really?' I asked with the innocence of the uninformed. 'What do you do with it?'

'Either write "return to sender" on the envelope and give it back to the postal worker, or simply toss the thing, unopened.'

'Michael York' leaned forward to address us. 'In truth, since September 11, 2001, and the anthrax scare, publishers don't open mail unless it's from a reputable literary agent.'

'Are you a publisher?' I asked.

'No. A "reputable literary agent."' The man cracked a small smile, but didn't extend his hand. 'I hope you'll forgive me for not shaking hands, but I fear contagion.'

'Oh, I'm sorry,' I said, though he hadn't shown any symptoms. 'You're not feeling well?'

'No, no. I'm just fine,' the agent said, hands still rotating his hat like the steering wheel of a car doing perpetual doughnuts. 'Now.'

'Our Carson is not only a renowned agent, but a renowned germaphobe,' Potter said dryly.

Ahh, I got it. Not being contagious, the agent really *did* 'fear contagion.'

'I haven't shaken hands with anyone for over ten years,' Carson said proudly.

'Truly?' I was trying to imagine the business meetings and conferences, parties and receptions the agent must have been invited to during the span of more than a decade. 'Isn't that a little awkward in your line of work?'

'My clients understand,' the literary agent said, now with a genuine smile.

'They understand he's a nut job,' Prudence cracked out of the corner of her mouth.

'One that negotiates some of the biggest advances in our industry,' Potter countered.

I glanced at my seat companion in surprise. It was the first time I'd heard Laurence Potter say anything positive about anyone.

Except himself, of course.

'Well, it's a pleasure to meet you,' I said to the agent. 'And your costume is wonderful. Count Andrenyi, the Hungarian diplomat.'

'Costume?' He looked down at the hat in his hand.

Uh-oh. I got a sick feeling in the pit of my stomach. 'I'm sorry. I just thought ... umm, I mean, you look so much like Michael York, who played the role in the, umm...'

The man exploded with laughter. 'I'm sorry, my dear, but I couldn't help myself.' He held up a badge encased in a plastic sandwich bag. It read, 'Carson/Count Andrenyi.'

Oh, thank the Lord. At least the germaphobe had a sense of humor. 'So you *are* playing the count tonight.'

'I am, and apparently I've nailed the role.' Carson the agent/count was pleased with himself.

'Carson was originally on Broadway,' the man in the checkered sports jacket said from behind me. 'In fact, we worked together way back when. Rosemary Darlington was in theater, as well.'

'What interesting career paths,' I said, meaning it. 'Actor, agent, writer—'

'A lot of young people come to New York to study theater,' Carson said. 'Just as they flock to Los Angeles for the movie industry. Most of us end up doing other things. Only a very few can make a living at acting and even fewer become famous.'

'That's not so different to writing,' Markus said. 'How many writers give up their day jobs?'

'More than should,' Potter observed acerbically.

'That's true,' Carson agreed, whether because the reviewer had bolstered the agent a minute before or not. 'Writing fiction is, at best, project work. You start one book and hope you have a contract to publish another by the time the first is finished. And that the successor sells once it, too, is published. Nothing like a twice-monthly, automatically deposited payroll check, by any means.'

'Even the best writers have gaps between books,' Grace contributed. 'Look at our Rosemary. *Breaking and Entering* came out nearly five years after her last book.'

'Is she one of your clients?' I asked the agent. The more I learned about these bizarre people, God help me, the more I wanted to know.

'No, but she's represented by another

agent at my firm, Natanya Sorensen, who was supposed to be here and play countess to my count.' He directed a smile toward me.

I returned it. 'You're ... countess-less, then?'

'Natanya had the sniffles, and I insisted she stay home and take care of herself.'

'Good thing the woman listened,' I heard Prudence mutter. 'Or he'd have sealed her up inside a Baggie, too.'

Undaunted by the jibe, Carson continued his train of thought. 'I'm afraid Missy was very disappointed.'

'That's because she's a control freak,' Prudence said.

'That's unfair,' Grace protested. 'Missy's worked very hard to put this together for us.'

'I managed events for a large corporation up north,' I said, 'and I would've loved to include someone with Missy's initiative on my staff. Did you know she's driving Rosemary Darlington to the train station because the guest of honor didn't want to ride the bus?'

'Oh, dear,' our other guest of honor said, eyebrows knitting theatrically as he looked up from his magazine. 'I do hope it wasn't anything I said.'

What an ass. 'Didn't you realize you'd be doing this event together when you wrote that review of her book?'

'Of course,' Potter said. 'What would that matter?'

I shrugged. 'I assumed it would be just ... awkward.'

Prudence snorted. 'As you can see, Larry's not the sensitive type.'

'If authors can't take criticism,' Potter said, 'they shouldn't be putting their work out there for everyone to read. The same for so-called authorities writing on their subjects. Am I right, Markus?'

Markus shifted uncomfortably. 'Well, yes. Reviews are certainly a recognized part of the industry.'

'Are you a published author?' I asked.

'More of a fan.'

'Fan?'

'Oh, don't listen to his self-deprecating bullshit.' Prudence the Princess confirmed her potty-mouth. 'Markus is a librarian, as well as a writer in his own right.'

Markus glanced uneasily at Potter, once again engrossed in his magazine. 'Just non-fiction. Readers guides and the like.'

'Writers don't exist without readers,' Grace pointed out.

'Your attention, please!' Zoe was standing up in the front of the bus, her hand on Pavlik's shoulder. Just for balance, *I'm sure*. 'We're approaching the station and since we're running late, I'd appreciate everyone exiting the bus quickly and moving to the train.'

She broke off and leaned down to look out the window, her breasts practically fwopping against Pavlik's cheeks.

'Oh, thank God,' Zoe said, straightening up and tucking a boob back in. 'Rosemary has just arrived.'

'Oh, thank God,' Laurence Potter echoed, gathering up his briefcase. Then a sigh before the words: 'That woman will be the death of me yet.'

FIVE

'So what's the deal?' I asked Pavlik when I joined him outside the bus.

'How do you mean?' The sheriff seemed uneasy, like a man who feared he was walking into a trap. 'I guess this must be a tourist train. You know, like the wine one in the Napa Valley or that Tootsie railroad in North Carolina's High Country.'

I waved away the fact that we were standing in front of something that looked more like a movie set than a train station that actually transported people who needed to reach somewhere. 'In North Carolina, it's "Tweetsie," not "Tootsie," but I didn't mean that. I was talking about the obvious friction.'

'Friction? Between who?' Pavlik looked even more uncomfortable. And why? After all, I hadn't asked what you get when you rub a sheriff and a conference organizer together.

Instead, I said, 'It's "between whom," I think. Around writers, better get that stuff right. And the "friction" I meant is between Laurence Potter and Rosemary Darlington, of course.'

'Oh.' Pavlik's face relaxed. 'I don't have a clue.'

'It seems to go beyond professional. Larry seems to take Rosemary's new book as a personal affront.'

Pavlik was smiling now. '"Larry"? Are you going to call him that the entire time, just to provoke the man?'

Of course. And Zoe Scarlett will continue to call you 'Jacob' in that possessively arch way just to provoke me. It's what we do.

I shrugged. 'It seems to be what everybody calls Potter. And besides, from what we've seen so far, it doesn't look like much is required to provoke him.'

We were following Zoe through the deserted train station. It was then the light dawned on me. 'Ah, the dragon kimono. I get it.'

'Kimono?'

'In *Murder on the Orient Express*. Zoe's wrap dress has a dragon design on the back, see? It's a more modern' – and sluttier – 'version of the red kimono Christie gave to one of her characters.' I looked at Pavlik. 'You *have* seen the movie, right?'

'No, but I read the book, which will probably endear me to more people at a writers' conference.'

'Movies are written, too,' I pointed out. 'And I have to believe that every aspiring writer here would also love a movie deal – oh, this must be our train.'

Not much of a stretch, since there was but one. Missy, having delivered her charge safely to the station, was squatting down in her furs and evening dress, teetering precariously on her high heels as she tried to tape a banner to one of the cars.

'You go on,' I said to Pavlik. 'I might as well earn my keep by seeing if Missy needs help.'

'I'll save you a seat this time.' Pavlik gave me a quick kiss on the lips.

'I'd like that.' I felt rewarded for not making a big deal – or any deal at all, in fact – about Zoe and the seating arrangement on the bus.

As Pavlik continued on to the rest of the

group milling around on the platform, I skirted the crowd, noticing Danny the supposed sycophant talking again with the sports-jacketed former actor from the bus. The two were standing on the fringe of the herd, the plaid of the older man's jacket even gaudier in the lights of the station. He seemed to be pointing out people of interest – or more likely, of note – to the newcomer.

'Oh, dear!'

I reached Missy just in time to catch a corner she had just secured – or tried, with duct tape, to secure – before it peeled away and brushed the railbed. 'Can I give you a hand?'

'Oh, thank you,' Missy said gratefully. 'I'd planned to have this all done before your bus arrived, but the traffic on my "shortcut" was heavier than I expected.'

'It was good of you to drive Rosemary Darlington,' I said, smoothing the banner. 'Given what I've seen, the farther apart you keep her and Laurence Potter, the better.'

Though admittedly not nearly as much fun for onlookers like me, who always appreciated being witness to a train wreck.

Not that I wanted to jinx the poor young woman's project.

'I didn't mind driving.' Missy swept her hat off and swiped her forehead with the back of the same hand. Wearing a fur coat in eighty degrees Fahrenheit must have been taking its toll, even on a Floridian. 'Rosemary suffers from motion sickness and buses are the worst. I hope she'll be all right on our trip tonight.'

'Eric – that's my son – gets car sick, but he's fine on trains as long as he's facing forward.' Which made me recall that passenger cars often had half the seats facing rearward.

'I suggested that to Rosemary,' Missy said, replacing her hat. 'Facing forward and, as you say, as far away from Laurence Potter as possible.'

The last was said under her breath and she glanced over at me, just seeming to realize it'd been said aloud. 'They...' Missy hesitated, '...have a history.'

Hmm. An affair gone wrong would certainly explain the venom with which Potter had criticized Darlington's literary side-trip to the erotic. Maybe I'd read the book just to see if one of the characters was a tall, bald man. 'So Larry Potter and Rosemary Darlington had a personal relationship?'

But Missy had colored up. And, apparently, decided to clam up as well. 'Conference rumors, I'm sure. Please don't say you heard anything from me, Maggy.'

'Of course not.' I was thinking about my dentist husband and the years of conferences he and his hygienist had attended so the office could 'stay current.' Undoubtedly there'd been 'rumors' in the dental community back then. I only wish somebody had bothered to share them with me. 'What happens in Fort Lauderdale, stays in Fort Lauderdale, right?' I said, echoing my earlier words to Pavlik in the hotel lobby.

Missy's eyes went wide. 'What do you mean?'

My turn to blush. I had no business inflicting my hard-earned cynicism on the next generation. Besides, if Laurence Potter – or anybody else – was playing musical beds, it was none of my business. I changed the subject. 'Are you a writer yourself, Missy?'

'No, not really. More a researcher.'

'That must be interesting. For authors?'

Missy moved the scissors aside with her toe and bent down to pick up the roll of duct tape while still holding up her end of the banner. 'Almost exclusively now. At first, I didn't get paid or anything, I just helped authors whose work I enjoyed.'

'That was certainly nice of you.'

'I was having a tough time getting a job in library science, what with all the budget cuts, and this gave me something to do – something I loved.'

'Library science,' I repeated. 'So how did you end up in event management?'

'You mean helping with the conference?' Missy looked surprised. 'Oh, that's just a volunteer post. It's not what I do for a living.'

'You don't get paid?'

'I get my hotel room comped, and I don't pay for the conference, of course. Plus, I meet such interesting people.'

An increase in the chatter coming from the 'interesting people' milling about on the platform drew my attention. The natives were getting restless. And Zoe Scarlett, of course, was nowhere to be seen to settle them down. 'You couldn't pay me enough to take orders from that woman.'

'Zoe?' Missy shot me a smile. 'She's not so bad, truly, though I think her divorce has left her a bit off balance.'

Not surprising, given the size of the woman's new breasts. I refocused my attention on Missy. '...has contacts everywhere, which is crucial,' she was saying. 'She really put this conference together.'

'If you say so.' I'd had experience with 'idea' people who were only too happy to hand off their ideas to other people – like Missy – to implement. And guess who'd take all the credit? 'But you seem to be the one who gets things done.'

'It's mainly logistics. Which is why, between you and me, I'm so excited about tonight.' She lowered her voice. 'I want to show everyone, including our guests of honor, that I'm capable of more creative things. Who knows where that might lead?'

Probably to Zoe dumping even more work onto her unpaid assistant. 'But how do you pay the bills? You said you didn't get paid for the research either.'

'That's changed, happily. A girl has to earn a living.' Missy tried a longer piece of tape, this time attempting to wrap it around a rope attached to the top of the banner.

Well, that was good, at least. 'Can you say who your clients are, or is that kept confidential?'

'I always ask about the confidentiality issues, because it varies from writer to writer. Everyone here, though, knows I've worked for Rosemary Darlington.' Missy took her hands away from the precariously hung banner. 'That's why she agreed to come to Mystery 101.'

'Wow, that's impressive. Zoe apparently isn't the only one with contacts.'

The girl looked pleased and not only because the banner seemed to be holding. 'Oh, it was nothing, really.'

'Not true. As you said regarding Zoe, contacts are crucial in event planning.' But I wanted to hear more about the research, especially in regard to Rosemary Darlington. 'Did you work on *Breaking and Entering*?'

A quick sidelong look. Missy seeming uncertain about my motives for asking. I held up my hands. 'Hey, I haven't read the book. I'm not judging.'

'Oh, not *that* kind of research,' Missy said with a slightly embarrassed smile. 'Heavens, I'm sure Rosemary ... well, I don't mean to say she has more experience, but ... Oh, dear, I'm still making a mess of this.'

The banner took another dive and I made a grab for it. 'I'm not sure even duct tape is up to this job.'

But I was also fairly certain the banner-hanging wasn't what Missy thought she'd messed up. Or, at least, not the only thing.

She was happy to follow my differing lead, though. 'You're right. I didn't ask the banner company to attach these ropes and they make it ever so much heavier. Maybe I should cut them off.' She was eyeing the scissors.

'Uh-uh.' I scooped up the scissors before she could and stepped back to look at our options for securing the signage to the side of the train. 'How secure does the banner have to be?'

'What do you mean?'

'Are we moving or staying right here in the station?'

'Oh, no, we'll be leaving in a few minutes. It's very exciting. I've managed to get us a sneak preview of a brand-new excursion into the Everglades.'

I surveyed the 'excursion' train. There were four cars and ... 'We have a locomotive on each end.' And facing opposite ways.

'Of course. The west one,' Missy pointed at the locomotive to our left, 'will take us into the Everglades. The east one will bring us back to Fort Lauderdale.'

Seemed like kind of a waste to me. 'Don't they usually have just one locomotive and then circle it around to the other end at the station so it can go back in the direction it came?'

'Yes, if there *was* a station. We'll be stopping on the single track in the Everglades and simply reversing back the other direction.' A gust of wind ruffled the banner. 'I hope the storms will hold off until after our three-hour tour.'

'Three-hour tour,' I repeated, the theme from *Gilligan's Island* dancing through my head. Not to mention the photograph of what was left of Flagler's Railroad after the 1935 hurricane. 'Isn't the route through the Everglades called Alligator Alley?'

'Well, the driving one, anyway. However, we'll be on a railroad bed that has just been completed – or almost completed – quite a bit north of the highway. We won't even see Alligator Alley. And besides,' Missy picked up one of the banner ropes and eyed it with evil intent, 'you don't see quite as many alligators anymore. The pythons are eating them.'

I reflexively glanced west toward the Everglades, imagining ominous clouds building in the dark. Despite the Florida heat, I felt a chill. 'Pythons? As in ... snakes?'

'Yes, of course,' Missy said. 'Burmese pythons.'

She said it as casually as Wisconsinites would say 'Canada geese.' But geese don't eat alligators. The worst they could do is poop all over them. *'Burmese* pythons? How in the world—'

'—did they get to Florida?' Missy was trying to unstick the tape she'd attached to her edge of the banner. 'Until a couple of years ago it was legal to have them as pets.'

'Pet snakes.' Snakes in their natural habitat scare me enough, but in the house? Brr. And what did you do with them? Take Fido out for a slither? Play fetch the squirrel? A snake didn't even have ears to scratch.

'...ball pythons,' Missy was saying. 'People who had Burmese pythons before the law was changed are grandfathered in and can keep the one – or more – they already have, assuming they get a "reptile of concern" permit.'

One or *more* 'reptiles of concern'?

'Unfortunately,' Missy continued, 'permitted or not, if the snakes get so big they're not cute anymore, people tend to dump them into the Everglades.'

I was kind of stuck on her choice of 'cute' when describing snakes in general, but especially those that could realistically consider alligators 'snack-size.'

'Isn't that like ... I don't know, biological littering?'

'I suppose. And, maybe even worse, Hurricane Andrew back in 'ninety-two destroyed animal and reptile "breeding greenhouses" and pet stores, freeing their inhabitants. I've even heard there were panthers and monkeys and gazelles running free for a while. The panthers are encouraged – they're a native species and quite rare – but the rest of the animals were rounded up, supposedly.'

Supposedly. I knew where this was leading, unfortunately. 'But the pythons are still out there.'

'Yes, a nearly eight-foot female was caught recently and she had eighty-seven eggs inside her, can you believe that? I've heard that we could have tens of thousands – even a hundred thousand – pythons slithering around the Everglades these days.'

Missy looked west as I had, but kind of wistfully, I thought. 'It's very hard to be sure. What they do know is that reported sightings of white-tail deer have dropped by ninety-four percent, and the entire population of rabbits in the Everglades has been wiped out.'

Jesus. 'The pythons are eating them, too?'

'Yes, which you'd think would be good news for the alligators.'

'But it's not? Good news, I mean.'

'No. Alligators eat rabbits and deer – in addition to birds, turtles and fish, of course – so both the alligators themselves and their food supply have been affected by the pythons.'

Missy looked up from her work. 'Did you know that nearly sixteen-hundred people signed up to hunt Burmese pythons last year to bring down their numbers? But all those hunters managed to kill only sixty-eight in a month. Apparently pythons are slippery devils.'

Or their hunters didn't have enough incentive. 'Maybe they should send Fendi and Jimmy Choo in there after them,' I said.

'For designer handbags and such?' Missy looked thoughtful. 'In fact, a couple of local places are paying fifty or a hundred dollars a snake. After processing and all, a custom-made python purse can bring, like, twelve hundred dollars, shoes easily a thousand, and jackets nearly five thousand.'

Maybe I should go into the snake-catching

business – or better yet, processing. 'Word gets out and the pythons will be wiped out in no time.'

'That would be a very good thing,' Missy said absently, her attention seemingly back on the banner.

'I'm sure the alligators would appreciate it.' Not to mention Thumper. And Bambi.

'I'm sure they would,' Missy said, looking up, 'but I don't want you to think there aren't consequences for the pythons, too.'

'Beyond being turned into Giorgio Armani stilettos?'

'No, no,' Missy said, a little impatient with me. 'I was talking about the snakes eating alligators, especially after they've had a big meal of their own. If you go on YouTube you can probably pull up photos and even a video or two of some pythons that have exploded during the digestive process.'

Oh, my. In my head, I'd been visiting the designer shoe floor of Barney's – and actually being able to afford something – and here was Missy yanking me back to the smorgasbord that the Everglades had become.

And with thoughts of rabbit, inside alligator, inside python, no less. The concept of turducken – a de-boned chicken, stuffed into a de-boned duck, in turn stuffed into a de-boned turkey and baked – had always seemed exotic enough, without imagining the

Everglades own sushi version of the same. The one remaining comfort being that human beings weren't on the menu.

At least until the pythons ran out of rabbits, deer and alligators.

SIX

'If you want to get technical,' Missy Hudson snapped me out of my snake-themed reverie, 'pythons don't really eat their prey so much as crush it so they can swallow it whole and digest it.'

Lovely. 'And this differs from "eating" in what way?'

Missy looked up, apparently startled by the edge in my tone. 'Well, no chewing, of course.'

'Oh.'

'That's nothing, though. You want to know something really scary?'

I hadn't realized that what we'd already been talking about didn't qualify. 'Sure.'

'They've found a number of African rock pythons in the Everglades. Including a pregnant one.'

'And that's worse than a Burmese python?'
Or tens or hundreds of thousands of them?

'Oh, yes. The rock pythons are Africa's largest snake – over twenty feet long. And the fact one was pregnant means they're reproducing here.'

'And not-too-tightly-wrapped people kept those things as pets, too?'

'Yes, can you believe it? The herpetologist at the Florida Museum of Natural History in Gainesville said the species is so aggressive they come out of the egg striking. His theory is that breeders didn't expect them to be so vicious – and hence so unmarketable to consumers – that they released them into the wild, too. The fear is the African rocks will mate with the Burmese and spawn a large and powerful population of hybrids – like a kind of Super Python.'

Just gets better and better. 'You sure seem to know a lot about these creepy-crawlies.'

'Well, most Floridians who live near the Everglades have heard the news reports, or at least should have. Knowledge is power. Besides,' Missy was back to picking at the tape, 'I needed to research them for *Breaking and Entering*.'

'There's a snake in the book?' Other than the trouser variety, I meant.

'Well, yes. Rosemary wanted Kat, the umm, heroine to have an, umm ... encounter with one. Or was it two?' The corner of the tape came loose. 'Damn.'

The subject of our conversation had gone from bad to worse. It was one thing to exchange views with someone my own age, but Missy couldn't be more than six years older than my son Eric, who was in his second year of college.

'Why don't I hop up into the train and open the window?' I suggested. 'You can hand me the rope and I'll secure it to something.'

'That's a wonderful idea! This is the passenger car, so—'

In my haste to get away from the images in my own mind, I didn't wait to hear the rest of Missy's instructions.

Entering the train, I turned right and nearly ran into a broad-shouldered man. He was wearing a boxy three-piece suit with a gold watch chain, presumably leading to a pocket watch in the vest. 'Can I help you?' he said, holding open a sliding door into the next car.

'Oh, I'm sorry,' I said. 'I was just looking for the passenger car.'

'This is the club car,' he said, hiking a thumb behind him. 'I'll be serving coffee and espresso drinks in a few minutes.'

'So our Orient Espresso will really have espresso?' I asked, spotting a brewer on one of the bars.

'That's the plan. Though it's not ready yet.'

'Oh, not a problem. I'm actually working on setting up myself.' I glanced out the window and saw that Missy was sorting out the ropes on the banner. 'I'm Maggy, by the way.'

The big guy wiped his hand and shook mine. 'Boyce. Or,' he pointed to his badge, 'M Bouc – the head of the railroad.'

Ah, Boyce/Bouc. 'I understand you run the coffee concession at the hotel. I own a coffeehouse in Wisconsin and there's no way I'd have the nerve to try to serve espresso to this many people at once. I'm impressed.'

'Don't be. I'll have brewed coffee, but I sure can't do hot espresso to order, given the space restrictions and the fact there's also a full bar next to me.'

'So, the espresso machine is just a prop?'

'Not at all, though I have to admit I considered it,' Boyce/Bouc said with a wry smile. 'But Missy was so excited about the *Murder on the Orient Espresso* theme she came up with that I knew I had to work something out. My plan is to pull shots ahead and let them cool down for espresso martinis.'

'Pulling a shot' was our trade expression for grinding espresso, tamping it into a small filter and then brewing the shot.

Boyce was looking a bit embarrassed. 'Not

72

ideal, I know, quality-wise. But...'

'Hey,' I said, waving off his professional discomfort. 'I think it's brilliant.'

'Thank you. Where did you say your coffeehouse was?'

'Brookhills, Wisconsin. It's near Milwaukee.'

'Oh, sure, I know the area. I went to college in Madison,' he said, referring to the University of Wisconsin's flagship campus in the state's capitol. 'And my parents still live in Milwaukee. Maybe I've seen your place. Where is it, exactly?'

'Originally in Benson Plaza on the corner of Brookhill and Civic. These days we're in the old train depot.'

'Brookhills Junction? Great area, but I remember it being pretty much abandoned.'

'It was, but we've rehabbed the station, which is the westernmost stop for the new commuter train to Milwaukee.'

'Sweet,' Boyce said, recognizing the value of being able to serve five-dollar cups of coffee to bleary-eyed workers before they were fully awake. 'How long have you been open?'

'About two years.'

'Two locations in two years? I can't imagine having that kind of energy.'

'Believe me, it wasn't by choice. Our first place kind of collapsed.'

'Collapsed?'

'Yes, but we already knew we needed to relocate. Our landlord had decided not to renew our lease. That was before he had the run-in with the snow blower.'

'Snow blower?' Boyce repeated. 'What did he run into it with?'

'His head. But we think he was already dead.'

Boyce's eyes narrowed. 'Wait a second. Now don't tell me you own Uncommon Grounds.'

'Oh,' I said, surprised. 'So you *do* know it.'

'Only through my parents. Wasn't one of the owners found dead in a pool of skim milk the morning you opened your first place?'

'Well, yes, but—'

'And, just recently, a body in the basement of the new location?'

'Under the boarding platform, technically, but—'

I was interrupted by tapping from outside the train.

'I'm sorry,' I said, grateful for the interruption. 'I promised to help Missy hang the banner. Do let me know, though, if I can pitch in later with your espresso brewing or anything.'

'You bet.' He said it automatically, though his expression was more in the vein of, *Right about when hell freezes over.*

'Great.' I was all too aware that trying to explain would only make matters worse. The truth was that Uncommon Grounds had more skeletons in its closet – and other environs – than Boyce had already mentioned.

The coffee man cleared his throat, probably eager to get rid of me. 'Did you say you were going to the passenger car?'

I nodded.

'Dining is next,' he said, pointing toward the sliding door opposite the one he was standing in, 'and the passenger car beyond that.'

We were standing in a vestibule, kind of an airlock with a metal floor and a sliding door on each of the four walls. Two of the doors – the one Boyce was standing in and the slider he'd indicated I should use – led to the adjacent train cars. The other two were exits to the platform on both sides of the train.

The dining car was through the slider, just as Boyce had promised. Eight white-clothed tables with C-shaped banquettes faced the aisle, four on each side. At the far end of the car, another table held a sheet cake frosted to look like a man sleeping. A knife protruded from his chest and red decorating gel with sparkles had been used to simulate other slashes.

I paused to admire the effect. The knife

was real and had a brown staghorn handle, reminding me of a three-piece set that my grandmother had passed down to me. I pulled the knife up a bit and, sure enough, there was the same 'Hollow Ground Stainless Steel' stamp as the blade of my set. I'd managed to trace those knives back to the fifties. Well after the era of the book, certainly, but nonetheless, I thought it was a nice touch.

More tapping, increasing in insistence. I replaced the knife, but then turned back to swipe my finger across the cake frosting on the culinary victim's foot, where nobody would notice. I plopped the sweet icing in my mouth. It had been hours since Pavlik had bought me lunch and I was starving. Needless to say, with our last-minute hanky-panky under the blankie, we hadn't had time to grab a snack from the newsstand as he'd suggested.

Believe me, I wasn't regretting it. I'd take Pavlik over a granola bar anytime. Even a sandwich.

Through the next vestibule, I found a regular passenger car with rows of seats. At the end of that car was a restroom. Stopping just short of it, I slid open the window.

'Sorry,' I called out to Missy. 'I stopped to introduce myself to Boyce.'

She passed me the rope. 'No need to apologize. You're helping, after all. And as a guest, you should be relaxing. I'm sorry I got a little impatient with you before.'

The girl obviously had no idea of the heights – or depths – I'd seen true impatience reach.

I caught a glimpse of Pavlik walking toward the platform with Zoe, each carrying something in one hand. Behind them was a gaggle of what I guessed to be writers, probably eager to pick the sheriff's brains about gore and mayhem. I told myself that wasn't the part of Pavlik I was most interested in.

At least not this weekend.

'It's nice to have something to do, since I'm a little out of my element here.' I opened the next window and tied the rope around the post between them with a double knot. It wouldn't get me a merit badge, but it should hold. 'How's that?'

'Genius,' Missy said. 'Will you be able to close the window, or at least nearly so? I'd hate for it to get too hot in there.'

What a difference a few hours and fifteen hundred miles can make. In Wisconsin on the first day of November, you'd slam the window to keep out the cold air. Here it was the opposite.

'Good idea. That way the rope will be more secure anyway.' I slid down one of the windows to prove it. 'Is that far enough?'

'Perfect,' Missy said.

I moved a few rows forward and tied the other end of the banner the same way. By the time we had the banner secure people were already boarding the train, which made the point moot, when you thought about it. I mean, once everybody was on the train and we were in the Everglades, nobody would be able to appreciate the legend on the banner. And I didn't think the alligators and pythons – whether they were Burmese or African rock – would need help identifying us as boxed-car lunches. Or dinners, adjusting for the time of day.

'I have to take tickets,' Missy was saying through the open window, 'and hand these out.'

She held up a playbill, sepia-toned, so as to seem older. 'See? The cast of characters is on this side and,' flipping it, 'here's the diagram of the train.'

I took the playbill through the window. 'Very clever. If I remember right, the book had a diagram, too.'

'Correct. I'm not sure how readers could have kept the plot straight without a cheat sheet. Our diagram shows this little train, of course, not Christie's Orient Express. I've put "Murder on the Orient Espresso" here, see? I think the playbill will make a nice keepsake, don't you?'

'I do,' I said honestly. Missy had pulled out all the stops to make tonight a success. I hoped, for her sake, people took notice. I offered the playbill back to her.

'No, no – you can have the very first one.'

'Thank you.' I smiled and tucked the souvenir in my non-python skin handbag. For the first time in a long while, I had a hankering to do events again. Even if you're not on Broadway, opening night of anything presented to the public is a rush. 'But can I help you with the tickets and all?'

'Oh, no, I'll be fine.' Missy said, waving me off. 'But thank you so much and please – after you close this window – do mingle and enjoy yourself. These are fun people. And, who knows? Maybe by the end of the week-end you'll decide to kill someone.'

My face must have betrayed my thought.

Missy Hudson giggled, suddenly realizing. 'Fictionally, of course!'

SEVEN

Making my way up to the front of the train, I found Pavlik already in the dining car, sitting in one of the C-shaped booths. Zoe, naturally, was butt-to-buns next to him.

'Join us,' he said, waving me to slide in on his other side.

I was about to when I noticed that they both had drinks in front of them. 'Wait, where'd you get the wine?'

'There's a bar next door to the station,' Pavlik said. 'I'm sorry – did you want a glass?'

Did I want a glass of wine? Exactly how long had this man known me?

'Not a problem,' I fibbed. 'Do I still have time to hop off and get myself one?'

'Certainly,' Zoe said, before turning back to Pavlik and ignoring me. 'That's fascinating. As county sheriff—'

I didn't bother to hear more, despite my fascination with her sucking up. Instead I tried to thread my way to the nearest exit through the gaggle of people still boarding.

'You're not helping things, swimming against the tide like that,' Princess Dragomiroff, aka Prudence said. She was pushing up the bracelets on her sleeves like she wanted to sock someone. I hoped it wasn't me.

'I'm sorry.' I gave up and allowed myself to go with the flow. 'I just wanted to jump off and grab a glass of wine before we leave.'

'I wouldn't chance it if I were you,' Prudence said. 'Zoe told me we were leaving at precisely eight p.m. and it's just past that now. Once they fire up this baby, anyone not onboard will be left behind.'

'But she's the one who told me I had time,' I protested.

'I'll bet she did.' Prudence nodded toward the booth where Pavlik and Zoe still sat, heads together. 'The bar in the club car just opened and if I were you, I'd get whatever crap they're serving and hightail it back before our host inhales that sheriff of yours alive.'

I decided to take Prudence's advice. It required me to push my way past the exit to the front car, but at least I wouldn't risk getting off and being left behind.

Unfortunately, I wasn't the only one in search of libations. In fact, the line for the lone bartender was past Boyce/Bouc's espresso bar and out onto the platform. This

81

seemed a problem in light of both Prudence's warning and the 'All aboard!' that somebody was shouting.

As I moved to the end of the line, a crack of thunder echoed. 'That bitch would have left me here in the rain,' I muttered under my breath.

'I'm sorry?' Markus/MacQueen stood on the platform.

'I just said "the ... weather's a bitch."'

'Sure you did.' With a grin he stepped back and waved for me to get in line in front of him.

'Thank you, but there's no need. I'll just get a coffee for now.'

'All aboard!' again.

I beckoned. 'We'd better get on before the train starts to move.'

'You think the bitch will leave us in the rain?' Markus flashed me a grin.

I smiled sheepishly as he and I both part pushed and part edged our way into the train vestibule.

With multiple apologies and explanations, I continued on, bypassing the queue for the bar to get to the espresso station where there was no line at all.

I hesitated, not sure how welcome I'd be given our earlier conversation, but Boyce greeted me like an old friend – a sure sign he was bored. 'I'm afraid it's going to be a long night. Pete's doing gangbuster business, though. I'm thinking I should give him a hand rather than standing here twiddling my thumbs.'

'Pete is the bartender?' I asked, taking in the dark blue uniform the good-looking young man was wearing.

'Not really, but that's what Missy is calling him. He's also the conductor.'

'What?' I didn't get it.

Boyce laughed. 'Missy needed a bartender who could play "Pierre Michel," conductor of the Orient Express. Tomorrow, Pete/Pierre Michel goes back to being Brandon, a server at the Olive Garden.'

Pete, it was. 'Do you want to help him while I staff the coffee bar for you?'

'I think I will, but there's no need for you to stay. If somebody does show up, I can always slide over and handle it.'

Old friend, perhaps, but this man had no intention of letting me get near his equipment.

Which was fine, I reminded myself. This was my vacation, after all. 'I'm sure there'll be a stampede for coffee once the cake is cut.'

'That's not going to be until after the program,' Boyce said. 'In the meantime, can I get you liquored up on an espresso martini and you can show these people what they're missing?'

'Gladly. And better make it a double.'

'Yes, ma'am. Double espresso or double vodka?'

'Both, please,' I said as Boyce tipped the espresso shot into the plastic martini glass. 'Do you know what kind of program is planned? Are we going to get clues and skulk around questioning suspects?'

A shake of the head. 'I'm not sure how elaborate it's going to be,' Boyce said, adding the clear alcohol. 'Missy told me her boss was willing to go along with the theme, but pointed out that the majority of the people – who are repeat attendees – would want to have a drink and catch up with each other on the first night.'

'Well, she's certainly right about the drink part,' I said as the train lurched away from the station. I was relieved to see that, though the exit door was still open, nobody was marooned on the platform. 'Let's hope the engineer goes slowly enough that we don't lose anyone.'

'I believe "slow" is part of the arrangement, given the train route isn't officially open yet. I have my fingers crossed we don't run into something unexpected.'

'You've heard about the pythons?' Apparently Missy wasn't overblowing this, either.

'Oh, yes. It's a real problem. Whipped

cream?' Boyce held the spray can poised over my incipient drink.

'Load me up,' I said, sliding over a twenty. 'I hate snakes.'

He laughed, stuck a swizzle stick in my drink and slid the twenty back. 'My treat. One professional to another. And don't worry about the wildlife. They're out there and we're safe in here.'

'Thanks, for both the drink and the re-assurance,' I said, raising the former. 'Let me know if you need help.'

'Will do,' Boyce said, sounding like he actually meant it this time. 'And have fun.'

'Hey, gigantic reptiles that eat each other, an untested train track, and a storm raging toward us?' I turned with my double-double, finishing over my shoulder with, 'If that doesn't spell fun, what does?'

EIGHT

Getting back to the dining car, I stepped inside its door. Zoe Scarlett was still to Pavlik's left on the banquette, but Rosemary Darlington and Laurence Potter had joined them. Potter was seated next to Zoe and Rosemary was on the other side of Pavlik, effectively putting her diagonally as far away from Potter as possible.

Bookended by the two most important men at her conference, Zoe was understandably incandescent. I wanted to smack her one upside the head.

This despite knowing full well I should be more threatened by Rosemary Darlington. As the author of the most erotic work of popular fiction since *Fifty Shades of Grey*, she'd certainly know all the moves. Still, the woman managed to come across as a class act.

As the 'Mary Debenham' of the book, Rosemary was wearing a light gray coatdress. The vintage garment crossed over at the front, forming a 'V,' like Zoe's, but in contrast to the red wrap Rosemary's dress was entirely risqué-free. A row of demure buttons fastened the panels of the dress, supported from below by a belt at her waist. The fullish sleeves of the dress ended in bands just below the elbow and, on her head, she wore a matching beret.

As I drew even with the banquette, Potter was talking. 'I'm not saying, Rosemary, that you haven't done all of us a service by ... shall we say, enlivening our sex lives? I have to admit that even I learned a trick or two from your book.'

'How lovely,' Rosemary said with a tight smile. 'Shall I expect a thank-you note from your wife?'

Good deal. I may have missed the preliminary bouts, but it appeared I was still in time for the main event. Setting my espresso martini on the table, I slid in next to our female guest of honor.

'Big enough for you?' Pavlik was nodding at my drink.

'No, but it was as much as the glass would hold.' I clamped on the plastic stem as the train swayed and picked up speed.

'What *is* that?' Rosemary Darlington asked. Her tone didn't convey disdain so much as envy. Rosemary didn't have a glass in front of her, but looked like she could use one. Our female guest of honor was a tad green.

The way the tables and banquettes were set up – in that 'C' shape with the open ends facing the aisle – Pavlik was sitting dead center and therefore sideways to the motion of the train, with Zoe and Potter facing forward on one side of the semicircle and Rosemary and myself facing backward.

'This?' I said, gesturing toward my glass. 'An espresso martini.' Then, lowering my voice, 'Do you think if you sit on the other side, the motion of the train will be easier to tolerate?' I nodded toward the patch of unoccupied bench next to Potter.

'Thank you,' Rosemary said, matching my tone. 'But I'd rather projectile vomit.'

I laughed and took a sip of my drink.

Just then Missy came by. 'Oh, our signature cocktail! I love how you're embracing the theme, Maggy.'

If all it took to 'embrace the theme' was to imbibe caffeine and alcohol, I was her poster girl. I flicked my tongue to lick cream off my upper lip.

'Speaking of *Murder on the Orient Express* – or *Espresso*, I should say,' Missy continued, virtually chirping like a bluebird and tentatively settling on the very edge of the bench to Potter's left, 'can we talk about our program?'

'Excuse me, my dear,' Laurence Potter

interrupted, 'but would you mind standing? I find my left knee aches if I can't extend it.'

Looking mortified, Missy jumped up and tugged at her evening dress. 'Oh, I'm sorry. I just—'

'No harm done, I'm sure.' Potter flexed his legs and extended them into the aisle, the multicolored toes of his wing-tip shoes ducking under the white cloth of the table across from us.

'Somebody's going to trip over Gumby's legs and sue,' I murmured automatically. One of the reasons I'd been happy to leave my role as events manager behind and open a coffeehouse was to escape the stress of being responsible for the safety and well-being of people who couldn't be trusted to behave responsibly.

Rosemary giggled. 'Gumby. Good one.' She had my martini in her hands.

I thought about reclaiming the drink but figured our female guest of honor needed it more than I did.

'Pardon me?' As if the vodka gods had heard me, Boyce, our onboard barista, was in the doorway behind me. But before I could order an espresso martini to replace the one Rosemary had commandeered, he said, 'Missy? There's someone who needs to speak with you.'

Missy, who'd been awkwardly standing in

the aisle downstream of Potter's long, un-
gainly legs, looked grateful for the interruption. 'Of course.'

She stepped over Potter's wheels and kept
right on going, Boyce on her silvery heels.

As the vestibule door to the club car slid
closed, I caught a glimpse of Potter's 'sycophant,' Danny/Col. Arbuthnot, talking to a
blonde woman I'd not seen earlier.

'Damnation,' Potter said, both hands
reaching into his jacket, one pulling out a
pack of cigarettes and the other a striking
black and silver book of matches.

'No smoking,' I snapped as Potter knocked
a coffin nail out of the pack. If I wasn't going
to get my drink, he sure as hell wasn't going
to enjoy *his* vice at our second-hand expense.

'What?'

'I said, no smoking is allowed inside the
train cars.' Technically, I didn't know if that
was true. But if not, it should be.

'Fine.' Laurence Potter dropped the loose
cigarette and its pack back into his pocket,
leaving the matchbook on the table's surface. 'I can't smoke and there's nothing to
eat but that ridiculous cake. And even that,
only after,' – air quotes – '"the crime is
solved." What, pray tell, am I supposed to
do until then?'

'Chat with attendees and be pleasant?'
This from Rosemary Darlington. 'Seems the

least you can do, given we are both being paid a fee for being here.'

Potter turned on her. 'And exactly who would you have me "chat" with? You?'

'Heavens, no. But perhaps that hero-worshipping mop-haired boy you seem to be avoiding.'

'Ridiculous,' Potter said. 'And I'll thank you to mind your own business, Rosemary.' He turned away from us.

If they *had* been lovers, they'd certainly perfected the 'quarrel' part.

'You seem to have struck a nerve with him,' I whispered to Darlington, who had simply smiled and gone back to her – or *my* – drink.

'I did, didn't I?' Rosemary was obviously pleased with herself. 'To be honest, I'm not sure what Larry has against the kid, but I'm happy to needle him, regardless.'

I resisted the urge to probe further into the Potter/Darlington milieu. 'So you've never seen Danny before?'

'Danny? Oh, the kid himself? No.' Rosemary was absently swirling what was left of my martini in its picnic-quality glass, like it was crystal from the Reidel collection. 'Maybe Larry's planning on stealing his book and foisting it off as his own. You know, like Agatha Christie's play, *Mousetrap*.'

'I think you mean Sidney Lumet's film, *Deathtrap*.'

She drained my glass and set it down. 'Christopher Reeve, Dyan Cannon, Michael Caine?'

'Yes, that's *Deathtrap*. I can understand your confusion, though, given the title and the fact that Lumet also directed Christie's *Murder on the Orient Express*. That was 1974, though, and *Deathtrap* was 1984, based on Ira Levin's play by the same name.'

Rosemary waggled her finger. 'Washed-up playwright decides to kill aspiring writer and stage his play as his own?'

'That's the one,' I said. 'Though the twists and—'

'Excuse me.' Missy was standing in the aisle behind my shoulder.

I turned.

'Surprise!' A blonde woman in a fur jacket nearly identical to Missy's – except this one looked more fox than faux – jumped out theatrically from behind her. I was fairly certain it was the same blonde I'd glimpsed through the door when Missy had answered Boyce's summons.

Laurence Potter's feet retracted like the Wicked Witch of the West's after Dorothy squibs the ruby slippers. 'Audra! Uh – my dear! Whatever are you doing here?'

I swiveled my head to Rosemary. 'Don't tell me.'

'You got it.' Rosemary lifted and tipped my

glass before tapping on the base to dredge the dregs. Then, 'All passengers, fasten your seat belts for Act Two. Wifey's here.'

NINE

'You didn't really think I'd miss your 'guest of honor' stint, did you?' The new arrival kissed Laurence Potter on the cheek and perched awkwardly on the sliver of bench Missy had vacated earlier. 'Do slog over, my love, so I have some room.'

His face capturing the concepts of gloom and doom in one portrait, Potter obliged, starting a chain reaction counterclockwise, which ended with me. I stuck out my hand. 'I'm Maggy Thorsen. And you must be Mrs Potter?'

I got an icy look and a cold hand for my efforts. '*Mrs* Potter is Larry's mother. I'm his wife, Audra Edmonds.'

'A pleasure.' I'm sure.

'Hello, Audra – this really *is* a surprise,' Zoe said. 'Wherever have you been hiding?'

'Do you mean in general? I do have a job, you know, so I'm not free to travel to *all* of Larry's book events. Though I have to admit

I learn something new each time I do.' She gave our other guest of honor a significant look.

Rosemary, my double-down martini probably making serious inroads on her consciousness, just shrugged.

From the exchange, I assumed Audra knew about whatever relationship Rosemary and Potter had enjoyed in the past. And maybe 'surprising' her husband was Audra's way of staying abreast of any new potential dalliances.

As if she'd read my thoughts, Zoe pulled her gaping wrap dress demurely together over her own breasts.

Audra idly picked up the pack of matches Potter had left on the table. 'But if you're asking, Zoe, where I was hiding, literally? The bartender – a lovely young hard-body named Pete or Pierre or something on his nametag – was kind enough to let me stow away to surprise Larry.'

She gave her husband a rather over-the-top adoring look. 'And you *were* surprised, weren't you, my love?'

There was something about the woman that reminded me of an early Katherine Hepburn. Even when Hepburn played a softer role, you sensed her strength.

'I certainly was,' Potter said, putting an arm around her shoulder and giving it a squeeze. 'You are my rock, and I must say you've gotten into the spirit of the occasion beautifully.'

'My outfit, you mean? Well, thank you. Even if you don't read your emails,' she surveyed her husband's lack of costume, 'I do. Though apparently,' she gestured toward Missy, who hadn't moved, 'is it...'

'Missy.' The girl nodded.

'Yes, well, apparently Missy and I had the same idea.' Audra shrugged out of her coat, revealing a period dress of deep blue silk chiffon, the waist cinched in and defined by crisscrossed ribbons. The skirt fell from a low inverted 'V' into what we now call a handkerchief bottom, but I had a feeling this was, like Rosemary's, a genuinely vintage dress. 'Coming as the fabulous Mrs Hubbard, that is.'

Missy gulped. 'I ... we did. Can I make you a nametag?'

'No need,' Audra said. 'I won't be mixing much, and the only people I care to know of my presence have already been informed.'

'All right.' Missy drew herself up. 'Zoe? Would this be a good time to talk about the program?'

'Program?' Zoe, on Potter's right, looked a bit adrift.

For his part, I wondered how Potter felt about being sandwiched between his 'rock'

95

and a potential new 'hard place.'

'Yes.' Missy seemed undeterred by her boss's marked lack of enthusiasm. 'I know you'll want to welcome everyone. You can use that intercom.'

She pointed toward the vestibule at the front of our car. 'After that, Markus – *not* as 'MacQueen' – will give a short talk on Agatha Christie's body of work and loads of lore. Once everybody's absorbed that, Mr Pavlik – sorry, I mean, Jake – Zoe will give you a signal. That's your cue to sneak into the first roomette on the left in the sleeping car at the back of the train. Oh, and assume the position of corpse.'

She giggled and I joined in to support the events woman, since you could cut the tension – or maybe bored disinterest was more accurate – with a blunter instrument than Missy's cake knife.

My stomach chose that moment to growl and Rosemary Darlington helped out by dropping her head on my shoulder. As the beret fell off her head and into my lap, our female guest of honor let out a snore.

'Oh, dear,' Missy said. 'It must be the Dramamine.'

'With a booster shot of my espresso martini.' I was craning my neck to confirm, indeed, that the illustrious author was drooling on my sundress.

'Perhaps Rosemary should take a little nap,' Missy suggested.

'Perhaps Rosemary already *is* taking a little nap,' Laurence Potter mimicked.

'Now, now, Larry. Be nice,' Audra Edmonds scolded her husband. Then, to Missy: 'Is there anything we can do?'

'Not really,' Missy said. 'If Maggy will just help me with Rosemary?'

'Of course.' I picked up Rosemary's hat and slid out, careful not to let her topple face-first into the banquette seat.

Our female guest of honor roused. 'Huh?'

'Dramamine and vodka apparently don't mix,' I said to her. 'Why don't we go and let you sleep it off?'

'Okey-dokey.' The woman slid out and stood up, albeit swaying. As I clamped on her left arm, a gust of wind hit the side of the train, driving rain against the windows.

'Storm's here,' I said, stating the obvious while trying to stabilize Rosemary.

'Oh, dear.' Missy had grabbed Rosemary's right arm. 'Laurence, if you could just lead everyone back to the sleeping car after Jake has been gone five minutes?'

'Why would I do that?'

Missy blinked. 'Well, because you're Hercule Poirot. You don't need to do much – just stroke your mustache as you solve the crime. I brought a fake one,' she dropped what

97

looked like a woolly caterpillar on the table, 'but you don't—'

'Solve the crime?' the critic repeated. 'Who among us hasn't read the novel, after all? We certainly don't need to reenact it. Don't you think that's a little childish ... is it Melissa?'

For the second time on the trip so far, Missy looked like she was going to cry.

I slid the mustache toward Pavlik. 'It's Missy, Larry. And if you'd prefer – and it's all right with Missy, of course – I'm sure Sheriff Pavlik would be happy to play the part of Poirot. You might prefer the role of Ratchett.'

Potter's eyes narrowed. 'The victim? I think not. Besides, I'm happy to pay homage to Dame Christie. She stood the test of time without prostituting herself. Unlike some writers any of us could mention.'

I felt Rosemary Darlington stiffen. 'And what do you mean by that?' was what I thought she said, though it came out more 'Mmmmoooomeeedat.'

'I'm sure Laurence didn't mean anything, Rosemary,' Missy said quickly. 'He—'

'I'm perfectly capable of speaking for myself,' Potter overrode her. 'Your new book, Rosemary, is not only pornography, but badly written, ineptly imagined pornography at that.'

'Larry!' This from his wife, of all people. I wondered how much of Potter's outburst was to convince Audra that he was no longer interested in Rosemary Darlington.

'I can't help it, my dear,' Potter said. 'This woman has – or *had* – talent, and she's gone and flushed it down the toilet.'

Rosemary shook off Missy and me, grabbed her beret and replaced it on her head. Almost.

'You know what happened to me, Larry? *You* did. Your criticism destroyed my confidence. I won't ever let anyone – and especially *you* – do that to me again.'

And with that, Rosemary Darlington stalked alone, and unsteadily, toward the back of the train.

TEN

Missy Hudson, cheeks flaming, followed Darlington.

Zoe Scarlett cleared her throat. 'Well, well. If you can let me out, Larry and Audra, I need to welcome our attendees and introduce the players.'

Whatever she was taking to stay so calm, I wanted some. I eyed my martini glass, which only served to remind me that it had been drained earlier by our female guest of honor in absentia.

Audra Edmonds stood up in the aisle, followed by Potter, who snagged the matchbook as he did so. Our hostess emerged and went to the front, where she slid open the vestibule door, amplifying the track noise, and appeared to push a button on the wall.

'Hello, mystery writers!' came through the sound system as I retook my seat and Audra Edmonds slid back in across from us. 'I'm Zoe Scarlett and I am so pleased to welcome you all to the first event of our glorious weekend, "Murder on the Orient Espresso."'

Applause, though sparse and, to my ear, jaded.

'As those of you who are Floridians may already have noticed, we are *not* heading north to Palm Beach nor south to Miami, but *west* on the new excursion spur into the Everglades. So much spookier, don't you think?'

As if the heavens had heard, there was a crack of thunder. Everyone applauded again, this time more enthusiastically, except for me. I shivered.

'Of course, the extra bonus,' Zoe continued, 'is that we won't be sharing our route with the Tri-Rail commuter train and Amtrak. No, no, we have these tracks all to ourselves. That's important, you see, because we have a *murder* to solve.'

Cue dramatic music, literally. The guy in the checkered jacket who had been seated behind us in the bus piped up with the Dragnet '*Bmmmm, bmp-bmp-bmp*' from the table next to Zoe.

'Thank you for the accompaniment,' she managed with a forced smile. 'I'd like to introduce our featured players for the evening, which you'll also find on your playbill.' She held up Missy's sepia-toned handout. 'And do feel free to ask participants to sign them as a remembrance of tonight's inaugural event.'

Heads nodded in approval of what I suspected was Missy's good idea. I feared, though, that given the number of people attending and the players listed, there weren't many fans/audience members on the train beyond the cast itself.

'First,' Zoe continued, 'as Mary Debenham, our guest of honor, Rosemary Darlington.'

Genuine applause, even though Rosemary Darlington was nowhere to be seen. Wherever she was, though, I trusted she was snoring and drooling blissfully.

Zoe plunged on. And not a bad strategy, since people listening to her in the other cars would assume Rosemary was in ours and

101

vice versa.

'And, as Hercule Poirot, our second guest of honor, mystery reviewer and critic extraordinaire, Laurence ... Potter.'

Applause, this time more tepid.

Not that it mattered. Potter/Poirot was nowhere to be seen, either.

'This is going well,' I whispered to Pavlik. I kept my voice down so Audra, the un-Mrs Potter across our booth, couldn't hear. I probably didn't need to worry, since Edmonds was pushing buttons on her phone and looking frustrated. I hoped she'd forgotten to charge it.

'What do you expect?' Pavlik asked in my ear. 'This isn't a "Maggy Thorsen" production.'

'For which I'm very grateful, since this threatens to become a train wreck.' Maybe I really *had* jinxed Missy's event with my earlier thoughts on enjoying train wrecks. 'Not literally, of course,' I added, hoping to undo any psychic damage.

Pavlik gave my shoulder a squeeze. 'Don't lose hope. The evening's young yet.'

At 'yet,' we hit a dip, sending me bouncing up off the banquette.

Zoe Scarlett droned on. '...our other players. As MacQueen, please welcome our Agatha Christie expert, Markus, um...'

A roar went up and Markus waved from

the table next to us. Zoe went on to introduce, sans last names, Grace as Greta Ohlsson, the Swedish Lady, germaphobic literary agent Carson as Count Andrenyi, Prudence as Princess Dragomiroff, somebody named Big Fred as Foscarelli, and Harvey – the guy in the loud sports jacket – as Hardman.

I noticed that besides not knowing her longtime conference attendees' last names without the aid of the badges she'd harangued Missy about, Zoe didn't bother introducing the help: Boyce as Bouc, the director of the railroad, and Pete the bartender as Pierre Michel, the conductor depicted in Christie's *Murder on the Orient Express.*

Missy slid into the seat next to me, wiping her hands on a paper towel. She also looked like she'd put on lipstick and combed her hair for the occasion.

'Is Rosemary all right?' I asked.

'Sleeping like a baby,' Missy said, head directed toward the towel in her hands. 'It's probably for the best.'

'The best for your event. No question.'

'And now,' Zoe was saying, 'a special and heartfelt thank you to someone who has gone above and beyond for us. As Mrs Hubbard, played so elegantly by Lauren Bacall in the movie, I give you...'

Missy's head jerked up, her face shining.

She slid over to the aisle and dropped the paper towel on the table, preparing to be introduced.

'Audra Edmonds!'

'You had to have seen that coming,' Pavlik said as I nursed the new espresso martini he'd brought me as Markus took over for his talk on Agatha Christie. 'Nothing has gone right for poor Missy.'

'Through no fault of her own,' I pointed out. 'And what did go well will be ignored anyway. That's the plight of the special event planner.' I sighed and gazed into my whipped cream.

'Poor baby,' Pavlik commiserated. 'Good thing you've left behind the drudgery for the exciting new world of coffee.' He nodded toward my martini. 'How is that, by the way?'

'Delicious, thank you. And your wine?'

'Awful, but if I switch I'll be sleeping it off next to Rosemary Darlington.'

'Ah, no, you won't, actually,' I said, swiping a finger into the whipped cream and offering it to Pavlik. 'That woman knows too many moves.'

'So I hear.' Pavlik licked the cream off my finger.

Engagingly slowly.

I gave a little shiver. And, happily, not

because I was either cold or scared. In fact, it might be raining cats and dogs, alligators and pythons outside, but inside the train it was comfortable and I was here beside my sheriff.

Life was good. I sighed.

'Something wrong?' Pavlik asked.

I laid my head on his shoulder and closed my eyes. 'Not a thing.'

I should have known it couldn't last.

ELEVEN

'Excuse me,' a voice said.

I opened my eyes to see Danny/Col. Arbuthnot's name badge sidle into sight. Tilting my head, I saw the tousled dark head.

'Danny.' I sat up and self-consciously slid the spaghetti straps of my sundress back onto my shoulder like we'd just been caught making out in the back seat of a Chevy. 'Have you met Sheriff Pavlik?'

'Jake, please,' Pavlik corrected.

'Jake,' I repeated. I wasn't used to all this first-name stuff. In fact, given Pavlik's position as Brookhills County Sheriff, I made a real effort to use his title when addressing him in front of others, especially his deputies.

'Thank you, Jake.' Close up, the young man looked older than I'd thought earlier, maybe mid-twenties. 'And please, call me Danny.'

'Danny it is.' Pavlik turned to me. 'And, obviously, you two have already met?'

'I don't believe so.' Danny's matte brown eyes showed no recognition.

'The coffeehouse owner?' I reminded him. He squinted at me.

'I told you I wasn't a writer?' I tried.

'Oh, yes.' Danny turned back to Pavlik. 'Well, it's a real honor to meet you, sir. I'm looking forward to your workshop tomorrow on "How to Kill Realistically with Guns, Knives and Bare Hands."'

'That's the name of your panel?' I asked Pavlik.

'They edited it. My title was longer.'

Figured. So many weapons, so little time.

'And it's a workshop, not a panel,' Danny corrected, this time. '"Hands-on," the program says.'

'I'll be calling up volunteers and demonstrating some techniques,' Pavlik said, looking pleased by the younger man's enthusiasm.

For my part, I was imagining myself – a convenient 'volunteer' – being tossed around like a crash-test dummy. Maybe I'd sleep in tomorrow morning. Catch Pavlik's second panel. 'What's the other one you're doing?'

'"The Ins and Outs of Firearms,"' Danny supplied eagerly. 'All about guns and ammunition. And entrance and exit wounds, of course.'

Even better. The hotel probably had a nice pool. I'd hide there.

'You'd be surprised,' Pavlik said, 'at the number of mistakes in books – or in television and even movies, too. And it's not complicated stuff. Simple terminology, or the difference between a semi-automatic and a revolver.'

Danny was nodding. 'The protagonist of the last book I read – or tried to read, I should say – put a silencer on a revolver.'

Pavlik looked skyward. 'See what I mean? That's as bad as a having a revolver that ejects brass.'

'Everybody knows that it's semi-automatics not revolvers that eject casings.'

'And, of course, that revolvers can't be silenced.'

The two men – and I bestow that mantle of maturity loosely – cackled at the stupidity of it all.

'I understand you've written a book,' I said

to Danny, trying to participate in the conversation. 'What's it about?'

'I'm afraid it's much too complicated to describe at a gathering like this,' he said, dismissing me again.

'Well, then it's much "too complicated" to sell, as well.' Zoe Scarlett slid onto the bench Audra Edmonds had abandoned after her introduction. 'If you can't describe your book, how do you expect publishers to categorize it and wholesalers and booksellers to display and sell it?'

'Then I'll publish it myself,' Danny said. 'Ebooks and on-demand publishing have changed the world for authors.'

'You're absolutely right,' Zoe said. 'But with something like a quarter of a million books being self-published a year, how is anyone going to find yours?'

'Because I'm good.' Danny's face was sullen, like a five-year-old who's been told he can't have a cookie before dinner.

'Yeah, you and two-hundred and forty-nine thousand, nine hundred and ninety-nine other authors who think the same thing.'

Disheartening words, I thought, from someone whose own conference was dedicated toward teaching people to write and, presumably, get published.

'But there obviously are success stories,' I

pointed out. 'I've seen books on the *New York Times* bestsellers list that are obviously self-published. The authors' names and the publishers' names are the same.'

'Sure, it can happen,' Zoe said. 'But lightning has to strike. Even today, with all this opportunity, books become bestsellers the same way they always have. One person likes a book and tells somebody else. The only thing that has changed is the medium used to have the conversation.'

Pavlik grinned. 'Zoe does a panel on changes in the publishing industry.'

'And another thing,' she continued her rant. 'Even if you self-publish, you need to come up with a pithy hook. One sentence that sells your book in the time it takes us to scroll on by. What's yours?' She stabbed a finger at Danny.

The boy's eyes widened. 'Well, I—'

'*That's* what you'll learn this weekend,' Zoe finished triumphantly. 'Now, go do your homework.'

'You've got a tough-love approach to promoting your conference,' I said, watching Danny slink, chastened, toward the passenger car.

'Can't coddle these writers.' Her head was swiveling like a lighthouse beacon. 'If you want something, you have to go out and get it.'

Which, of course, raised the question of what something – or *somebody* – she wanted.

I slid my hand off the table and onto Pavlik's thigh slowly, so Zoe would notice.

He glanced at me before asking, 'Umm, are you looking for somebody, Zoe?

'Larry,' she said. 'I *told* him I was going to introduce our players.'

Which was most likely why the man had disappeared.

'The last I saw of Potter was when he got up and stepped back to let you out,' Pavlik said, laying his hand on top of mine. 'He didn't pass us to go forward to the club car, so he must have headed toward the back of the train.'

'Well, we'd better find him before Missy's "program" starts. Thank God Markus can be counted on to drone on and on.'

The librarian was still at the intercom, presenting his talk.

'Larry's probably in the bathroom,' I suggested. 'Has Audra seen him?'

'No,' Zoe said. 'And he's been gone for half an hour.'

I shrugged. 'Maybe he took his magazine in there with him. He's obviously quite the reader.'

'Huh.' Zoe seemed to be thinking it over. 'Perhaps I should go tap on the door.'

Pavlik watched her leave. 'Was that a

thinly-veiled knock on male bathroom habits?'

'Hey,' I said, smiling, 'if the stool fits.'

Pavlik laughed and raised my hand to kiss the palm. 'You're one twisted woman, Maggy Thorsen.'

'Not as "twisted" as I'd like to be,' I said, sliding even closer. 'Bet even Rosemary doesn't have any wings in her boo—'

'Have you seen Zoe?' Prudence was standing at our table now, fingers twisting in the ropes of princess pearls around her neck. 'Missy is going batshit because she can't find Larry.'

And these people called themselves *mystery* writers? The train was four cars long, not counting the locomotives – first and last – so how tough could it be to find someone?

I had a thought. 'Maybe Larry's standing in one of the vestibules between cars smoking. I saw him grab the matches when he got up from our table.'

'Great,' Prudence said. 'Markus is done with his soliloquy and we're all supposed to gather here in the dining car before trooping back to solve the crime. Wait a minute.' She squinted at Pavlik's nametag. '"Ratchett." Aren't you supposed to be dead?'

'Zoe didn't give me the—'

'Well she *should* have,' Prudence said, looking more like the imperious Princess

Dragomiroff. 'How are we supposed to view the body in the sleeping car if you're out here, obviously still alive?'

'Well, I don't know. I—'

Raucous laughter erupted from across the way. Grace/Greta was trying to climb up onto the table in a manner not befitting her role. In fact, the blouse and skirt somehow invoked more Naughty School Girl than Swedish Lady.

'Damn it,' Prudence said. 'We need to get some food into these people.'

'There's cake,' I said, watching Grace gain her footing and release her hair from its bun, shaking out the wild curls like Raquel Welch in *One Million Years B.C.*

'To be served when the crime is solved, from what I understand,' Pavlik said. 'Though maybe if you ask Missy—'

'Any sign of Laurence?' It was Missy herself, magically appearing but looking concerned.

'No, but Zoe went to check the bathroom,' I said.

'I've already done that.' Tears were welling up in Missy's eyes again. I couldn't help feeling sorry for her. 'Twice.'

'OK, let's look at this logically,' Pavlik said. 'He has to be in one of these cars. You're just missing him because people are milling around.'

A whoop came from the unincorporated mob as Grace slid butt-first off the table.

'We're coming to a stop already,' Missy said as Prudence shook her head in disgust. 'Now the rear locomotive will pull us back the same direction we came from.'

Since there were no lights outside to judge our speed by, I had to take her word for it.

'So, are there two engineers, or does the guy in front have to come through the train to get to the other locomotive?'

'Oh, dear,' Missy said, putting her hand to her face. 'There *is* no interior connection. Our engineer is a lovely older man – retired, in fact, and a bit eccentric. He'll have to go out in this rain and wind. We didn't think of that.'

'Would you like me to go out and check on him?' Pavlik asked.

'That's so kind of you.' Missy was trying to peer out the window. 'I'd be afraid, though, that you'd miss him somehow and accidentally be left behind. The Everglades is a dangerous enough place in the daytime. At night, and in this weather?' She shivered.

I was right there with her. Meaning inside the train was safe and sound, which is where I wanted Pavlik to stay.

But I knew the sheriff wouldn't be deterred by concern for his own safety, especially when somebody else might be in danger. It wasn't in his DNA. I wasn't sure I had that kind of grit myself – to run toward disaster, rather than away – but I was very grateful there were people like Pavlik who did.

So, I tried another tack. 'You're right, Missy. We certainly can't chance losing your main forensics speaker. There would be no one to teach the panels – or workshops – tomorrow.'

Pavlik looked at me.

'Imagine the disappointment if you didn't show up,' I said to him. 'You know, to teach killing and guns and bullets and such.'

'Oooh, that reminds me.' Missy turned away from the window to address Pavlik. 'Did you bring your own weapons or do you need mine?'

'You have ... weapons?' I asked.

'Of course,' the two of them chorused.

'I meant Missy.' When it came to Pavlik, personal experience had taught me that asking Mae West's come-hither question, 'Is that a pistol in your pocket or are you just glad to see me?' wouldn't get me the answer I'd hoped for.

'Oh, yes,' the young woman said. 'But only props for the workshop. Rubber knives and the like.'

That was a relief, at least. Maybe I would attend, after all.

'...shipped everything I needed, along with

114

my handouts,' Pavlik was saying.

That explained what was in the UPS box that had been waiting for us in the hotel room.

'My Glock Forty semi-automatic,' he continued, 'and a Colt Detective Special, a revolver designed for a six-chamber cylinder. I also have a variety of cartridges – standard, hollow-point, Hydra-shok, the Glaser Safety Slug—'

Suddenly the Flagler Suite wasn't looking quite so romantic.

'You *will* talk about caliber versus millimeter, won't you?' This from Prudence, whom I'd forgotten about. 'That always confuses people and we really need to know those things in order to write intelligently.'

'I'll have thirty-eight, forty and forty-five caliber cartridges as well as nine millimeter, to illustrate,' Pavlik assured Prudence, then turned to me. 'What we're talking about, Maggy, is the diameter of the ammunition. A forty-five caliber bullet or cartridge – the same thing, for our purposes – is forty-five one hundreds of an inch in diameter, or nearly half an inch across. A nine millimeter is, as you might guess, nine millimeters across.'

'And nearly equal to the size of a thirty-eight caliber,' Missy contributed brightly. 'If you do the conversion from metric, I mean.'

'A nine is a bit smaller than a thirty-eight,' Pavlik said with an approving nod. 'But very close.'

Obviously gratified, Missy asked, 'And did you bring – or ship – a variety of knives as well?'

'I have a rubber knife with a five-inch blade to use in the hands-on demonstration, of course. For show-and-tell, I shipped a switch blade, and gravity, pocket and buck knives.'

What, I thought, no death by butter knife?

'Oh, and my assassin's dagger, of course.'

So I *would* hang out at the pool tomorrow. Or maybe go to the beach. There was an original thought, given I was in South Florida. From rainforest tonight to sand castles tomorrow. And I'd thought Wisconsin was diverse.

'Gravity,' Prudence said. 'Is that the one with the button on the handle?'

'Exactly,' my personal weapons expert said. 'When that's pushed and you flick out to the side with your wrist, the weight of the blade opens the knife.'

'But isn't that a switchblade?' Missy seemed puzzled.

I, for my part, was completely lost.

'Not at all,' Pavlik said. 'When you thumb the button – or 'switch' – on a switchblade, the blade flicks out automatically.'

'So no gravity needed.' Prudence was nodding.

'Correct,' Pavlik said. 'The pocket knife, on the other—'

'We're moving,' I interrupted, feeling the train hiccup in the other direction. *And* with Pavlik still safely inside. My delaying tactic had worked.

'Oh, thank goodness.' Missy was back to the window. 'The engineer has already moved to the other locomotive. We must be starting back toward Fort Lauderdale.'

'Spry old fellow,' Prudence said.

'The engineer? Oh, he's quite the character.' Missy checked her watch. 'I do worry that we'll get back to the station too early, though. You know, before the crime is solved?'

'Maybe someone should make an announcement,' I suggested. 'Requesting that Potter and the rest of the "cast" come to this car.'

There was a flaw, of course, in my plan: Laurence Potter obviously didn't want to appear. Missy, however, didn't seem to see it. 'That's a wonderful idea, Maggy. Zoe should—'

'Zoe? Why not you?' Prudence prodded. 'You do most of the work, anyway. Why let her take all the credit?'

Missy blushed, tugging down her dress.

117

'Oh, no, I prefer to work behind the scenes. I couldn't.'

'You couldn't what?' Zoe, perhaps instinctively, had magically turned up, too.

'Maggy suggested that we make an announcement...'

'Maggy?' Zoe repeated.

I raised my hand. The woman was either stupid or trying to rile me. I was betting on the latter.

'Oh, right,' Zoe said distractedly, her attention drawn to the commotion in the corner, where a huge man dressed in a zoot suit was trying to climb onto the table.

Pavlik, having been thwarted in his effort to save the day by venturing into the Everglades, slid out of the booth. 'You!' he said in a thundering voice. 'Down! Now!'

The big man ignored him. With the train's swaying movement he looked like an overweight, overdressed mob surfer trying to position his feet for one last Big Kahuna of a wave. Worse, he was a decade off in his costume. The high-waisted trousers and long coats with wide lapels and padded shoulders were popular in the forties, not the thirties.

'Off the table, Fred!' Zoe bellowed.

'Fred' got off. Pavlik shrugged and returned to our table.

'Zoe, we think you should cut the cake,' Prudence suggested. 'Sop up some of the alcohol.'

'Too late,' Missy said mournfully.

'Too late to sop up the alcohol or too late to cut the cake?' One more Orient Espresso martini on an empty stomach and *I'd* be up on a table. Or under it.

'Maybe both.' Missy was agitatedly tip-tapping her foot. 'But what I mean is that someone took a big hunk out of our cake and made off with the knife. Can you believe that? What are we going to use to cut the rest of it?'

I looked down at my swizzle stick, hungry enough to give it a good-faith try.

'I'm sure we can come up with something,' Pavlik said. 'If all else fails, I have my trusty Swiss Army knife.' He reached into his pocket and pulled out yet another knife in addition to the ones that apparently awaited us in the Flagler Suite.

'But the original cake knife was also meant to be the murder weapon. We need it for the "reveal."' Missy was near inconsolable. 'Somebody has ruined everything!'

'Oh, for God's sake, don't be such a child,' Zoe snapped, adjusting her dress. 'It's not the end of the world.'

By this point I desperately wanted to do something to assist poor Missy, and if it got me closer to food then all the better. 'Show me the cake, Missy. Maybe the knife just fell off the table after someone messed with it. If not, we'll come up with a substitute.'

'Good idea.' Zoe seemed to be glad to be rid of her overly emotional assistant. And, perhaps, me. 'In the meantime, we can't wait any longer to solve our little crime. I was going to have you go back to the sleeping car, Jacob, but without Larry I wonder—'

I wanted to hear more about Zoe Scarlett's plans for Pavlik, but Missy had my arm and was pulling me toward the cake at the far end of the car.

TWELVE

'Hmm,' I said, looking at the hacked-up corpse that had been part of the cake. 'Somebody amputated the left foot.' Including the big toe, where I'd swiped the bit of frosting earlier, resulting at least in my tracks being covered there.

Missy looked forlorn. 'Didn't I tell you?'

'He or she might have taken the knife blade to carry the piece of cake on,' I glanced around. 'I don't see any plates.'

'I didn't put them out yet. So no one would get ideas of cutting it early, for all the good that did.'

'The best-laid plans,' I commiserated. 'By the way, I loved that knife – what a loss. My grandmother left me a carving set that contained one just like it.'

I was thinking about the gift, which I only brought out for special occasions like Christmas and Thanksgiving. The hinged brown box contained two large knives and a serving fork. One, with an eight-inch blade, was a twin of the missing knife.

'That's so nice,' Missy said. 'I got this one on eBay for fourteen ninety-five.'

$14.95. Apparently, I wouldn't be retiring on the proceeds from the sale of my family heirloom. But then if it *were* a collectible, Missy would hardly have put it in the cake. Unless ... 'Maybe somebody *did* think it was valuable and stole it. I believe the handle is staghorn and—'

'Your attention, please.' Zoe Scarlett's voice came over the speakers.

The sudden lurch of the train coupled with a metallic grinding made me grab for a pole. Apparently the new tracks were adding a few more kinks for the return voyage.

'Hercule Poirot requests that all guests assemble,' Zoe continued, 'in the forward dining car. It seems there's been a murder.'

At the words, most of the costumed guests started to head in from the next car.

A clap of thunder was followed almost immediately by a searing flash of lightning outside the window. Although we'd been traveling through the blackness for more than an hour and a half, this was my first glimpse behind that curtain of darkness.

'My God,' I said, leaning down to peer out the window. 'There's nothing out there except low brush and the occasional clump of trees.'

'And sawgrass, as far as the eye can see. The Everglades is a "slow-moving river of grass,"' Missy quoted, seeming to relax a little. 'Over three million acres originally. It really is striking when you fly into Fort Lauderdale at night. You'd swear you're soaring above the clouds or over the ocean because you can't see anything and then, suddenly, the lights of South Florida pop up beneath you.'

Then Missy tensed again as people continued to file past us. 'I still don't see Laurence. Would you help me search while the rest of the group is occupied?'

My eyes lingered longingly at the cake, but I said, 'Of course.'

Missy turned, and I managed a last swipe at the frosting before following. 'Aren't you going the wrong way? You said the sleeping car is the last one, right?'

'Yes.' Missy stopped. 'Except that we've

reversed direction, so it's the first car after the locomotive, which used to bring up the rear of the train, but now is the front.'

I think my eyes must have crossed, because Missy waved for me to come along. 'I'll show you.'

We passed from the dining car into the vestibule, where the noise of the track passing below the metal plates beneath our feet made conversation difficult until we opened the next door into the passenger car. It was empty except for Danny and Audra Edmonds. They were seated side by side, curly dark hair and blonde waves close as they chatted in low tones.

'Excuse me,' Missy interrupted. 'But we seem to have lost track of Mr Potter.'

Audra looked up. 'Have you checked with Rosemary?'

'She's not feeling well,' Missy said. 'She's lying down in the sleeping car.'

Danny's eyes flickered. 'Rosemary Darlington? I saw you go by with her before. I'd love to meet her.'

I bet he would. I'd also bet that if I quizzed the star-chaser he'd have no memory of meeting me once, much less twice.

'I'm afraid she's unavailable at the moment,' Missy said in the voice of an experienced gatekeeper. 'But I'd be happy to introduce you sometime during the conference,' she glanced at his badge, her nose crinkling, 'Danny.'

I caught the sign of displeasure, probably at Danny/Col. Arbuthnot's lack of alliteration.

'He signed up late and barely caught the bus,' I told her. 'You and Rosemary had already left, so I assume the conference registration person just assigned a character to him randomly.'

Danny glanced down at the badge self-consciously. 'Is there a problem? Like I told Zoe, I did pay.'

'No, no – it's fine,' Missy said and, to my surprise, smiled brightly at the young man. 'We're happy to have you.'

The two were probably close in age. Could love be in the air?

'Thank you,' Danny said. 'Are you an author?'

Before Missy could answer that she was 'just a researcher,' and thereby render herself invisible, I jumped in. 'Missy is one of the conference organizers. She knows everyone.'

That piqued his interest. 'A pleasure to meet you, Missy. You must have a very interesting job.'

Missy blushed. 'I suppose so. I—'

'Missy works closely with all sorts of famous authors,' I said encouragingly. 'And publishers, too, I'm sure. Right, Missy?'

'Well, I ... No—'

'All guests to the dining car,' Zoe's voice thundered over the intercom again.

'Oh, dear,' Missy said. 'If we don't find Laurence, who's to solve the crime?'

'If it helps, Mr Potter passed through here not long after you and Ms Darlington did,' Danny said. 'He had a pack of cigarettes and was headed the same way.'

Toward the sleeping car. Having walked a mile in the cheated-upon spouse's shoes myself, Danny's statement would have raised a red flag for me. It apparently did for Audra as well.

'"The same way,"' she repeated, not seeming at all surprised. 'What a coincidence.'

'He may have gone out on the landing – or whatever you call it, between cars – for a smoke.' Danny seemed to sense he'd said something to upset her. Why he cared, I didn't know.

'It's called a vestibule,' Missy said. 'And there's no smoking on the train, anywhere.'

So I'd been right.

'Like I said,' Danny continued, 'I wasn't sure where he was going, only that he had his cigarettes. I was going to follow, see if we could talk, but I saw Mrs ... um, Audra, and thought I'd introduce myself.'

I frowned. Something wasn't right. 'I'm sorry, but didn't I see the two of you speaking in the club car before Audra surprised everyone?'

'Just for a second,' Danny said. 'I didn't know who she was then.'

Well, that explained it. I had to admit Zoe Scarlett was right. It *is* hard to know who to suck up to without a scorecard – or, at least, last names and titles on nametags. I was curious about this kid. Hell, about *all* these people. 'You sent your manuscript to Larry Potter, why—'

Missy tugged on my arm. 'We really need to find Laurence, Maggy.'

'Oh, of course,' I said and then to Danny, 'I'm sorry. We can talk later.'

'Umm, sure. Anytime,' he said distractedly. Then to Missy: 'I'd love to hear more about you. Maybe you and I can get together for a drink.'

Missy giggled and tugged at her dress. 'Maybe.'

As we pressed on toward the restroom at the end of the car, Missy was walking taller, with a sexy little wiggle that threatened to send her careening off her shiny spiked heels as the train chugged along the track.

Ahh, amour. And ambition. And always the twain shall meet.

Which brought me back to our guests of honor. Missy had said that Rosemary Darlington and Laurence Potter had a 'history.'

126

I took that to mean an affair and Audra Edmonds's reaction to Rosemary seemed to bear that out. But was this affair truly 'history' or more current events? As in, the two of them shacked up in the sleeping car at this very moment.

If so, I had to give both Potter and Darlington props for acting ability. The disdain he professed for her – and her new writing endeavor – seemed very genuine. Ditto, our female guest of honor's feelings toward the reviewer, not to mention her own reaction to the motion of the train, her medication and my espresso martini. If Rosemary Darlington was faking, I'd eat her beret.

As Missy and I reached the back of the car, wind was whistling through the opening in the windows I'd been forced to leave in order to secure her banner.

For all the good the thing was doing. Not only, as I expected, was there no one out there to see it except for the denizens of the Everglades, but the vinyl banner was slapping rhythmically against the side of the train, occasionally being lifted by a gust to cover the windows.

The sign might not survive the trip. I just hoped the windows would.

Hesitating at the restroom door, I said to Missy, 'I suppose it won't hurt to check again.'

She shrugged. 'Sure, maybe third time's the charm.'

'Speaking of charm,' I said casually, as I tapped on the restroom door, 'Danny is kind of cute.'

'You think?' She cocked her head. 'He seems awfully young to me.' She must have seen the surprise on my face. 'Oh, don't get me wrong, Maggy. What girl doesn't like a little male attention, but...'

'But?' I gave another knock.

'But he's really not my type. I don't like users.'

'Losers?' Still no answer from inside, I tentatively slid the restroom door open.

'No, *user*. Somebody who uses other people to get what they want. True love should be more than that.'

Not wanting to get into a discussion of 'true love' with the starry-eyed girl, I stepped my jaded self into the empty restroom. 'Huh, this is larger than I expected.'

Missy came in after me. 'Do you think so?'

'Well, bigger than an airplane restroom, certainly. I mean, we're both standing in here, not exactly comfortably and it smells like a flaming bag of dog poop, but—'

The door slid closed.

'Hey,' I said, grabbing the handle and giving it a shove. 'That's not funny.'

'Oh, I'm sure nobody did it on purpose,

Maggy. It was probably just the motion of the train.'

We did seem to be slowing. 'The door is stuck.'

'I think you locked it.' She pushed the handle the other way and yanked open the door. 'Here we go.'

We stepped out into the hall and I let out the breath I'd apparently been holding. 'Thank God for South Florida's insistence on over air-conditioning.'

'It *was* a little stuffy in there. Now, where were we?'

'Heading that way,' I pointed, proud that I was getting the hang of this front-is-now-back, back-is-now-front reorientation. At least I had a sense of which way we were going, which was more than I could say of my one and only cruise. I'd spent the entire four days wandering the halls and punching up information on the computerized 'You are here' maps. And eating, of course.

My stomach growled again.

Beyond the restroom was the vestibule leading to the sleeping car. I had a hard time seeing why someone would come here to smoke. The exit doors on both sides of the vestibule had no outside platforms, the floor was a rumbling metal ramp and the space was noisy and smelled.

Come to think of it, it probably wasn't

unlike a lot of places smokers had been banished to.

'What's that?' Missy said, pointing to something in the corner to my left.

'An empty book of matches.' I picked up the black and silver pack. 'Potter's, do you think?'

Missy took them and read, 'Titanium.'

'What's that?'

She looked embarrassed and handed them back to me. 'A ... gentlemen's club?'

'Ah, then definitely Potter's.' I slipped the match book into the pocket of my sundress.

Missy looked around the cramped space again. 'He came this way, then.'

'But probably not to smoke,' I said, looking around myself. 'Unless he did it in the restroom. Maybe that's why it smelled like that.'

'I think that was just train smell and toilet. There are a lot of us onboard and we've all been using that restroom. I think the other is at the far end of the sleeping car.'

'So if Potter isn't in this bathroom, maybe he's in that one. The only other option is...'

'Oh, dear. Do you think he's with Rosemary? I wondered if that's what his wife was insinuating.'

'Insinuating' was putting it mildly. 'Could Potter have snuck in there after you left?'

She shrugged. 'I hate to think he'd do that, but, well, I'm starting to believe no one is

130

what they seem to be.'

As far as I was concerned, Laurence Potter was exactly what he seemed – a pompous sleazeball, but then I tend to be judgmental. 'Where is Rosemary sleeping it off?'

'The farthest roomette – that's what the train company calls the little sleeping compartments – from where we are. On the left. I knew we'd be using the nearest one to the passenger car for solving our program's crime, so I wanted Rosemary to be as far away as possible so she wouldn't be disturbed.'

'Good idea,' I said, not bothering to add that it was also the room where, like the last one on a hotel corridor, two people could fool around with less likelihood of being discovered. 'We know Potter came through here, because of the matchbook. Is there an outside platform anywhere that he could smoke?'

'You mean like on the back of an old-time campaign train? I doubt it, though I suppose he could open an exit door.'

Yikes. 'Haven't you seen the news stories about people disappearing from trains?' I asked. 'Granted, many of them were older or ill but the authorities suspect they got confused and thought the door led to the bathroom or the next car. Once opened, with the velocity of the train, they—'

'Oh, dear. But then why aren't the exits kept locked?'

'Because there are also safety issues arguing against that. People need to be able to get out quickly in case of an emergency.'

Could Potter have opened the exit door to have a smoke and somehow, perhaps when the train hit a rough section of track, tumbled out?

Leaving the question and the vestibule behind, I opened the first roomette door on the left and peered in. All I saw was blackness and all I felt was warmth. Someone had opened the window. 'Hello? Is anybody in here?'

Missy reached past me and felt for a light. 'I think—'

As I took a step forward, she screamed and grabbed my arm.

At first I thought the scream was because my sandal had landed in the mutilated left foot from the cake left lying on the floor, grinding buttercream into the carpet.

But then I saw the body, knife protruding prominently from the chest.

THIRTEEN

'We have to get the sheriff,' I said, backing-pedaling and pulling Missy with me. 'He'll know—'

The body sat up, and Missy's scream nearly deafened me. But the corpse wasn't the critic, of course. It was Pavlik in the fake mustache.

'Damn it, Pavlik.' Deafened but not mute, I stomped my foot into a second smear of cake icing on the floor. 'You scared the living hell out of us.'

Missy was crying. 'How did you get past ... ohhh.' Realization dawned on her tear-streaked face. 'Did you shut us in that bathroom?'

'I'm sorry.' The sheriff was smiling and didn't appear a bit apologetic. Perversely desirable, though. Made me want to jump right in that bunk with him.

Missy, however, was not as easily mollified. 'That was cruel.'

Pavlik held up his hands. 'Truly, I am sorry. I couldn't resist, but it was a childish thing to do. Please forgive me?'

Now it was Missy who was smiling, her toe doing little coy circles. 'Well, I suppose so. If you promise not to do it again.'

With luck, the opportunity to shut two women in a train bathroom in order to scare them by playing a fictional murdered villain come-to-life wouldn't pop up on a regular basis.

'Promise.' Pavlik crossed his heart.

Oh, please.

The sounds of a crowd and sliding doors opening and closing were getting closer.

'Can I hope those are the frenzied villagers, coming to burn you at the stake?' I asked pleasantly.

'Merely to solve my heinous – or not so heinous, given my character's own crime – murder.' Pavlik lay back and repositioned the knife.

'Is that my cake knife? You took it?' Missy demanded, eyes narrowed.

'Uh-uh.' The sheriff held it up. 'My Swiss Army knife. With the blade closed, of course.'

'Ohhh.' All appeared forgiven again.

'Did you send that with the rest of your "weapons"?' I asked. 'I didn't think you'd opened the UPS box.'

'This?' Pavlik held it up. 'It's more tool than weapon. I brought it with me. In my luggage, of course.'

In truth, the thing did look like some gadget you'd see on an infomercial. 'But wait!' I said, mimicking the medium's pitchmen.

Missy teetered on her heels. 'I wasn't going anywhere.'

'No, I meant ... never mind. Does that thing have a corkscrew?' I asked Pavlik, thinking we might snare a bottle of wine for the room on the way back to the hotel.

'Of course not. This is a *classic* Swiss Army knife. Not one of those fru-fru all-in-ones.' Pavlik closed his eyes. 'Now get out, you two, before you blow my cover.'

'Will do, Sheriff.' I went to follow Missy into the corridor, but as she reached to slide the door closed behind us, I held up my hand.

I stuck my head back into the roomette. 'By the way, did you open the window?'

'Me?' He opened one eye. 'No, it was open when I came in, though I'm grateful for the warmth. Dead men don't shiver.'

The eye closed.

'He's so funny,' Missy said as we made our way down the corridor, quickly checking each roomette as we went. Behind us the participants were gathered around the door to Pavlik's chamber. 'And nice.'

'He is,' I agreed, closing the second to last door. 'Most of the time.'

Missy stopped and looked at me, disbelieving. 'Please don't tell me he's a louse, too.'

Louse. Great word, and probably fitting of the era we were supposed to be in. 'Oh, no. Pavlik is a very honorable man.' Which I'd found to be a problem at times. Like when he suspected yours truly of murder.

'Well, that's good.' Missy stopped at the door to the last compartment. 'This is where I left Rosemary. Shall I rap?'

Another genteel turn of phrase. 'Probably a good idea.'

She did, using just the tips of her fingernails.

'Huh?' we heard from inside.

I tried the door, which slid ajar. So the thing hadn't been locked from the inside. 'Rosemary? We're just checking to make sure you're OK.' And alone.

'Who's there?'

'Missy and Maggy,' my fellow quester said, flipping on the light.

Rosemary was on the bunk alone, arm up over her eyes. 'Jesus, are you trying to blind me?'

'Sorry, it's because the Everglades are so dark. You can even see the stars at night.' Missy leaned down to point out the window.

'I don't see any stars,' Rosemary said. 'In

fact, isn't that rain streaming down the glass?'

'I'm afraid it is,' Missy said, looking again. 'Oh, dear. It's coming down in torrents.'

Oh, dear, was right. 'Well, we're on the way back, at least.'

'The train seems to be going quite slowly, though,' Missy said worriedly. 'I hope there's no flooding on the tracks.'

Flooding? In the Everglades at the end of their so-called 'wet season'? Who would have thunk it, as my son Eric would say. But then he was a smart-aleck teenager and I, his more mature parent. Or I should be. 'Flooding? In the Everglades? Might we have foreseen that possibility?'

'Oh, don't be a worry-wart, Maggy,' Missy said a little sharply, which indicated to me that she herself was worried. Or, perhaps, didn't appreciate being criticized in front of an important client like Rosemary Darlington. 'We've already *had* record rains this year.'

I wasn't sure why her latest little factoid was supposed to reassure me.

Nonetheless, I kept quiet as Missy continued. 'The Murder on the Orient Espresso is being solved as we speak and our event is a success!'

Her statement made me think. 'But what about Poirot? Who's playing him?'

'Potter, of course,' Rosemary said.

Missy and I exchanged looks. Rosemary was out of the loop when it came to his vanishing act, but I wasn't going to be the one to fill her in if I could help it.

'I suppose it's possible he's been up front the whole time,' Missy said slowly. 'After all, Audra was able to stay hidden until she sprung herself on Laurence.'

'Audra,' Rosemary sniffed. 'That woman is hateful to me.'

'To be fair, she apparently has reason,' I countered. 'To hate you, I mean.' You can take the cheated-upon woman out of the state, but you can't take the state of being cheated upon out of the woman.

Rosemary, for her part, looked genuinely bewildered. 'Me? Why?'

'The affair?' I knew I should drop it, but my list of things I should do had probably filled three volumes by then.

Still a blank look, then changing to comprehension. 'Oh, you mean between her husband and me? There was never any affair.'

'But why would people say it if it weren't true?' Missy, trusting girl that she was, seemed sick at the thought. 'And his wife, even.'

'It's probably the percentage bet with Larry, though not in this case.' Rosemary looked at her researcher. 'Don't worry, Missy. I know there are rumors about an

138

affair and I truly don't care. In fact, at the time I preferred that people thought that than the truth.'

'Which was?' I asked.

'That my career was floundering and he offered to mentor me. I was supposed to be the "Next Great American Novelist," with his help. And for a percentage.' Rosemary was sitting on the bunk cross-legged, dress hitched up to her waist. 'Instead he nearly ruined me.'

'How?' I was remembering what Rosemary had said earlier about Potter destroying her self-confidence. I'd assumed she'd meant more personally than professionally.

'Oh, nothing horrible.' With her short cropped hair, Rosemary looked like a little boy. 'But Larry was relentless about my writing the book he had in mind, exactly the way he imagined it.'

'Why didn't he just write the thing himself?'

'That's what I asked him after the fourteenth or fifteenth draft. You know what he said?'

Missy and I both shook our heads.

'He said, "Happily. And I'll give you half the proceeds if you'll allow me to publish it under your name."'

'Rather than his own?'

'I'm a brand.' Rosemary shrugged. 'Or

was, back in the day.'

'You still are,' Missy said staunchly.

'What do you mean by "brand"?' I asked.

'As with products – or authors – that are "brand names," in and of themselves,' Missy said. 'Like maybe James Patterson or Janet Evanovich. The public has a nearly insatiable appetite for anything they write. It's hard for the author to keep up with the demand.'

'Sounds like a good problem to have,' I said.

'I suppose it is – or would be,' Rosemary said. 'Not that I would know. Back in my day, ebooks hadn't mainstreamed, so just the publishing and printing processes made it necessary—'

'In your day?' Missy scolded. 'Your last novel was only five years ago.'

'Might as well be five decades, given the pace at which publishing is changing.' The 'legendary lady of romantic suspense' sounded tired.

'I understand *Breaking and Entering* is doing very well,' I said, although I had no idea whether that was true or not. The book was certainly being talked about.

'That's right,' Missy said, with an approving glance toward me. 'Before you know it, Rosemary Darlington will top the *New York Times* bestseller list again.'

Rosemary smiled. 'Thank you. At the very

least, I'm hoping it gives me a running start at it.'

Missy looked pleased that she'd been able to raise the woman's spirits.

Me, I just wanted more dirt. 'So you decided to end it with Potter? The collaboration, I mean.' I'd taken Rosemary at her word about the affair. Or lack of one.

'Yes, and none too soon. My work needs to be more ... organic? It morphs as I go on and that gives me great pleasure – it's what keeps me writing. Things fall into place and every day brings a new "aha!" moment. Larry, on the other hand, is the ultimate planner. Or maybe a better word would be controller. Pages and pages of outline. It felt like an unavoidable school assignment and nothing I did seemed to please the teacher. By the time he approved the outline, I hated the book. Worse, I hated writing, period.'

'How long did you work that way with him?' I was thinking the story might explain why there had been such a gap between books by Rosemary Darlington.

'Nearly a year.' She shivered and put a hand up to the air-conditioning unit by her head. 'Happily, that's all in the past.'

'Absolutely,' Missy said. 'Water under the bridge.'

Another quaint expression, but I was examining what looked like an airplane tray table 'in the upright and locked position' on the wall inside the compartment next to the bunk. 'Hey,' I said. 'This flips down into a sink.'

Missy pointed. 'And below that is a toilet.'

'Huh.' I lifted the lid to see the blue water. 'So, each roomette has its own toilet and sink?'

'Apparently so, though I'm sure I saw...' She stepped into the corridor. 'Oh, yes – there are more facilities off the corridor, just like I thought.'

I followed her out. 'Seems like the sleeping car has cornered the market on restrooms. They couldn't have spared one or two more for the rest of the train?'

'Good point,' Missy said. 'We'll have to remind people they can use the lavatories back here. After the crime is solved, of course.'

'And by Potter, let's hope.' I slid open one of the 'lavatory' doors she'd indicated. 'There's no toilet in here, just a shower, sink and dressing area.'

Missy pulled open the matching door on the other side of the corridor and looked inside. 'This one, too. I guess that makes sense, given what you said about each room having its own toilet facilities. The only thing the sleeping car passengers would need is a shower and somewhere to dress before venturing out into the corridor again.'

Scattered applause came from the group down the hall, and they started to troop away from us and toward the dining car. 'Is it time to cut the cake?' I asked.

'Did someone say cake?' came from the roomette. Rosemary had slipped back under the blanket. 'Can you bring me a piece?'

'Certainly,' Missy said. 'Back in a flash.'

'Let's hope there's something left of it when we get there,' I said to Missy.

'We still don't have a knife,' she said as we approached the room Pavlik had used for his portrayal of the victim, Ratchett.

'True, but the sheriff does have his "classic" Swiss Army knife.'

'Oh, dear,' Missy said. 'We should have cleaned that up.'

The crowd had finished the job I'd inadvertently started, stomping the cake in the hallway to an unrecognizable blue and white mish-mash.

'Now it'll be tracked all over the train,' the event planner lamented.

I guiltily rubbed the edge of my own shoe against the carpet.

The door of the roomette had been left open and I stepped in. 'Just let me see something.'

'What's wrong? Did Jake forget to close the window?'

I noticed that using Pavlik's first name was no longer a problem for the girl.

'No, it's closed.' And a good thing too, since the wind was pummeling rain against the glass. I went to where the sink was located in the other roomette and, sure enough, it seemed to be standard equipment. I let the thing down, then re-secured it in its original position.

Next I lifted the lid over the toilet.

A cigarette butt floated in the blue water.

FOURTEEN

'I don't get it,' Missy was saying as I slid the door closed. 'How did you know that Laurence had been smoking in that room?'

'Easy.' I was feeling smug. 'The cake in the doorway, for one thing. He must have dropped it opening the door. And then there was the open window. Potter must have been worried about setting off any smoke detectors.'

'Wow,' Missy said. 'You really should write mysteries. How did you know Laurence wouldn't flush the toilet?'

'He's a man. I'm surprised he didn't leave

the seat up, too.'

In truth, the floating cigarette butt had been a lucky break. Not that I was going to admit it.

Missy screwed up her face. 'But if Laurence was smoking in the roomette, he wouldn't have needed to open the exit door. So, what was the matchbook doing on the floor next to it?'

'Beats me. But since the book was empty, we know Potter dropped it *after* he had his smoke,' I said as we passed the spot in question.

'And on his way to rejoin the rest of the group in the dining car?'

'Exactly.'

'That's wonderful reasoning, Maggy,' Missy said, nearly walking between my heels like my sheepdog, Frank. 'You're a genius.'

'Not really,' I said modestly, stopping to look around in the passenger car. No sign of Potter, nor of Audra Edmonds and Danny, but Prudence and Grace were sitting in adjacent seats, talking to Markus. Fred, the table-dancing behemoth, was nearby, as was Harvey/Hardman in his checkered sports jacket. All five of them had hunks of cake in their hands and a trail of crumbs leading from the dining car and ending in their respective laps.

I couldn't tell if the commemorative cake

had been cut with Pavlik's Swiss Army knife or just gnawed off.

'Oh, dear,' said Missy. 'I never did put the plates and forks out.'

Oh, dear, indeed. 'I hope the cleaning team has a vacuum.' Or a sheepdog. My Frank would make quick work snuffling up the leavings. Hell, at this point *I* was nearly hungry enough to do it myself.

'We lose our deposit if we don't return the train spic-and-span, so I'm afraid that little task falls to me,' Missy said unhappily.

I knew I should offer to help, but the truth was I was downright exhausted. It had been a very full day since we stepped onto our plane at Mitchell International in Milwaukee. 'Shouldn't the train be pulling into the station soon?'

'Yes, but I fear the rain has slowed us down. Haven't you noticed we're barely creeping along?'

Honestly, no. But now that she said it – and I'd become accustomed to the train motion – it did seem as though the critters in the Everglades could probably have outpaced us.

Missy stopped at the cake to rectify the plate situation, though I wasn't sure why she bothered. The crumbs that were left in the flat box required a thimble at most.

Resigning myself to a not unpleasant – if

perhaps ill-advised – liquid diet, I continued on to what had been the first car on the train and now was the last: the club car. There I found Pavlik, Zoe and Audra standing at a high table with Carson. The agent stood a little apart, as if his need for personal space was greater than everyone else's and they were happy to cooperate.

At the adjacent bar, Boyce was serving coffee. I waved to him and sidled in next to Pavlik. 'I see the murder has been solved and all is right with the world.'

'It is now,' Pavlik said, sliding an arm around my waist. 'Would you like something?'

I weighed my options, trying to be an adult. Though I truly wanted a drink, another martini or even a glass of wine might send me over the top.

'I'll just grab a cup of coffee when Boyce has a moment. I heard the applause,' I said, turning to the others in the group. 'Did things go well?'

'Jacob was a marvelously villainous victim,' Zoe said. 'And we're very grateful to Carson for stepping in as Poirot.'

I turned to Audra. 'Wait. Your husband never showed up?'

Her eyebrows shot skyward. 'We all assumed you'd found him and he declined to participate.'

'It wouldn't be the first time.' Carson took a sip of what looked like bourbon in a small clear plastic cup. I wondered if he'd brought both himself. In a Baggie. 'Your husband – and my client – is a very stubborn man.'

Another wrinkle. 'You represent Larry Potter?'

'And Audra.' Carson nodded to the woman next to him. 'My very first husband-and-wife writing duo.'

Pavlik leaned down to whisper in my ear. 'You didn't see any sign of Potter?'

'Signs, yes.' I beckoned the sheriff away from the group. 'I think he went back for a smoke. We found his matches on the floor near an exit and a cigarette butt in the toilet of the room where you were playing dead.'

Pavlik looked surprised. 'Toilet? I didn't even see a bathroom.'

'Not a full one, just a sink that flipped out from the wall and a toilet. You might have thought the cover was a shelf.'

'Huh – some observer I am. I didn't smell cigarette smoke when I entered, but Potter would have opened the window to let it vent into the fresh air.'

'Exactly. We assumed he'd snuck in there to bolster his nicotine level,' I was saying as Missy joined us from the next car. 'Did you give up?' I asked her.

'On what?' asked Pavlik.

She waved her hand. 'Oh, nothing. Just all the cake crumbs.'

'There's no housekeeping service,' I explained, 'so Missy feels responsible for returning the train in the condition it was when we boarded. Meaning, mostly clean.'

'Well that's absolutely ridiculous,' the sheriff said.

'It is?' Missy was wide-eyed.

'Of course. We can't let you do that alone. We'll be glad to help, won't we, Maggy?'

I nearly groaned, but the fact was that despite my worst intentions, I wouldn't have left the girl to clean the train alone.

If Pavlik and I were scrubbing and vacuuming, however, I was going to make damn sure Zoe Scarlett did, as well.

Which reminded me. 'When Zoe announced the solving of the crime—'

'What are you saying about me?' Apparently feeling left out, the woman in question had pivoted in place, effectively abandoning Audra and Carson for our party without having to take a step.

'I was just saying that Missy and I assumed Potter had surfaced while we were at the back of the train.'

'I'm afraid not,' Pavlik said. 'Are you sure—'

A squeal of metal on metal, followed by a thud. I was thrown into Missy and the two of us slid down the wall. Zoe grabbed onto Pavlik, who struggled to keep his own balance as the train tilted precariously and shuddered to a halt.

The lights flickered, but managed to stay on. 'Everybody OK?' Pavlik asked in his command voice, putting out a hand to help me up.

I, in turn, pulled up Missy. 'Think so.'

'Did we derail?' Missy was rubbing her butt, probably where she'd landed.

'Is there any place to derail to?' I asked, thinking of Flagler's railroad trestle. 'I mean, without being at least partially submerged?'

'Is everyone all right?' Pavlik called out again.

Boyce was getting to his feet. 'I'm fine, although I'm not as sure about the espresso machine.'

'We've lost a few bottles from the bar,' Pete the bartender reported, 'but I'm OK.'

Both Audra Edmonds and her agent appeared shaken but also unhurt. Carson was holding his hands out like a skater trying to keep from falling or, more likely in his case, touching anything.

'I'll check on the others,' I said to Pavlik. I crossed the eerily quiet vestibule to stick my head into the dining car. 'Any injuries in here?'

'Just bounced around a bit,' Prudence said.

She was braced in the aisle, pearls askew and her dress ripped at the hem, as if she'd stepped on it while trying to steady herself.

Markus and the rest of the group that had been chowing down in the passenger car were filing in behind her. Greta had a smudge of icing on her nose.

'What happened?' a sleepy-looking Rosemary Darlington appeared and, behind her, Danny.

'We're not sure,' I said. 'But—'

The vestibule door opened behind me, admitting Pavlik. Now everybody started firing questions. Or comments.

'Did something blow up? I thought I heard an explosion.'

'Don't be silly. We must have run into something.'

'Or, perhaps, might the engineer have had a heart attack, thereby rendering him unconscious and leaving us hopelessly stranded in the Everglades?'

This last soliloquy was delivered by Harvey, whose palm was dramatically placed over his checkered heart.

Sheesh. No wonder Broadway had spit him back out.

Pavlik held his hands up in twin stop signs. 'I'm going forward to the locomotive to investigate. In the meantime, everybody please stay where you are.'

I touched Pavlik's arm. 'Speaking of the engineer, are you at all surprised he didn't come to check on his passengers?'

'I am. Though maybe he already has his hands full.' My sheriff looked grim as he continued on toward what was now the front – or east-facing – end of the train.

I went back the other direction, retreating to the club car, where Boyce was hoisting his espresso brewer back into place.

I helped him settle it on the bar and then leaned down to pick up the metal frothing pitcher. 'You didn't get burned, did you?'

'Not a bit, thank you. I'd finished brewing the last of the espresso and was letting things cool down. You need a hand there, Pete?' he called over to the young bartender.

Pete turned around from the closet behind his bar, a bottle in each hand. 'No, I'm good. Luckily, we have reinforcements.' He raised the liquor over his head.

'Something tells me we're going to need it,' I said. 'Or at least some people will.' God forbid anyone think that would include me.

'What happened?' the bartender asked. 'Did one of the passengers pull the brake?'

'The brake?' I repeated. The thought had never occurred to me.

'Right here. I saw the thing when I boarded and asked about it.' Pete pointed to a cord dangling from the ceiling. At the end of it

152

was a red ball and on the wall next to it a sign warned, 'For emergency use only.'

'Each car has one,' Pete explained. 'But you're only supposed to pull it if someone gets caught in a door or dragged or something. The train stops right where you are – in its tracks.' He smiled at his railroad joke. Cute kid.

'As we just did,' I said.

'Correct.' Pete was straightening the bottles on the back bar. 'So if the guy next to you is having a heart attack or something, it's the last thing you want to do because it could take even longer for help to come.'

I looked at the guy next to me, who happened to be Boyce. 'I suppose that could be what happened.'

'We'll find out.' He gestured toward the direction Pavlik had disappeared. 'We're lucky to have some law enforcement with us, regardless.'

'Amen,' I said. 'Usually I have to deal with these things myself. Until the police or sheriff's department arrives, of course.'

Boyce shook his head. 'So you've been in a lot of train derailments, too?'

I felt myself blush. 'No, not really. Just the other ... emergencies.'

'Uh-huh.' Boyce glanced at Pete and apparently decided not to pursue the subject. At least for the time being. 'Is everyone up front safe?'

'So far as we can tell.' In truth, everyone I'd *seen* was all right. I couldn't be certain that all of the passengers were accounted for. Maybe it would make sense to take a roll call just to be sure.

'Pavlik is going to check on the engineer,' I continued. Then I frowned.

'What's wrong?' Boyce asked. 'I mean, beyond the obvious.'

'According to Missy,' I was already heading for the vestibule, 'there's no inner connection between the locomotive and the passenger cars. The sheriff is going to have to go outside.'

'Do you want—'

I didn't wait to hear the rest, letting the connecting door close behind me.

The dining car was empty, the rest of the group still congregated in the passenger car, chattering. Pavlik must have been delayed by further questions, because I was just in time to see him slip into the vestibule beyond.

Before I could catch up, he'd slid open the exit door and disappeared.

FIFTEEN

'Wait!'

Pavlik was standing on the gravel bed beneath and sloping away from the tracks. 'What?'

The bed was narrow, but it was there, which was a relief. I'd imagined we were traveling on some sort of elevated trestle like that in the photograph of Flagler's ill-fated railroad. In actuality, though, our tracks were mere inches above the swamp.

This was good news because we needn't fear falling. Bad, because we were within serving distance of whatever creatures were making dinner plans.

At least, though, I thought as I jumped down after Pavlik, the warm rain had slackened to a steamy sprinkle. 'Do you have your knife or, even better, your gun?'

'Knife, yes. Gun, no. Why?'

'There are alligators and pythons and, umm ... lions.'

'Lions?' Pavlik looked skeptical.

'I may have that part wrong.' I was frowning again. 'But definitely the rest.'

'Well, then, stay close.' Pavlik was walking along the outside of the sleeping car toward the locomotive. 'That way, if something drags me away, you can properly identify it for the local authorities.'

I scurried along behind. 'Is it my imagination, or is that pitched down?'

'You mean the front of the locomotive? Sure looks like it to me, too.' He grasped a vertical bar and swung himself up and into the already open door of the engine car.

'You know,' I called up, 'there are emergency cords in every car that can stop the train, if they're pulled. Maybe that's what happened.'

'I noticed the cords,' the sheriff's voice came from inside the cab.

I shouldn't have been surprised. The man was aware of everything. And revealed nothing, damn it.

A hoarse *sqwaaak* pierced the air and hung there, followed by a series of raspy *wok, wok, woks.*

'Shit!' I edged closer to the train. 'It's like we're in a Tarzan movie.'

'Funny you should say that.' His head appeared. 'Apparently at least a couple of Johnny Weissmuller's Tarzan movies of the thirties and forties were filmed somewhere in Florida. Legend has it that some of the rhesus monkeys used in the movies escaped. Supposedly it's their descendants that run wild here today.' Pavlik jumped down from the cab. 'Cool, huh?'

Well, I certainly had goose bumps, if that confirmed his opinion.

The big front headlight of the train illuminated the Everglades in front of us, which was a good way to capture a black hole of nothingness. Oh, I could see water, scrub grass – sawgrass, presumably – and some sort of foliage, but nothing else except low, shapeless shadows as far as the light could pierce the gloom.

'Holy mother of God,' a male voice said.

Startled, I saw the figure of a man standing next to the nose of the locomotive. I didn't remember noticing him earlier.

'Oh, dear,' I said, sounding like Missy, even to my own ears.

Pavlik and I strode toward the man. Well, Pavlik strode. I scurried fearfully in his wake.

'Jake Pavlik,' the sheriff said, sticking out his hand to the other man. 'I assume you're the engineer. Nobody onboard seems to be hurt. What happened?'

The engineer turned. His name was 'Theodore B. Hertel, Jr,' according to the embroidery that covered nearly the full width of the pocket on his bib overalls. It probably didn't improve my first impression of our train pilot that he shared a first name with my ex-husband, but his appearance didn't fill me with confidence either. The man looked close to eighty, and if the denim overalls had been striped and matched with a hat and red bandana, I'd have said he was in costume for the event. I only hoped he wasn't as 'fictitious' as our bartender/Wagon Lit conductor, Pete. Or whatever his name was.

'Did we derail?' I asked anxiously. 'Or someone pull the emergency brake?'

Hertel shook Pavlik's hand, but virtually ignored me. 'Well, sir, I certainly did pull on that brake my own self. Have to say, I'm glad to hear the people *in*side the train are OK.'

A shiver crawled up my back. I didn't like the way the engineer had said that, given that Pavlik and I were standing *out*side.

Was that banjo music I heard? In addition, I mean, to the feral monkeys and God knew what else.

Pavlik seemed unconcerned. 'Looks like the track is flooded.'

The nose of the engine was tilted down and the tracks in front of it gone. Or at least submerged under water blacker than a crow's wing.

'You're right about that, for sure,' Hertel said, rubbing his chin. 'But I'm thinking that might be the least of somebody's worries.'

I put my hand on Pavlik's sleeve, trying to pull him away from the engineer who even *Missy* thought was 'eccentric.'

'What?' Pavlik glanced over at me. Hertel was watching me, too.

'DoodooDOOdoo—' I tried shakily.

'Maggy, use your mother tongue, please?' Pavlik went to shake off my hand.

'Dueling banjos,' I hissed, hanging on. 'Ned Beatty. Squeal like a pig?'

The engineer was eyeing me suspiciously. Hertel had abnormally long earlobes, like he'd been hanging heavy earrings on them for years and years. He pulled at one lobe, a more likely cause of the droop. 'No, ma'am. That just ain't right.'

'It's not?' I was backing away. Pavlik could fend for himself.

'No, ma'am. It weren't *Dueling Banjos*. That was the name of the music. The movie was *Deliverance*. But I'm scratching my head wondering why you're trying to sing about anything when we've got this mess on our hands.'

Pavlik cocked his head, probably wondering which of his two companions was crazier. Then he turned to the engineer. 'I'm a county sheriff up north, but I don't know a whole lot about trains or the Everglades. I assume from your exclamation that we're stuck pretty good?'

159

'My "exclamation"?'

'"Holy mother of God"?' I was trying to be helpful.

'Oh, that. No, it weren't the flooded track got me down. I seen worse. It's that what sort of took me by surprise.' He pointed.

Pavlik and I both followed Hertel's index finger. On the other side of the dip in the tracks and not ten feet away from us was the biggest fucking snake I'd ever seen.

With a pair of custom-made wingtips protruding from its jaws, the knees and shoes flicking up and down in a primeval two-step.

SIXTEEN

'Holy mother of God!' I screamed, echoing the engineer's sentiments. Except I had more information to add: 'It's Potter!'

Pavlik and Hertel just looked at me.

'Those are Potter's legs sticking out of that thing.' Even as I said it, I was backing-pedaling as far and as fast as I could.

The snakes I was accustomed to sunned themselves in my flower bed. They were maybe two feet long and an inch thick and *they* scared the bejeebers out of me. This one

... this one, it could be a whole different species. Not a snake at all. This monster was big enough to devour—

The limbs sticking out of the thing did a scissor-kick. 'Oh-my-god, oh-my-god,' I said, as my back slammed into the locomotive. 'He's still alive!'

'Well, ma'am,' Hertel said, 'I suppose that's possible. I didn't spot the snake until I climbed down to examine the tracks, but I think we've got us some kind of python. They like to squeeze their victims mostly to death and then swallow 'em whole to digest later. Sort of nature's doggy bag.'

I think I liked the guy better when I thought he was going to murder us. 'Enough with the nature lesson!' I screamed. 'Do something!'

Pavlik was already pulling the knife out of his pocket. He flipped out the blade and started forward. Then, over his shoulder, 'Maggy, go get help from the train.'

I screamed 'Help!' at the top of my lungs and forced myself to move away from the relative protection of the train's engine. I might be shaking like a leaf, but there was no way I was leaving Pavlik with only Euell Gibbons for back-up.

'Can you tell how deep the water is?' I asked the sheriff as he waded in, knife in his hand.

'To the bottom? I'm not sure. But I can feel the ties seven or eight inches below the water. I'm standing – and staying – on what's left of them.'

'I'm coming with you.' What was I thinking? Clearly, I wasn't. The words were out of my mouth before I *could* think.

'I appreciate the offer, but you're afraid of snakes, remember?'

I was, but then I used to be scared of spiders and mice too – things that my then-husband dealt with at home when we were married. If divorce has taught me anything, it's that a person is as brave as she needs to be.

I puffed out my chest. 'Not anymore,' I said, hoping that saying it would make it true. I turned to Hertel. 'You have anything I can hit this thing with?'

The engineer pulled a long flashlight from a loop on his belt. 'This do?'

I took it, my hand sagging under the unexpected weight. 'Geez, yeah. This should be good.' I was imagining hitting the snake with the flashlight and having it bounce off like a rubber mallet on a concrete block. 'Listen, can you call for help?'

'Happy to, though it'll likely just be coming from the train. Cell communication's down.'

Lovely. I had started to follow Pavlik,

wondering what the hell we were going to do once we got there, when I heard Hertel again. 'They say to stay away from the pointy end.' He chuckled. 'I hear tell these big fellers don't like to be disturbed during supper.'

I'd been noticing that the snake wasn't moving much, other than sort of gulping. And keeping a wary eye on Pavlik and me.

The good news for us, if not for Potter, was that there really wasn't a 'pointy end.' The snake's mouth was full – stretched impossibly like the thing had dislocated its jaw not only into two parts, top and bottom, but into four quarters in the effort to swallow a human being.

'I've got this friend who brags he can eat a steak as big as his empty head, but these critters are the only things I've ever seen that are actually capable of doing it.' Hertel was just chock-jolly-full of culinary lore.

My foot had found the first wooden crosspiece under water and I stepped unsteadily out onto it. 'Could you please get help from the train? Let them know that it's Lar ... Laurence Potter.' The least I could do was to call the man by the name he preferred, given the indignity of his current circumstances.

'Hey, isn't that the big-shot reviewer we had onboard?'

I forced myself to look more at the wing-tips than the snake. It wasn't much of an improvement. 'We think so.'

'Now how in the hell do you figure he got out here?'

'That is a very good question,' Pavlik said, not looking around. His tone indicated that messing with him would be even worse than messing with the snake at this point. 'One we'll try to answer once we get him out of *that*.'

He hiked his thumb at the snake and, as if on cue, I swear the monster burped.

Potter's leg slid in to the ankle.

I gagged.

'One down,' I heard Hertel say. 'One—'

Ignoring the rest of it, I waded anxiously over to Pavlik. 'Can you cut him out of there?'

'I think so. With so much of Potter inside of this thing, I'm betting it can't constrict anything else.' A glance my way. 'Like me or you.'

He looked at my flashlight. 'Any part of that snake gets near you, wallop it hard with the business end and run.'

'Gotcha.' Now that I was closer, I realized what I had imagined was Potter's movement was the snake's mouth and head absorbing the actually still body. Almost like a curtain being worked onto a rod – the snake the curtain and Potter as rod. 'Please, God, he can't be alive in there, can he?'

'Don't know, but I'm sure not leaving even a corpse inside that thing's digestive system.' Pavlik was not eighteen inches from the snake, stepping up on the wooden crosspieces that looked like the rungs of a macabre ladder with one end submerged in the water.

The snake did a kind of shimmy, assuming the shimmier was the length and girth of an I-beam. I splashed back into the water. 'Be careful!' I called to Pavlik, who was trying to circle behind the snake as best he could, given the narrowness of the railroad bed.

Hertel began talking again. 'I hear tell that these fellers tire easy. Or at least the Burmese do, though this beauty looks to be one of those bigger devils.'

'You mean an African rock python?' I was trying to steady my nerves, though conversing with the engineer might not be the best way to do it.

Pavlik gave a backwards glance at my question, probably wondering how I'd know anything about snake species in the Everglades.

'The very ones,' Hertel said. 'Surprised you've even heard of them, cuz we ain't seen many around here yet. But to my eye, this queen bitch looks pregnant, so I have a hunch that's going to change.'

Wonderful. If the snake in front of us wasn't, in itself, a super hybrid between the

Burmese and Rock pythons, we were messing with the mother ship.

'Don't touch it!' I yelled at Pavlik, panic rising. 'Did you hear what he said? If you cut the thing open they'll all come crawling out.'

'No, no, no.' Hertel was practically chortling, like he'd been yanked back to his days of reading The Hardy Boys and Tom Swift. 'This ain't no *Aliens* movie, you know. Snakes lay eggs. All you gonna find inside that one is what looks like the floor of a hen house.'

'Chicken eggs,' I managed in a squeaky voice.

Pavlik turned around and put a hand down to help me. His words, though, were more for my psyche than physical well-being. 'Steady, girl.'

'You know what you might say?' Hertel went on. And on. 'You might say this snake's done bitten off more'n she can chew.'

Honest to God, if I were within batting distance of the man, I'd have beaten him to death him with his own flashlight.

Hertel laughed at his own sick joke and rubbed his chin thoughtfully. 'Last year, I spent some time with guys that went out on that python hunt. Which is how come I know so much, case you've been wondering.'

Slowly the snake stretched and then seemed to coil back on itself, the one leg and both multicolored shoes still protruding. I had a flash of my Uncle Gus after a huge Thanksgiving dinner, sucking on a festive toothpick.

And contemplating dessert.

Pavlik jumped back.

Hertel said, 'If I was you, I wouldn't be practicing my dance steps on that—'

'If you know something that will help, tell us!' I screamed at Hertel. 'Otherwise, just ... shut ... up!'

Instead of being hurt or incensed, the engineer seemed gratified, even complimented. 'Well, Sheriff, appears to me you've got yourself a feisty one there. But yes, ma'am. I guess I will leave you to it. Though they do tell me that these snakes – well, the Burmese, at least, and like I said, I don't know if this one—'

'*Now!*'

Honest to God, it was like I was talking dirty to Hertel in bed. The nastier I got, the more he seemed to like it.

'Yes, ma'am.' Now he was smiling widely. 'Well, like I said, these snakes get tired out easy. In fact, the trappers treadmill 'em.'

'"Treadmill"?' Pavlik asked, coincidentally saving my sanity.

'Yup, they hold the tail of the snake and run their hands up along, under its belly. Makes the python think it's the one moving – escaping – so it tuckers itself out trying.

Once that snake's exhausted, you can grab 'em by the base of the head and dump them in a pillow case.'

I looked at the snake. 'Would have to be a big pillowcase.'

'I don't intend to capture this one, so I wouldn't worry.' Pavlik had positioned himself behind the snake once more. Or, more precisely, behind the snake's head. If he was fully behind the snake he'd be standing another twenty feet down the railroad track. 'Maggy, try and get his attention.'

I wondered if snakes could smell fear. If so, I figured I already had the python's undivided attention.

Heart thudding, my legs like jelly, I tried to get a grip of myself and moved to the front of the serpent's head, but as far away as I could get without stepping back into the water and inadvertently becoming some other critter's quarry. You know, like the goofball who steps into the street to evade a pickpocket only to be mown down by a truck.

'Oh, and the other thing I found real interesting.' Hertel kept spewing his grisly little *bon mots*. 'Snakes go dormant when they're digesting.'

Pavlik was watching me. 'Ready, Maggy?'

I met his gaze and nodded. Since one eye was on each side of the creature's head, I had to pick left or right. Choosing the former, I waved at it. The snake turned the other way and looked at Pavlik, as if to say, *Is this broad serious?*

Meanwhile, Hertel was still compulsively sharing. 'Feller told me if you scare 'em right after a big meal, they—'

'Try making noise,' Pavlik said out of the corner of his mouth. He was stone still, the knife unwavering in his hand.

'Hey!' I yelled, jumping up and down. 'Anaconda. Over here!'

The snake reared its head like the cobra in Kipling's *Rikki-Tikki-Tavi*. Even though my brain told me this wasn't a venomous snake, my feet didn't believe it.

In fact, they had recovered impressively from their previous jelly-like state and were now backpedaling rapidly into the water, demanding to know why we believed Hertel's claim that this was a python at all. After all, we'd just met the man, and—

'Blaaaaaaaah!' An explosion in front of me.

A full lower-third of Potter was now hanging out of the snake's mouth.

'Holy shit,' I said, taking another half-step back. 'What's—'

'Blaaaaah!'

Now I could see Potter's belt.

'Kill it, kill it!' I screamed in horror as I fell backwards onto the bank. 'It's spitting out

Larry Potter so it can eat me!'

'Blaaaaah-blaaaaah.' The snake's eyes were huge and it looked ... well, concerned?

'Like I was saying,' Hertel had come from behind to help me up, 'I hear tell you scare one of these things after a big meal and—'

'Blaaah! ... Blaaah ... Blaaaah!'

Pavlik had the knife poised, but was holding fast. 'Sounds like it's got something stuck in its throat.'

Under the circumstances, I couldn't think of anything to say other than, 'the whole damn monster *is* its throat,' and anyway, speech had momentarily left me. I kept my mouth shut.

'Yup,' Hertel said, 'kind of like he's hockin' up a loogie. Or a "Larry" maybe?' The ancient engineer was laughing as he offered me his hand.

I pushed his helping hand away and got up under my own steam. 'That's in poor taste.'

'Taste,' Hertel was still chuckling. 'Now there's another good one.'

I weighed the flashlight in my hand, considering which critter I should knock senseless – or more senseless, in Hertel's case – with it.

'Blaaah – blaaah! ... Blaaaah ... BLAAA-AAAH!'

I turned around in time to see the entire body of Laurence Potter erupt from the snake's mouth and land in the water, face-down, not two feet away from me.

'Holy shit.' My stomach was heaving and I pleaded with whatever was in it – a little cake icing and a lot of espresso martini, probably – to stay down there.

'No wonder the poor bitch had trouble getting your reviewer in. And out,' Hertel said, coming up beside me. 'That thing there had to get hung up somewhere along her gut.' He pointed.

'That thing there' was a staghorn handle, buried past the base of the blade in Laurence Potter's back.

SEVENTEEN

'I guess we can eliminate "accident" as the cause of death.'

The statement was my weak attempt at bravado as the python – Burmese or African rock, with my money on the latter – shuddered its last on the opposite bank.

With me refusing to touch any part of Potter that had been inside the snake, the sheriff and I managed to drag Potter's body

171

onto what passed for dry ground on the railway bed near the locomotive. We stood and watched while Hertel – finally, and mercifully – left us to climb onto the train in search of help, Pavlik instructing him not to provide any details to even the hoped-for helpers.

'Unless that snake managed to hop up into the train and steal the knife from the cake,' Pavlik said, 'I think we can assume Potter was stabbed and either fell or was tossed off well before it got hold of him.'

I shivered and glanced toward the gaping snake carcass. The python had split its sides – and not in the good way – during the final effort to urp up the reviewer.

Pavlik, who'd been crouched down examining Potter's body, rose to his feet. 'The knife is plunged in so deeply a good portion of the handle isn't even visible. We won't know for sure until the autopsy, but I can't imagine a person being strong enough to do that.'

I lifted my eyebrows. 'So we're back to the snake as cause of death?'

'Not necessarily.' Pavlik waved toward the road bed. 'If our decedent, knife already in his back, hit the ground a certain way, his own weight might have punched the blade deeper. Or, as you say, the snake's constriction might have forced the knife farther into the body.'

I felt sick again. 'And that's what killed him?'

'We don't know that yet.' Pavlik put his hand on my shoulder. 'Potter might have already been dead from the wound. Or from drowning.'

You know you're in a bad place when the thought of somebody dying sooner rather than later cheers you.

But here we were. Welcome to the Everglades.

'What's that?' I asked, moving closer to Pavlik.

'The water dripping off the leaves and grass, probably.'

'I hear that, as well, but this is kind of a tick, tick, tick.'

'You mean like a clock? Inside a crocodile perhaps?'

Captain Hook's crocodile. My sheriff was channeling Peter Pan. 'I know it's silly, but – there! There it is again.'

Pavlik listened. 'Probably some kind of night bird. They have a lot of species down here that we've never heard or seen.'

'And, of course, alligators, not crocodiles,' I said with a self-deprecating laugh.

'No, they have crocodiles, too.' Pavlik was crossing the flooded breach back to our friend the python. 'Just not as many as they do alligators.'

More great news. With a nervous look around, I followed him.

'Did you get a good look at this thing's teeth?' I pointed a cautious toe at a portion of the snake's head. 'They tilt backwards like those one-way exit spikes in parking lots. You know – the ones that cause "severe tire damage" if you back over them.'

'A very efficient creation of nature. And from the looks of the maternity ward, Hertel was right about one thing: she was eating for about eighty.'

I looked into the belly of the beast and could swear that some of her eggs were rolling against each other. 'We're not going to leave them here, are we?'

Pavlik eyed me. 'Please tell me you're not that hungry. Or maternal.'

Ugh. 'No, thank you very much, on the former. As to the latter, just the opposite. I know everybody down here is concerned about the population of pythons in the Everglades, and I think the 'ticking' noise might be coming from inside the eggs. Maybe we – or better, *you* – should smash them or something.'

Pavlik shook his head. 'I get your point, but outside of what Hertel told us, I have no proof that's a python. Nor that it's legal to kill whatever it is or its eggs.'

'Pavlik, it was eating another member of our species, and you're going to risk letting its offspring grow up to slither in Mommy's footsteps? Not to mention following her dietary habits?'

The whole thing was starting to feel surreal. Whatever were we doing stuck *here*, talking about *this*, while standing next to ... *that*? I averted my eyes.

'I get it, Maggy. And if the creature hadn't ruptured, I would have happily slit the thing's throat if I could find it. As it is, though, I'm not sure I feel right about smashing the eggs. We'll let the authorities decide on that when they arrive.'

'Unless the eggs hatch first, overrun the cars and *Murder on the Orient Espresso* gets made into a sequel to *Snakes on a Plane*,' I muttered. 'Then all the "authorities" will find of us is our shoes. Maybe.'

'Good flick,' Pavlik observed as the rain started to fall heavier again. 'A classic, in fact. But I have to say, if these eggs can hatch themselves, make their way up and into the train and then kill us all, we deserve what we get.'

Terrific. Now Pavlik was Charles Darwin.

On the opposite side of the breach, the engineer came around the locomotive's corner. 'I tapped the first two I saw. Will they do?' He hooked a finger toward Boyce, the coffeehouse owner, and Markus, the librarian.

'Jesus,' Markus said. He was looking at the flooded track. 'What do we do?'

'I didn't tell them nothing,' Hertel said to Pavlik. 'Like you said.'

Pavlik nodded. 'Sadly, the track's not our biggest problem.' He gestured toward Potter's body in the shadow of the locomotive.

Boyce stepped forward. 'Isn't this one of our passengers?'

I realized the coffee man wouldn't necessarily know Laurence Potter by face.

'How in the hell did Potter get out here?' Markus asked, not seeming to know what to make of it all.

He could join the club.

'Apparently he fell off the train and,' Pavlik waved toward the python in front of us, 'was attacked by a snake.'

It was true as far as it went, but it didn't fool Boyce, who had begun to circle the body. 'A snake carrying a knife?'

Pavlik's eyes narrowed, as if he was appraising Boyce. 'Time on the job?'

'Military police, two hitches, one tour in Iraq.'

I didn't quite see why it took a specialized background to notice a knife in a man's back, but I'd grown accustomed to the fact that people who've served in the military or law enforcement seem able to recognize each other. Pavlik had explained it to me as an awareness, displayed by a way of carrying oneself and cold calmness in being ready for anything.

My opinion? This was a *big* anything.

'That's a python – African rock, I think,' Markus said, coming to join us on the opposite bank. 'Did he explode?'

'She,' Hertel corrected. 'But "explode" is a fair description. Full of eggs, I might add.'

Since Markus seemed to know something about pythons, I was hoping he was willing to share the facts, sans Engineer Hertel's colorful embroidery. 'Can those eggs hatch?'

'You mean right this second?' Markus pursed his lips, squatting down to get a better view of the snake. 'The female would need to lay them first and then coil her own body into a nest to keep them warm.'

'Doesn't look like that'll happen,' Boyce said.

'A good thing, too,' Hertel said. 'You don't want to be around a Mama Python protecting her eggs, 'specially if you and me are right and this is one of those African rock jobbies.'

'Bigger and meaner,' Markus concurred. 'Do you think Potter was protecting himself with the knife and somehow got it in the back during the struggle?'

For a second I thought Pavlik might go along with the theory for expediency, but then he seemed to reconsider. 'Pretty un-likely, I'd say. He—'

'What in the world are you all doing out here?' Zoe Scarlett had rounded the locomotive and come up behind the engineer and Boyce. She stopped short and Missy, following on her boss's heels, nearly rear-ended her.

Then both of them looked down at Laurence Potter.

'Oh, dear,' Missy Hudson, the mistress of understatement said. 'Is he...?'

'Dead,' Hertel said, flatly. 'Stabbed and squeezed, then swallered and *ree*-gurgi-*tated* for good measure.'

Missy turned green, but it was Zoe who fainted dead away.

EIGHTEEN

I registered a benefit of the train having already reversed on the tracks so it now pointed east and back toward the station in Fort Lauderdale: the sleeping car, where Pavlik wanted to stash Larry Potter's body, was the closest one to us.

Leaving Missy, Markus and the recovering Zoe to continue on to the club car entrance at the rear of the train, Pavlik and Boyce had carried Potter's body to the exit where I'd found the matchbook. They stood waiting while I slid open the door.

'You may just have to count to three and sling 'im up there,' Hertel said from behind them. 'This train doesn't have no steps to pull down, because the station's got high platforms and that's the only place people will get on and off.'

We all looked down at Potter. Pavlik had hold of the reviewer under his arms and Boyce had hold of the feet. I couldn't see how they were going to "sling" him – one-two-three, heave! – and have him land inside the train as opposed to splattered up against it.

'Fireman's carry is the best,' Boyce said, setting down his end. 'I'll get him.'

'You sure?' Pavlik asked. 'We can—'

'Yup.' Boyce leaned over, wrapped his arms around Potter's waist and levered him up onto his shoulder. 'Gotta keep in shape.'

Straightening up, the coffee man swung himself and his burden up and into the train, seemingly effortlessly.

'Your tongue is hanging out,' Pavlik growled to me. 'Put it back where it belongs and climb in.'

'Yessir,' I said, swinging myself up ahead of him. Zoe's swoon at the sight of Potter's body, while understandable, had made me feel absolutely plucky by comparison.

'Don't you want a ... pristine room?' I asked, as Pavlik slid past me to open the first door on the left for Boyce, who was waiting patiently. 'This is where you – and Potter, if my theory is right – were earlier.'

'Which makes it the perfect place now,' Pavlik said. 'Any evidence was already trampled over during our little play and this way we don't chance contaminating another possible scene.'

'Murder scene?' I asked, as Boyce went to deposit his load.

'He was stabbed somewhere,' Pavlik pointed out. 'There must—'

'Oops,' Boyce said as Potter slipped off his shoulder and onto the bunk. 'He's kind of slippery.'

'Probably python tummy juices,' Hertel said from the doorway. 'Not to mention the rain. It's coming down cats and dogs again out there.'

As if the Everglades themselves were writing our stage directions, lightning flashed through the window, illuminating the body.

'Let's keep him up on his side,' Pavlik said, assisting. 'We don't want to jam the knife any deeper into his back.'

'Not going to matter much now,' Hertel opined, clicking on the roomette light.

We ignored him as the two other men settled Potter onto the bunk, facing away from us toward the window.

I suppressed a shiver. Given my new-found 'pluck,' I attributed the reaction to the fact that my sundress was rain-damp. With the window closed and air conditioning on, the sleeping space felt like an icebox. And it smelled none too sweet, as well. 'What do we do now?'

'I asked Markus, Missy, and Zoe to keep this to themselves, but have everyone convene in the passenger car.' Pavlik hooked a finger in the direction of the next car. 'We'll need to explain the situation and outline our options, assuming there are any.'

Then, to Hertel, 'I assume, since the track is underwater, we're stuck here?'

'You're plumb right about that. We can plow through a little water, but it looks to me like the railroad bed might've washed away under the tracks and sunk 'em, which is why we have that gulley between us and where the snake had ahold of him.' He nodded at Potter.

I looked at the dead man, who could easily have been curled up in bed 'with his trousers on,' as the old nursery rhyme goes.

One shoe off and one shoe on. Diddle, diddle, dumpling, my son John. 'Should we cover him or something?'

'I'd rather not,' said Pavlik. 'The less we tinker, the happier the crime-scene people are going to be when they get here. In fact, we should clear this car and post a guard to keep everyone out.'

He looked at Boyce. 'Will you take first watch?'

The coffee man née military policeman nodded.

I was relieved Pavlik had found a comrade-in-arms in Boyce, especially since his next choice probably would have been me. Much as I appreciated the trust, being left alone guarding a dead body – especially one that had been headfirst in the digestive tract of a very pregnant nightmare – was beyond creepy, even bordering on sci-fi.

Besides, I told myself, much better that I be present when the sheriff briefed the rest of the passengers. That way I'd know what he had and hadn't told them and, therefore, what I was free to say. That was the kind of judgment – or lack of judgment – call that had gotten me into trouble before.

Moving to the warmer corridor, Pavlik waited for the rest of us to follow him out before sliding the door closed behind us. Then he and Boyce went room to room – one opening the door, the other entering, then alternating for the next one just like you would see in the movies.

Satisfied no one was in the sleeping car besides us, Boyce asked, 'Do you want me posted here in the hall?'

'Let's go through to the next car,' Pavlik said, leading the way into the vestibule.

'Wait a second,' I said, backtracking. 'I don't think we closed this exit door completely when we brought the body in. That's probably why it's so toasty warm in the hallway.'

'Stop!' Pavlik barked, but I'd already grabbed the handle and went to slide the door closed.

My hand came away, sticky.

NINETEEN

The rumble of voices could be heard as Pavlik slid open the door of the passenger car.

'It *must* be blood,' I whispered to Pavlik as I slipped past him into the restroom to wash my hands. 'That's also the area where I found Potter's matches.'

'Time and forensics will tell us just what the substance is,' the sheriff said, maddeningly reasurred. 'As for the matches, are you sure they're his?'

'Yes.' I dried my hands on a paper towel before plunging one of them into the pockets of my sundress to retrieve the empty matchbook. I held it up. 'See? These were the matches he had at the table in the dining car. At first, Missy and I thought he might have opened the door to smoke and fallen out.'

Pavlik took the matchbook. '"Titanium"?'

'Apparently it's a "gentleman's club," or at least that's what Missy called it. Knowing her gift for sugar-coating, it could be a brothel, or even an S&M dungeon, for all we know.'

'I think we'll position you in here for now,' he called back to Boyce, who was still in the vestibule talking with Engineer Hertel.

The two men joined us. 'I assume people can use the restroom here in the passenger car?' Boyce asked.

'Yes, but nobody goes through the vestibule into the sleeping car.' Pavlik nodded toward the door that had just closed behind the engineer. 'I'll see if I can find you a chair so you can sit with your back up against the door to the vestibule, facing into the rest of the passenger car.'

'Yes, sir,' Boyce said, taking up the position. This time even I could see the military in his bearing. I felt, rather than saw, his hand itching to rise in a salute.

Guard stationed, Pavlik, Hertel and I paused. I could hear the buzz of speculation coming from the rows of seats beyond the restroom.

'After we settle down the passengers,' Pavlik told the engineer, 'you and I will go to the locomotive, where we'll call the authorities. You'd have a better idea than I do which jurisdic—'

But Hertel was shaking his head. 'Sorry, but as I told your girl here,' he hooked a thumb back to me, 'we're purely in-communicado out here.'

185

'What do you use?' Pavlik asked. 'Radio?'

'Well, now, this being a new line and our being a little off the grid, official-wise, I have this.' He held up a cell phone, and not even a very smart one.

I was still trying to translate 'off the grid, official-wise' to plain English. 'What exact-ly—'

We were interrupted by Missy, who had added the wringing of hands to her reper-toire. 'We're doing our best, but people are getting very impatient for answers. We ... we haven't told Audra.' Missy's voice broke. I could see tears.

Pavlik squeezed her shoulder. 'I'm sorry – this shouldn't all fall back on you.'

'He's just wonderful,' she whispered to me as Pavlik strode to the front of the car.

While I couldn't echo the worshipful tone, I did the sentiment.

'Excuse me,' Pavlik said, standing in the aisle at the front of the car. Zoe was seated in the first window seat, twisted around to Markus behind her. I wondered how much help either had been to Missy in keeping a lid on things.

At least they'd herded the group as in-structed into the passenger car. There were just a few seats to spare, including the one next to Zoe. I took it, feeling charitable. 'How are you?'

'Better,' she said, looking surprised that I'd asked. 'Though I'm not sure why. We're in a terrible fix.'

'What's happened?' Prudence called from a few rows back. She was sitting next to Rosemary Darlington. 'Why have we stopped?'

'According to our engineer,' Pavlik pointed at Hertel, but didn't give him an opportunity to speak, 'a portion of the railroad bed has been washed away by the storm, temporarily stranding us here.'

'Isn't Jacob going to tell them about Larry?' Zoe whispered to me.

'Got me,' I said. 'All I know is that *we* shouldn't.'

'Where is he? I mean ... Larry?'

'In the sleeping room where the "crime" was solved.' I used my index fingers to fashion air quotes.

'But what happens if someone goes in there to lie down or something?' Zoe persisted. 'Or he starts to smell?'

I was afraid that ship had sailed, but didn't see how my answer could give her any comfort. 'Don't worry. Pavlik will handle it.'

Zoe was looking at me quizzically. 'Why do you do that?'

'Do what?'

'Call Jacob by his last name?'

'I don't know,' I snapped, charity out the

window. 'Why do you call him "Jacob"?'

Zoe shrugged. 'He was listed as "Jacob Pavlik" the first time he spoke here. I was in charge of the nametags and program materials and I guess it just ... stuck.'

It could be the truth, I supposed. Zoe was looking for an explanation in return, so I obliged. 'He suspected me of murder. Believe me, "Pavlik" was the nicest thing I called him.'

Zoe's eyes flew open and she managed a weak, 'Oh.'

'So,' I said brightly. 'How long have you known Larry?'

'I, uh ... about five years, perhaps?' She was edging away from me as best she could, given the constraints of the side-by-side seats.

'You needn't worry about me,' I told her, feeling a little hurt. 'I didn't commit the crime then and I certainly didn't have any reason to kill Potter now. But somebody must have.'

'Must have what?' Zoe was looking a lot like she did before she passed out. Happily, if she toppled, she couldn't go far.

'A reason to kill Larry Potter, of course.' I slid closer and in a confidential tone whispered, 'So who do you think it was?'

'How would I know?' The conference organizer was back to the window.

'But you *know* these people. For example,' I nodded toward Rosemary Darlington, 'could the legendary author have finally snapped when her rumored former lover trashed her new book? Or maybe,' I hooked a thumb over my shoulder at Danny, 'it's the aspiring young writer who's the killer. He's practically been stalking the victim, after all, since the critic refused to read his work.'

'Then there's the literary agent.' A head tilt toward Carson, seated with Markus across from us. 'Could he have had a reason to kill his client? Or what about the librarian? I'm pretty sure he was one of Potter's "victims" in the past. And what about the long-suffering wife?' I couldn't see Audra Edmonds, but plunged on anyway, still keeping my voice down. I was on a roll. 'Might Don't-Call-Me-Mrs-Potter have done away with her cheating mister?'

'I ... I don't know.'

'Of course not. How could you?' I turned back full-face to Zoe. 'The only person who *does* isn't talking.'

'You mean Larry?' Zoe's voice was raspy, as if she couldn't draw in enough air.

'And the killer, of course.' I swept my hand to encompass the entire assemblage. I couldn't help myself. 'Or killers.'

Zoe was surveying our fellow passengers warily, so I left her to it and turned my attention back to Pavlik's question-and-answer session, chewing things over in my mind.

'...say, we're stuck here,' Carson was saying. 'But for how long?'

'Has someone called for help?' came from Grace, who looked a little worse for wear. Hopefully she hadn't been dancing on top of a table when we'd come to our abrupt stop, but her body language did project an aching head.

'Unfortunately, it appears the only communication is by cell.' I noticed that Pavlik didn't elaborate. 'And there seems to be no service here.'

Cell phones magically appeared in hands.

'Huh,' Markus said, looking at his. 'Not a single bar.'

'We're still deep in the Everglades.' I tried to look out the window, but all I could see was my own reflection against the black backdrop of rain riveting down the glass.

'There are no cell towers. Or at least not many.' Zoe slipped her phone back into her pocket. 'And I'm sure the storm didn't help matters any.'

'I hear the Everglades is like twice the size of Rhode Island,' Danny contributed. 'Some hunter got separated from his friends a while back and they didn't find him for four days.'

Prudence sniffed. 'Must have been decades

ago. Now—'

'You'd think,' Danny interrupted, 'but this was like three years ago. And just this past spring a whole family got lost. They were found a day later, but the newspaper story I Googled said they got lucky. They could have been out here a week.'

'A week?' Missy's voice squeaked from somewhere in the back of the car. The assistant event coordinator was probably keeping a low profile.

'Please,' Pavlik said, holding up both hands. 'I'm not familiar with the area. But once it's light, we'll have a better idea of what we're dealing with. For tonight, stay in this car and the two behind it – the dining and club cars. The forward one is off limits.'

'The sleeping car?' Rosemary asked. 'Why?'

'See?' Zoe hissed, elbowing me. 'I knew they'd ask.'

'At least a few of us should be allowed to catch some zzz's in there,' Prudence contributed in support of our surviving guest of honor.

'I'm afraid that's not possible,' Pavlik said flatly. No explanations, no apologies.

I dug an 'I told you so' elbow into my seatmate's ribs.

'Oh, yeah?' demanded the big guy who'd followed Grace onto the table earlier. 'Who says?'

'Can it, Fred,' Zoe said, rubbing her side. 'The sheriff is in charge.'

'Some cop from Hicksville, Wisconsin?' The guy surfed tabletops – I guess it figured he had more nerve than brains. 'That doesn't give him any authority here.'

'And you are...?' asked Markus.

Fred got up and unsuccessfully tried to hike up his belted pants over his enormous paunch. 'I'm in South Florida law enforcement. I should be in charge.'

Geez, just what were we being treated to, *'Lord of the Flies: Their Boomer Years'*?

Though in truth, I'd prefer that classic over the Donner Party experience in the Sierra Nevadas, given that this guy looked like he could give the python a run for its money at an all-you-can-eat buffet.

'You're a gate guard at a senior housing complex,' Zoe said, cutting him off at the knees. The woman still had some fight in her. 'When was the last time someone was stabbed to death there, huh?'

Uh-oh.

'Stabbed to death?' someone echoed, sounding more than a little horrified.

'And,' a firm, also female, voice from the back, 'just *where* is my husband?'

192

TWENTY

I wouldn't say the writers with us on the Orient Espresso were ghouls exactly, but they did seem loathe to let a forensic learning opportunity pass by unexploited. However impromptu and even if the corpse was, in a vertically integrated sense, one of their own.

'I don't see how it would hurt,' Prudence was saying. 'I mean, you said the man is already dead.'

'And, outside a funeral home, I've never seen a dead body,' Grace whined. 'This may be my only chance.'

'You said he was stabbed?' Harvey – the man playing Hardman, the American detective disguised as a 'flamboyant American' in Christie's book – was taking notes. 'How many times?'

Obviously thinking about the number and variety of blade wounds in Christie's original, he winked at me.

I'd been bombarded with nonstop questions since Pavlik had taken Potter's wife away to break – or, thanks to Zoe – elaborate and maybe soften the news for Audra.

I wished the sheriff good luck on the last, especially since at least one paragraph of his explanation would have to include the expressions 'cake knife' and 'exploding python.'

I was twisted around in my seat to face the crowd, one knee tucked under me and my patience wearing thin. 'I told you. I can't—'

'So the cause of death is a stab wound or wounds, plural?' from Danny, who seemed to be tapping notes into his iPhone.

'The knife was stuck in his back,' Missy piped up. She was still a little green around the gills, but determined to be helpful. 'Though the python—'

'Python?' Prudence interrupted. 'Nobody mentioned a python.'

'There's a snake on the train?' Grace was glancing around like the thing was going to slither down the aisle.

'No, no,' Missy said, seeming to realize the firestorm she'd just sparked. 'And I didn't say it was the cause—'

'There *is* no python – or snake of any type – on this train.' Pavlik had entered from the dining car, shooting a dark look at the young woman. 'You have my word on that.'

I knew the drill all too well, but Missy looked like the sheriff had slapped her. The bottom lip trembled and I knew she was seconds from another round of tears.

'Oh, look,' I said, holding up my cell phone to distract the group. 'I have service!'

A dozen phones promptly reappeared and then disappeared as their owners realized I was mistaken. Or lying.

'Sorry, phantom bar,' I said, tucking my prop away. 'Anyway, you're welcome to ask the sheriff, but I can't imagine that the authorities in any state would want us traipsing in and out of that sleeping car before they have a chance to examine it.'

A surge of muttering waved down by Big Fred, of all people. 'Folks, the sheriff's tootsie has it right. The crime scene must be preserved.'

'It's in all the books,' someone else said. 'And TV shows, too.'

A third piped up. 'But we could go one by one. Or just send a representative to take a few photos we can share.'

OK, maybe they *were* ghouls.

'It'd be like a press pool,' Prudence said. 'Back in the day—'

Pavlik held up his hands. 'I appreciate your *concern*,' I had to hand it to him, he managed to sound more commanding than sarcastic, 'but I think your – and our – time here is better spent trying to figure out how Mr Potter spent his last hour or so on this train.'

I shot Pavlik a look of disbelief and, since he was standing in the aisle next to me, I tugged on his pants leg.

He held up his finger to the assemblage and leaned down. 'What?'

'You're encouraging witnesses to discuss the things they saw?' I whispered.

'You really think we can stop them?' He shrugged. 'At least this will keep them busy and away from the body. We can make a record of what they claim to have seen and done before their memories are further compromised.'

Hmm. My 'tootsie' was a smart cookie, too. God knew when the local authorities would arrive and by then this group would have written their own storylines and re-arranged their memories to match. Not to mention using their cell phones as we drew sufficiently near civilization to sew up book and movie deals before we left rail for pavement at the station.

'Maggy, I have to ask you to serve as secretary,' Pavlik said, raising his voice so the rest of the group could hear and pulling a notebook out of his pocket. 'I'll conduct the interviews and record them on my smart phone.'

Even without the ability to make a call, we could do that. 'Good idea.'

'Oooh,' Grace squealed. 'This is just like

Murder on the Orient Express. Do you want to interrogate us in the dining car?'

Pavlik said, 'I think that will do nicely. Just give us a few minutes to set up.'

A tired-looking Zoe Scarlett stood and tugged closed her perpetually gaping dress. She was looking less like a bombshell and more like its crater. 'What would you like me to do, Jacob?'

'Stay in this car and Maggy will let you know who to send in next.'

The woman, who an hour ago would have thrown me a scathing look, just nodded resignedly and turned away. 'I can't believe this,' I thought I heard her say. 'I just can't believe this is happening to me.'

'Do you think it's odd there was just one real railroad employee on the train?' I asked Pavlik as we prepared the same table in the dining car where we'd sat earlier in the evening. It was just past midnight. 'Shouldn't there have been a conductor and ... I don't know, a brakeman or steward or something?'

'Got me,' Pavlik said, sliding into the booth. 'We'll ask Zoe and Missy when they are in here, but it sounds to me like corners were cut, probably because of budget limitations.'

'Missy did say she'd hoped more people would attend.'

'And now there's one fewer.' He handed me his smart phone.

'I thought you wanted me to take notes.' I held up the cell. 'What do I do with this?'

'Changed my mind.' Pavlik took back his pad and flipped it open. 'You video and I'll take notes. I need to be looking at their faces directly, not paying attention to a screen.'

Made sense. My ex, Ted, had been a camera bug and I swore the man never experienced any place that we went except afterwards on video and photos. Always had his eyes glued to a lens, following the strategy of 'make camp and break camp: we'll look at the pictures when we get home.'

'Did you bring a charger?' I slid the control on the phone to 'video.' 'I'm afraid this could take all night.'

'Yes, I did, and I hope it will. Take all night, I mean.' Pavlik was jotting down a list of buzzwords toward his questions. 'The longer we can keep these people engaged the better.'

'You mean the less trouble they'll be to us?'

'That's exactly what I mean. You saw it. Their imaginations are already running away with them.'

I found it hard to believe that the imaginations of even a bunch of mystery writers could measure up to the reality of what we'd just witnessed.

'The minute Missy mentioned pythons,' Pavlik continued, 'they started fabricating. That's what I want to avoid.'

'That's not really fair,' I protested. 'There was a python. A big one. And eggs, filled with little bitsy pythons. Remember?'

'But not on the train.' Pavlik spaced each word as though it were a separate sentence.

'True.' As far as it went.

'Remember, Maggy: we obtain information, not provide it. The detail of the python's involvement is better kept among those of us who are already privy to it.'

The detail of the python's 'involvement'? I was starting to feel like I'd fallen down the rabbit hole with Alice. 'You've reminded Missy, Zoe, Boyce, Markus and Engineer Hertel to keep mum?' Our privy wasn't very private.

'I have.'

'Then consider the snake off the table,' I said. 'What's next?'

'Any chance you remember the order of the witnesses called in *Murder on the Orient Express*?'

'No, but we do have access to a crib sheet.'

Pavlik, for nearly the first time since I'd known him, let a look of confusion cross his face.

TWENTY-ONE

Grace/Greta's copy of *Murder on the Orient Express* in front of us, we surveyed the chapter headings of 'PART II – THE EVIDENCE.'

'Let's see, first witness.' I looked at Pavlik. 'Pete the bartender is playing the role of Pierre Michel, the fictional "Wagon Lit conductor."'

'I can't imagine he has anything to tell us,' Pavlik said. 'He's been behind the bar in the club car most of the time. Besides, he's not one of the people we want to keep occupied.'

'Good point. What about Engineer Hertel? Should we call him to the stand?'

'I'm not sure we can keep the natives from getting restless out there while we get an encyclopedic lowdown on Wild Kingdom – The Everglades Franchise.'

Another good point. Hertel was probably more a bizarre Marlin Perkins than a carnivore's Euell Gibbons.

'Still,' the sheriff said. 'I do have one thing I need to clarify with him before we talk to anyone else. So yes, bailiff, please bring in the first witness.'

I grinned and got up.

Pavlik's hand stopped me before I could get any farther. 'I know this hasn't been exactly what you expected when I asked you to come along.'

I smiled. 'You mean when I invited myself?'

'Yeah, since you mention it.' His blue eyes flashed. 'But I'm glad you did. Even now, and maybe especially now, given what's happened. You were truly stand-up brave following me off the train when I know you were scared.'

'Try terrified.'

A grin. 'Yet when we confronted that goliath of a snake, you were nigh-on to heroic.'

'Just "nigh-on"?' I teased, giving him a quick kiss on the lips. 'And there's no one else *I'd* rather be with, either. Especially stuck in the Everglades with a murderer onboard.'

His hand stopped me again. 'That person *is* still here somewhere, Maggy. The only other possibility was that he – or she – bailed into the Everglades.'

I remembered what I'd been thinking earlier. 'Do you want me to take a head count and compare my tally to Zoe's passenger list?'

'Already done.'

'By whom?'

'By me, just now, when everyone was seated in the passenger car arguing with you. Nobody's missing.'

I shook my head. 'What a mess.'

'You're telling me. And God knows whose jurisdiction we're in. We could be on federal park land, the Seminole Indian Reservation or just county, state or private land.'

'Aren't you going to get in trouble with whoever the authorities are?' I blushed. 'I mean, you've scolded me often enough for sticking my nose in and mucking things up and now you've...'

'Become functionally you?'

'A civilian,' I tried.

'Technically, but I'm still law enforcement. And I'm the best we've got or will have until we can contact someone both official and local. I'd like to get what we can down on the record before people start swapping – and blending, and embroidering – their individual stories.'

'Like they probably are, as we speak.'

'Which suggests...' He gestured toward the door.

Got it: bring on the engineer.

'Well, golly, that's a real good question.'

202

Engineer Theodore B. Hertel, Jr was sitting across from us, pulling on his earlobe. I hoped, for symmetry's sake, not the one he'd been dragging down out on the railbed with Potter and the python.

He stopped and then went to his chin. 'What's this?'

I set down the camera/phone and leaned across the table. 'Looks like you missed a spot,' or three, 'when you shaved.'

'That's a relief,' he said. 'Thought it was a hairy mole. Those puppies can turn into cancer, you know?'

I didn't know. And I didn't want to know. Not now and preferably not ever, especially from this master of disaster.

'Back to the question,' the sheriff prompted.

'Which was?'

A trained interrogator, Pavlik didn't roll his eyes, though I feared I might be rolling enough for the both of us. 'Given that we found Laurence Potter's body on the opposite side of the flooded track from where we sit now, can you tell me when we passed through that area on the way out into the Everglades?'

I thought I knew where Pavlik was going with this.

'Before we reversed direction to go back east, you mean?' He was back to tugging on the lobe, but the one on the other side of his head.

'Correct.' Pavlik waited.

'Well, now. That's hard to say. You see, I'm not quite sure just where we are.'

'I can understand that,' Pavlik said mildly. My brain, on the other hand, was screaming in all capital letters, 'WHAT THE HELL DO YOU *MEAN* YOU DON'T KNOW WHERE WE ARE IN THE MIDDLE OF THIS—?'

'Let's start with the "when," then,' Pavlik continued, giving my nervously vibrating thigh a reassuring squeeze under the table. 'We know that tonight's event was to be a three-hour-long round trip. That would mean you turned the train around halfway through that time or ninety minutes after we departed the station, right?'

'Well, technically we don't turn around. Just stop and I take her back the other way.'

I could have smacked the man, but the sheriff apparently thought we were making progress. 'So you confirm that you "took her back the other way" ninety minutes after we left the station?'

'Probably that, like you say, give or take. This isn't an exact science, you know.'

Seemed like a hell of a way to run a rail-road.

'And how many miles into the Everglades

would that have taken us?' Pavlik was writing again.

'No way of telling.'

Pavlik looked up from his notes. 'You didn't glance at your odometer?'

Hertel looked puzzled. 'Odometer? Ain't got one. Leastways that's any use to the engineer. No, we just chug from one assigned stop to 'nother along the same track. What would I do with an odometer?'

I suppressed a grin as Pavlik seemed to ponder what Hertel could do with his odometer. 'So you don't know how far we traveled before we reversed directions.'

'No sir, that I don't.' Hertel shifted on the banquette. 'Not quite sure why it matters, tell you the truth.'

I saw Pavlik's knuckles whitening as he gripped his pen, so I took over before he decided to bayonet the guy's eye. 'Let's forget distance for now. If we know what time we reversed, and how long after that we came to a stop because of the damaged track, we'll know approximately when we passed this spot on the way into the Everglades.'

'Meaning that's when this Potter became snake-bait, huh? Well, that's real good reasoning, I have to say. Not sure it'll hold water, though.' Hertel was grinning.

'And why is that?' I asked between my own clenched teeth.

Mercifully, my tag team partner stepped in. 'We left the station a little after eight?'

'Correct-o-mundo. Eight-oh-four, to be exact.'

'And we've agreed we reversed ninety minutes after we left the station, so as to be back within the three-hour timeframe. That means, of course, nine thirty-four.'

'Give or take,' I added before Hertel could.

Pavlik's pen hovered over a sheet of paper he'd torn from his pad. 'And the train travels how fast?'

Hertel worried the errant patch of chin hair. 'We averaged about forty on our way out.'

'Good, good.' The sheriff wrote it down. 'So at forty miles an hour, we'd cover sixty miles in an hour and a half.'

I gave Pavlik an admiring glance. He'd get his gold star later.

The sheriff began chewing on the eraser end of his pen, giving me a glimpse of little Jacob Pavlik in grade school. 'We still need to know what time we were stopped here by the flooding. With all the commotion, I didn't think to look.'

'Maybe Missy or Zoe noticed,' I suggested.

'Well, now, I can tell you that,' Hertel said.

'You can?' Pavlik and I looked at him. 'Why didn't you say so?'

'You asked how far we chugged into the

Everglades, which I didn't know, and what time we left the station, which I did. You never did ask when we stopped out here.'

'I'm asking it now.' Pavlik's eyes were narrow slits. 'When?'

This time I patted his thigh.

'Why, a mite before ten p.m.'

I threw a smile at Pavlik. 'That means that Potter went off the train here about nine.'

'And "here" is approximately forty miles west of the station.' Pavlik leaned back against the banquette and stretched.

'And how do you figure that?' from Hertel.

'Easy.' I pushed Pavlik's paper in the middle of the tabletop so the engineer could see the sheriff's notes. 'We reached the place we reversed at nine-thirty and, according to you, our current position at ten. That's a half hour after reversal, meaning we must have passed this spot a half hour *before* reversal or nine p.m. That also means that at forty miles an hour we would have covered – you guessed it – forty miles between eight and nine p.m.' I sat back now, too, pleased with our paired reasoning.

But Hertel frowned. 'It sounds simple enough, but the problem is we weren't traveling at the same speed coming back east as going out west. In fact, I was keeping the throttle at near crawl because the track was flooding. And good thing, too, or I wouldn't have been able to stop before that wash-out.'

The engineer pulled the paper toward him and dug a stub of a pencil out of his bib pocket. Touching it to his tongue, he started to work. 'Now if a train's heading one direction at forty miles an hour, and another at, say, twen—'

I let my forehead hit the table and took the self-inflicted pain without whimpering.

TWENTY-TWO

Pavlik's eyes were glazed over the instant Theodore B. Hertel, Jr closed the door behind him. 'So the long and the short of it is that the later it got, the more the rain slowed us down.'

'There is no short, when it comes to our engineer.' I was holding my head in my hands. 'Only long. Really, really long.'

'Did you understand all that?' Pavlik asked. 'I feel like we just lost more ground than the road bed in front of the locomotive's nose.'

We had Hertel's chicken scratchings in front of us, but given that we hadn't maintained a steady speed, even he hadn't been able to calculate our location with any degree of reliability. And I wasn't sure we'd have understood if he had. The man had the presentational skills of your average batty theoretical physicist.

'Well, we have to start somewhere.' Pavlik drew himself up. 'We know we reversed around nine-thirty and got stuck here at ten.'

'Correct. What we don't know is where "here" is.' I checked my cell. One a.m.

The 'Dark Side of Midnight,' as legendary Milwaukee jazz DJ Ron Cuzner had dubbed his late-night show way back when. Ron had kept me company through countless hours spent rocking Eric when he was a colicky baby. And today...

I shook myself back into the present.

'...try to bracket the time of death,' Pavlik was saying. 'We know Potter was alive as Zoe got up to welcome people. Hopefully she'll be able to tell us exactly what time that was.'

Or, more likely, Missy would. 'So that time, whatever it is, will be the early end of our bracket. The latest has to be well before we reversed directions at nine-thirty.'

'Why "well before"?'

I chewed on my lip. 'I see your point. Since we don't know how slowly we've traveled since the turn-around – or "reversal," as Hertel insists – let's just say Potter went off the train before nine-thirty.'

'Why not after?'

'Because you said he'd fallen or been push-ed—'

'Let's use "exited," since we don't know. It'll be more consistent.'

Honest to God, Pavlik was nearly as maddening as the engineer. 'You said he'd *exited* when we came past this point on the way into the Everglades.'

'Actually, I didn't. You did.'

I tried to think back to the conversation with the engineer and who had said what.

'See?' Pavlik pointed at his notes. 'You took over questioning here and made the statement to Hertel.'

Son of a bitch, but the sheriff was right. 'Only that has to be how it happened. We're on *one* side of the break in the tracks—'

Pavlik interrupted. 'Let's call what lies in front of the train – to the east of the locomotive – the flooded track. We don't know there's an actual break or that the tracks are washed away, rather than merely covered.'

'So stipulated,' I said, though if I clenched my teeth any harder, I'd need to wear a mouth guard to spare my molars. 'But my point is that Potter's body was on the opposite side of *the flooded track* from where we sit right now. Remember? We had to wade through water to get there?'

Pavlik was writing. 'The *snake* was encountered on the opposite side, east of the flooded track.'

'With Potter's body *in* him.'

'Mostly.'

'Thank you.' I was one heartbeat away from—

'Maggy, you think I'm nitpicking, but this kind of detail is important.' Pavlik read from his notes: 'The snake was encountered on the east side of the flooded track, opposite the train's stopped position. The lower portion of the victim's body was protruding from its mouth.'

'The *African rock python* was encountered,' I corrected. Two could play this game.

'We have only the engineer's opinion that it was a python, and only,' the notes again, 'Markus's belief that it was, indeed, a rock python.'

I threw up my hands. 'Hey, maybe it isn't even a snake. Why don't you just say a really big worm with teeth dwarfing a great white shark's? Want me to go out and count them?'

'Sarcasm rarely becomes you, Maggy.' Pavlik was writing again.

'I was going for "facetious."'

'Well, you missed the target.' He still didn't look up.

I sighed. 'OK, I'm sorry. Obviously, this detecting is more complicated than I realized.'

'The record-keeping is tedious and using the same terminology to identify something may seem repetitive, but believe me, it reduces ambiguity and makes the detecting, as you call it, easier and conviction much more likely.' He raised his head and smiled. 'Apology accepted.'

I cocked my head. 'Aren't you going to tell me what word I should use instead of "detecting"?'

Head down again. 'I'm trying hard not to.' A beat. 'But "investigating" might be a good choice.'

Pavlik was just too cute and I laughed, genuinely. '"Investigating" it is, Sheriff. Now tell me what difference it makes to the investigation to say that both the snake and Laurence Potter's body were on the east side of the flooded track, versus the *snake* was on the east side of the flooded track with Laurence Potter's body inside it. Mostly.'

'Happily.' Sheriff Jake Pavlik, out of his jurisdiction or not, made steady eye contact. 'The difference is how Potter got there.'

TWENTY-THREE

'Are you saying Larry Potter didn't necessarily exit the train as we passed this spot on our way west?'

'Exactly,' Pavlik said. 'The—'

I interrupted. 'Do you know if pythons eat ... dead things?'

'Carrion? If you're asking whether they're scavengers or consume only what they've killed themselves, I don't have a clue.'

'We'll have to ask somebody.' My kingdom for Google. 'I'm sorry, I interrupted. You were saying?'

'Just that the snake could have retrieved the body – or Potter, still alive, if that's the way it went down – from another location.'

'Retrieved?' The word made the thing sound more like a loyal hunting dog than a repulsive, slithering man-eater. But then foxes probably weren't so fond of hounds, either.

'Yes. Retrieved the body and conveyed it to where we found them both on the east side of the flooded track. That means Potter needn't have exited the train on the *east* side of the flooded track, but anywhere in the vicinity.'

'And the time?'

'According to the engineer, he didn't see the snake – and Potter – until he'd brought the train, now eastbound, to a stop and climbed down to investigate,' notes again, '"a mite before ten."'

'So, this "mite before ten" would be the latest Potter could have exited one of the cars, and the start of Zoe's speech the earliest.'

'Agreed.' Pavlik wrote it down and gestured toward Grace's tattered copy of *Murder on the Orient Express*. 'Who's next?'

'"The secretary, MacQueen,"' I read. 'That would be Markus.'

'Have Zoe send him in,' Pavlik ordered. 'But first, and I should have thought of this earlier, grab some bottled water and a rack of clean glasses.' He hooked his finger to the club car behind us.

I stood up, too tired to question. 'Will do, boss.'

'Oh, and Maggy?'

I stopped and turned around. 'Yes?'

'Glass glasses, not plastic. And use a towel when you take them out of the rack.'

I got the glasses and, on Pavlik's orders,

poured the water into three of them. One for him, one for me and one prepared for our next witness. And that witness's fingerprints. Then I went to the far-end door and slid it to access the vestibule.

The train was eerily still without the clatter of the tracks passing below. I pulled open the door of the passenger car, half-hoping the whole lot of them would be asleep. If so, Pavlik and I could follow suit. It had been a long day.

But alas, Zoe was still awake and seated in the front row, with Prudence now next to her. The latter looked up.

I stepped in. 'Is Markus—'

'Here,' a voice said, and he stood up.

'See?' Grace popped up from the seat behind Prudence and Zoe. 'I told you we'd be called in the same sequence as the characters in the book were.'

'That means I'll be very nearly last,' Rosemary Darlington, aka Mary Debenham said. 'Wouldn't you rather go alphabetical? Perhaps start with "A" for Arbuthnot?' She hooked a finger toward the young man seated next to her. Danny had finally snagged an audience with the great lady.

'Andrenyi comes before Arbuthnot,' Carson, aka Count Andrenyi, pointed out. 'I should go first.'

'I think we'll stick with the book's order.' I

turned to Zoe. 'Is the only railroad staff on the train the engineer?'

She shrugged, as if it didn't matter, and called out, 'Missy?'

The first Mrs Hubbard half-rose from a seat next to Pete the bartender about three-quarters of the way back. I had to hand it to Missy, she certainly was being sought out by the young men on the train. But then we only had three passengers under the age of thirty – it shouldn't be surprising that they'd seek each other out.

Even from this distance, I saw Missy blush. 'Maggy, we had a very tight budget, you know.'

Which had managed to put us in a very tight spot. 'And...'

'And, well, the train people said we had to have a conductor and I told them we did.'

'Don't tell me,' I said. 'Pierre Michel?'

The line between fact and fiction was quickly blurring. Although for these people maybe they were the same thing.

'Yes.' She plopped back down in her seat and added miserably, 'They wouldn't let us go otherwise.'

'With good reason, Missy,' Markus said, not unkindly. 'The conductor is the person in charge.'

'Really?' I asked. 'I always thought they just took tickets.'

'Uh-uh.' Markus was shaking his head. 'My mother worked at Amtrak's headquarters in Washington, and my brother Kevin is an engineer. The engineer runs the locomotive and reports to the conductor, who communicates with dispatchers and oversees the train and its passengers.'

And *our* 'conductor' was a kid whose real name was Brandon and worked at an Olive Garden. Lovely.

'Then you're it, MacQueen,' I said to Markus, gesturing for him to go ahead of me.

As we entered the dining car, Pavlik looked up from his notepad and stuck out his hand. 'Thanks for your help out there. And for keeping the particulars of the situation to yourself.'

Markus shook and slid in on the opposite side of the semicircular booth. 'Not a problem. Zoe came to almost as soon as Missy and I began helping her back to the train. None of us was eager to spend more time out there with that Jules Verne creature split open on the opposite bank.'

Pavlik shifted over so I could sit next to him and passed the smart phone to me. 'Do you mind if Maggy tapes us? It'll help the investigators if we can get everyone's initial impression.'

'Not at all,' Markus said, his open face

217

curious. 'Are you going to read me my rights?'

'You're not a suspect.' Pavlik gave him a friendly smile. 'At least, so far as I know.'

I raised the phone and through it, saw Markus's gaze waver. 'Well, no. Of course not. But I'm happy to answer any questions you might have. Not that I necessarily can.'

Pavlik raised his hands. 'Understood. First off, could you state your full name and home address for me?'

Markus complied, giving an address in Washington, D.C.

'Just for the record,' Pavlik continued, 'could you detail your movements after you boarded the train?'

'Let me think.' Markus picked up the glass of water in front of him, then set it down again. 'I saw Maggy here,' he nodded at the camera/phone, 'when I was in line for a drink. From there I made my way back through the train, stopping to talk to people here and there until I reached the passenger car.'

Pavlik, who had been studying his notes, looked up. 'We do know that Mr Potter was in the dining car until Zoe Scarlett welcomed everyone over the speaker system. Would you know about what time that was?'

Markus pulled out a handkerchief – not the dainty square of initialed cambric in

Murder on the Orient Express, but a big honkin' one – and mopped his brow. 'I remember thinking it was later than I'd expected. When Missy asked me to speak after Zoe welcomed everyone, I assumed it would be right after we left the station, which was just past eight, as you'll recall.'

This last was directed to me and I nodded encouragement.

'I remember checking the time at nearly nine and thinking they thought it best to let people chat and get liquored up before they had to sit and listen to me talk.' A self-deprecating smile.

'From what I recall from the previous time I was at this conference,' Pavlik said, 'people come from all over and may not have seen each other for quite a while during the interim.'

'Exactly.' Markus was nodding. 'Everyone wants to catch up. Find out who got published. Who found an agent. Or even was lottery-blessed by receiving a film option.'

'So you looked at the time and it was nearly nine, you said. What time exactly?'

'Eight fifty-five, maybe?'

'What did you do then?' Pavlik asked.

'It suddenly hit me that perhaps the sound system could only be heard in the dining car and, for all I knew, the program had begun and they were looking for me.'

'Not true, though.'

'Correct. As I went forward to check, I heard Zoe greet the gathering.'

'Did you see Laurence Potter?' I asked from behind the phone/camera.

'Come to think of it, we did cross paths in the dining car. He was going toward the back of the train as I was moving to the front.'

'Did you pass him before the cake?' I asked.

Finally, a roll of the eyes from Pavlik. Unfortunately directed at me.

Markus looked confused. 'Are you asking if I saw Larry before I went past the table with the cake on it?'

I glanced at Pavlik. When there was no response, I nodded at Markus.

'We were coming from opposite directions,' the librarian said, 'but as I recall we crossed paths about halfway through the dining car.'

'So you'd already passed the cake, but he hadn't reached it yet,' I summarized.

'Correct.'

'Did you notice the cake as you went by?' Pavlik followed up.

'I did.'

My turn. 'Was the knife still in it?'

This time I got a glare before Pavlik turned to Markus. 'Can you describe the cake?'

It was only then I remembered that Pavlik

had been seated on the banquette at the front of the dining car for most of our ride. Except for going to the club car – the opposite direction – to get my second espresso martini, he hadn't left the table and therefore hadn't seen the cake before it was hacked apart. Nor the knife, until we discovered it in Potter's body.

'Umm,' Markus glanced nervously at me and then back at Pavlik before answering. 'I don't know ... shaped like a sleeping man? Blanket pulled up to the neck. Covered with icing, of course.'

'Of course.' This time Pavlik seemed to purposely not look my way. 'And did you see the knife?'

'Sure. Stuck in his chest.'

Pavlik did a double-take. 'You saw the knife in Potter's *chest*?'

Markus's eyes grew wide. 'Oh, no. No, no. It was in the cake's – I mean the "man" depicted in the cake's – chest.' He looked back and forth between us. 'You saw it, right?'

I turned to Pavlik. 'The cake knife was stuck in the frosted body's chest.'

'Explains the white goo,' Pavlik said to himself. 'Any idea where Potter was headed when he passed you?'

Markus shook his head. 'Since the bar was the other way, I assumed he was going to the bathroom or to see someone in the passenger car. Tell you the truth, I didn't even realize the sleeping car was there.'

'You've told us you knew you were to speak next. Did you also know Potter was about to be introduced?'

'Are you asking why I didn't stop him?' Markus asked. 'Believe me, Potter did pretty much whatever he wanted and no one had the nerve to mess with him. Or they'd pay.'

Pavlik's eyes rose. 'First-hand experience?'

'Me?'

'You're a writer, aren't you?'

'Markus writes—' I started, and slapped my mouth shut. 'Sorry. Go ahead.'

'I write non-fiction,' Markus supplied. 'Books on classics, mystery compendiums, readers' guides, like that.'

'So you've never had the pleasure of being reviewed by Potter?'

'No. Well, yes. Once.' Markus looked miserable. 'Maybe.'

'Maybe?'

'Umm, well, he did review a … well, sort of an encyclopedia I did of crime writers.'

'Sounds impressive,' Pavlik said. 'Did Potter like it?'

'Not exactly,' Markus directed the words toward his clasped hands on the table.

'Excuse me?'

'I said,' the man looked up, 'that while he praised the "effort," Potter found a bit of fault with it. Not at all unusual in a work of this length.'

'How long was it?'

'Three volumes.'

'And how many errors did Potter find?'

'One...' Markus, just murmuring, stammered anyway. 'One hundred and forty-eight.'

I remembered the interchange between the two men on the bus. I'd known something wasn't quite right there. Potter had seemed to take great pleasure spreading salt into that wound.

I said, 'It would take forever to read all three volumes cover-to-cover and fact check each page.' Being a lover of old movies, I had a couple of reference books on that subject that sounded like what Markus was talking about. Listing upon listing upon listing.

'It's what PotShots does,' Markus said simply.

'Apparently.' Pavlik made a note. 'Do reviews like the one Potter gave you affect sales?'

A throaty laugh. 'Any review is better than no review.'

Like any publicity is good publicity, but I wasn't buying it. 'Assuming libraries and schools use your books as reference material, wouldn't the inaccuracies present a real problem for them?'

This time it was Markus directing annoyed looks my way. 'Maybe sales weren't what they could have been, but this happened more than a year ago. I certainly wouldn't murder a man over it, if that's what you're implying.'

'Good to know,' Pavlik said as he tapped me on the shoulder so he could stand. 'Could you send in whoever it is who's playing the next person on the list...'

'Ratchett's valet, Masterman,' I supplied. 'If there is one.'

'Will do.' Markus slid out of the booth, too, but then stood his ground. 'You have no doubt in your mind that Potter was murdered?'

'If you can come up with another plausible explanation for the knife on this train winding up in his back, I'd be glad to entertain it,' Pavlik said.

'Now that you say it was the cake knife in his back, I'm at a loss. He sure didn't jump off the train with it between his teeth to fight pythons.'

'Agreed.' Pavlik swept his hand toward the door.

Taking the hint, Markus moved to the door and slid it open. 'Though that leaves us with what seems like an even more unlikely scenario.'

'What's that?' I asked.

Markus stepped through into the vestibule. 'That one of my friends is a murderer.'

The door slapped shut.

TWENTY-FOUR

'Do you think whoever stabbed Larry Potter is a threat to kill again?' I asked Pavlik as we waited for our next witness. While I'd been happy to point out to Zoe Scarlett that we were *all* murder suspects, I really hoped this crime was a one-off. So to speak.

'We have to assume that anyone who crosses that line has the potential to cross it again.' Spreading his fingers inside Markus's glass to lift it without compromising the fingerprints on the outside, Pavlik leaned over to place it carefully on the table behind us.

'But why?' I asked. 'This has to have been a personal attack against Potter. Someone followed him to the sleeping car.'

'And grabbed a hunk of cake en route?'

'Potter probably did that. Remember? He was complaining not only that he couldn't smoke, but there was nothing to eat onboard except the cake. I wouldn't put it past the man to take matters in his own hands and cut the cake.' I had sublimated my own swipe at the frosting into relative irrelevance.

'Potter certainly struck me as somebody who believed rules – of etiquette, in this instance – didn't apply to him.'

'So you think Potter was a ... sociopath?' I heard the far door of the vestibule open.

Pavlik was regarding me with a wry grin. 'Honey, I'm not sure there isn't a little sociopath in all of us – you and me, included.

'What? I—'

Before I could inquire further, the near door slid open.

The man who'd been taking notes earlier entered. Harvey/Hardman's checkered sports jacket might be loud, but his voice was even louder.

'Hope you folks don't mind,' he said, every bit the blustering American of Christie's novel. 'But I have things to do and people to see. I took a poll and nobody minded that I went next.'

I minded. With a sigh, I skipped over Missy as Mrs Hubbard, Grace the Swedish Lady, Prudence the Russian Princess, Carson as Count Andrenyi and Danny as Col. Arbuthnot on my neat list and put a grudging checkmark next to Mr Hardman the American. Then I checked the time. Nearly 2:30 a.m.

'Things to do and people to see at this hour, Mr...?'

'Hardman.' We all shook hands.

Before I could tell Pavlik that 'Hardman' was the man's fictional identity, Harvey blustered on. 'I know what you're going to say. Maybe it's *people* I should be doing and leave the seeing to others.' Cue hardy laugh.

You had to give it to the man – he raised the bar of 'Ugly American' to new levels, stereotype-wise.

'Have a seat. Maggy, would you mind getting Mr Hardman a glass of water?'

'Not necessary,' Harvey said, waving me to sit back down.

I ignored him, poured the water and handed it to him.

'His name really is Harvey,' I told Pavlik. 'He's just playing the part of Christie's "Hardman."'

Harvey accepted the glass, but set it down immediately. He glanced back toward the closed connecting door to make sure we couldn't be heard, then leaned in anyway. 'You do know the Hardman character is just a blind. I'm a private detective.'

'And *you* do know,' Pavlik said, 'that you're only a fictional character, right?'

Harvey sat back like Pavlik had punched him, a look of astonishment on his face. 'But this is just part of the show, right? The whole crazy man-eating snake story?'

'Take my word for it, Harvey,' I said. 'The python was real, Potter is dead and neither incident was in the script.'

Harvey cocked his head. 'Listen, you don't have to worry about me. I'm not part of this group – just an actor. I've been playing these kinds of parts for years, and—'

'For the last time,' Pavlik said, honing an edge in his voice that made me fear for all mankind. 'This is *not* a show. A man has been stabbed to death, more than half devoured by a snake the length of a fishing pier, and this train is stranded in the Everglades with no current means of communicating to the outside world.'

'Oh.' Harvey seemed to deflate beneath his flashy sports jacket. 'Well, that's not good.'

'No, it's not,' said Pavlik. 'Your real name, please, as well as your profession and address?'

Harvey wiped his forehead on a cocktail napkin and scribbled his answers on another.

'Thank you,' Pavlik said, after reviewing the details. 'How many of the people on this train did you know prior to boarding?'

'Know personally, you mean?'

'Personally, or via telephone, telegraph, carrier pigeon, email, Facebook, Twitter.' Pavlik was getting wound up. 'I really don't give a shit, Harvey. Just tell me if you know any of these people.'

'And therefore have a motive, huh?' Harvey leaned back. 'Well, let's see. Zoe Scarlett. And Missy Hudson, of course, was the one who invited me.'

'Who else?' asked Pavlik.

'Well ... no one,' Harvey said, trying to smooth down the independent-minded lapels of his God-awful sports jacket. 'I mean, not really.'

Even I could see that Harvey was prevaricating.

'How about Potter, Harvey?' the sheriff asked.

'What about Potter?'

Pavlik's eyes darkened. 'Cut the crap. Did you know anything about Laurence Potter before you boarded the train?'

'Well, well,' Harvey said. 'If you put it like that, of course I'd *heard* of Potter. What writer hasn't?'

'Then you're a writer as well?' I asked.

'As well as what?'

'As well as an actor.'

'Oh, yes.' Harvey dipped his head. 'I've tried my hand at the occasional screenplay or two, here and there.'

'And that's how you knew Potter?'

I could tell that Pavlik wasn't going to let go of his bone.

'I didn't say I knew him *personally*. A friend offered to show him one of my screenplays, but I ultimately decided against it.'

'Why?'

'A different friend warned me off. Said Potter had a reputation for...'

Pavlik growled, 'Giving unkind reviews?'

'Well, yes, that too, but my second friend was talking more about Potter stealing other people's ideas.'

'Like whose?' I asked.

'Rosemary Darlington, for one,' Harvey said. 'Word has it he was mentoring her a few years ago – professionally *and* personally, if you get my drift.'

I didn't bother to correct him. I was too busy thinking about Rosemary's slightly drunken suggestion that Danny was dogging Potter because the young man suspected the uber-reviewer had stolen his manuscript. Not to mention that I'd seen Danny whispering with Harvey on the bus.

'And that kid, Danny,' Harvey continued, like he'd read my mind. 'He's been pumping me for information on Pott—'

Two doors slid open in rapid succession and then Missy was standing there. 'I think you'd better come. And quick.'

'Why?' Pavlik and I answered in duet.

'Well, Audra has a gun and, oh, dear, she's going to shoot Boyce.'

TWENTY-FIVE

'I want to see my husband.' Audra Edmonds was, indeed, pointing some kind of pistol at Boyce, not three feet in front of her, Danny the Sycophant just to her side.

Boyce didn't look too worried. He was sitting on the stool we'd found for him, leaning against the door of the vestibule leading to the sleeping car, arms crossed. 'I'm afraid not.'

'Are you blind?' She waggled the barrel to prove her point. 'I have a gun.'

'And a permit for it?' Pavlik asked quietly from behind her.

Audra turned, startled, which is when Boyce stood and pushed down her wrist so the muzzle was pointing to the floor before he pried it from her hand.

'Of course I have a permit,' Audra said to the sheriff, rubbing her forearm and seeming dazed by his question. 'This is South Florida. Santa and his reindeer can carry concealed weapons.'

'Unfortunately, that's true,' Boyce said,

handing Pavlik the gun, butt first. 'It's easier to get a CCW permit down here than a driver's license.'

'Or a Resident Beach Parking permit,' contributed Danny.

Absently, I wondered how he hyperlinked to that connection. And which of the two permits Danny had attempted to get.

The young man stepped past me to take hold of Audra's non-shooting arm. 'She's really upset,' he told Pavlik. 'Can we go to the club car, maybe find her something to drink?'

'As long as she doesn't expect to get this back anytime soon.' The sheriff held up the gun and we watched Danny and Audra shuffle/stumble off.

'Interesting,' I said under my breath. 'A variation on the *Deathtrap* twist, perhaps?'

'What?' Pavlik asked.

'Never mind,' I said, linking my arm with his. 'We'll watch it together some time. What's next?'

'Excuse me, Sheriff.' Carson/Count Andrenyi was standing in front of us.

'Yes?'

I couldn't remember if Pavlik knew who the man was. 'This is Carson, the lit—'

'Of course,' the sheriff said. 'I saw you in the club car earlier. You're Mr Potter's and Ms Edmond's agent.'

But when Pavlik extended his hand, Carson leaped back like a two-legged gazelle.

'He doesn't shake,' I whispered to my lover.

The sheriff lowered his hand. Slowly, I thought, so as not to embarrass Carson any more than the man had himself. 'What can I do for you?'

'I do understand that you're interviewing people in order and I should wait my turn.'

'He's Count Andrenyi,' I said to Pavlik. 'In Christie's sequence, the second to last.'

The sheriff shrugged. 'It sounded like a good idea at the time, but I think that moment has passed. Why don't you follow us?'

I led the way and got Carson a glass of water while Pavlik settled in across from him and opened his notebook. 'Do you have something you'd like to tell us?'

I tried to hand Carson the water, but he just waved me off, refusing to touch the glass.

I set it down and picked up the smart phone. 'Do you mind if I video our conversation?'

'No, I suppose not,' Carson said. 'Though I'd appreciate both of you keeping this confidential unless it has a bearing on Larry's death.'

'I'll do my best,' Pavlik said, 'but you have

to understand that I don't have jurisdiction here. We'll need to answer the authorities' questions when they arrive, just like everyone else on this train will.'

Carson thought about that for a second. 'Understood.' He leaned forward. 'I'm a little concerned about Audra and that young man.'

Pavlik rocked three inches backward. 'That "young"...?'

'Danny,' I interjected. 'The one who was so interested in your workshops and who just escorted Audra to the club car.'

Mystery 101's principal forensics speaker shook his head. 'I'm starting to think you know more people here than I do.'

I shrugged. 'I get around. You've been ... monopolized.'

'And I'm sorry about that,' Pavlik said. 'When we get—'

Carson cleared his throat.

'Sorry.' Pavlik shook his head again. 'It's been a long day. And night.'

'I understand,' Carson said. 'I just want to get this off my chest before I have time to think better of it.'

'Shoot.' The sheriff raised his pen. 'Uh, Danny?'

'Correct. The young man saw a trade announcement about a novel that Larry and Audra are working on. Danny got it in his head that Larry stole the idea from him and sent me an email outlining his accusations literally chapter and verse.'

So Rosemary, even under the influence, seemed to have been right.

'How is Potter supposed to have come across this "idea"?' Pavlik asked.

'Danny apparently sent him the manuscript originally, hoping to get Larry's endorsement or perhaps a referral to an agent, like myself, or an editor. Larry says ... said that he didn't even open the package.'

'Did you believe him?' Pavlik asked.

'Of course. He's my client, after all.' An embarrassed smile. 'Or was.'

'So why has Danny been cozying up to Audra,' I asked, 'if he thinks she might have been in on this?'

'I have no idea. Perhaps he hopes Audra will confide the plot of their new novel, and therefore prove Danny right about the plagiarism.'

Or, I thought, maybe the two already *were* acquainted and had hatched a plot of their own. One that didn't include Laurence Potter lasting until the final chapter.

'So what's the book about?' Pavlik was asking.

'I can't really tell you that.'

'Carson, I'm certainly not going to steal Potter's plot,' Pavlik said. 'And even if I considered the possibility, I can't write.'

'It's true,' I told Carson as we heard the sound of the far vestibule door opening. 'The sheriff is addicted to redundancy.'

We all looked toward the door, but nobody entered.

Pavlik turned back to Carson. 'The plot?'

'The reason I can't tell you is because, well, there really isn't much of one.'

I mulled that over. 'So ... Potter couldn't have stolen it?'

Carson shifted uncomfortably. 'From what I could tell from Danny's email, his manuscript doesn't have much of a plot, either.'

I felt like banging my forehead on the tabletop. Again. 'I don't understand.'

'You've read Rosemary Darlington's most recent book?'

'No,' Pavlik said.

'I haven't either,' I said, 'but I understand it's very steamy. Erotic. Is that what you're talking about?'

'Pretty much.'

'And that's what Potter's new book was to be like as well?' Sounded to me like Rosemary had more of a case against the recently deceased than Danny did.

'Everyone's doing it,' Carson said, 'which is part of the problem. Larry and Audra's had the twist of being written by a man and a woman. The reader sees the scenes from two different viewpoints.'

'Top and bottom?' I guessed.

Pavlik stifled a laugh. 'And what about Danny's ... uh, "plot"?'

'From a man's point of view only.'

'Gay or straight?' I asked.

Carson cocked his head. 'You know, I'm not sure. But that might be a great twist for—'

This time Pavlik interrupted. 'Do you believe that Danny could have killed Potter over any of this?'

Carson shrugged. 'I wish I knew. These aspiring writers take everything so seriously. They don't understand that there are only a handful of basic plots with shoulders broad enough to carry the three-to-four hundred pages of a novel, and what we're all doing is re-imagining – no, more *spinning* – them. And even if someone did steal a concept, no two writers would come up with the same book.'

A gust of wind rattled the window next to us, making even our stationary train car sway.

Carson stood up. 'I've had my say, and thank you for the opportunity. Do with the information as you will.'

Pavlik stuck out his hand reflexively and then retracted it nearly as so. 'Thanks very much.'

After Carson left, Pavlik looked at me. 'Well, what do you make of his story?'

'Could be true, I suppose. According to Rosemary Darlington, Potter once tried to browbeat her into writing a novel to his specifications, with the further conditions being she'd publish it under her own name and split the proceeds fifty-fifty with him. Rosemary, smart woman, finally told him where to stick his book, but maybe Potter saw a brand-new opportunity when Danny's material landed on his doorstep. Except this time he had no intention of splitting the money or credit with anyone. Or at least not anyone but his wife.'

Pavlik nodded approvingly. 'Anything else?'

'Everybody seems to be writing dirty books.' I'd slid around to the back of the booth and was peering out the window.

'Makes you wonder where they're getting all their ideas, doesn't it?' Pavlik dug in his jacket pocket and produced the matchbook. 'Here, perhaps?'

'Here where?' I had my cheek close to the glass, a hand cupping my eyes in an effort to cut down on the glare of the interior lights so I might see into the natural gloom.

'You spot something out there?' Pavlik asked. 'Maybe a gremlin on the wing?'

'*Twilight Zone*, season five, *Nightmare at*

Twenty-Thousand Feet, starring William Shatner,' I recited, still looking out. 'And, if you think about it, trains don't have wings. Though current events have persuaded me that fins mightn't be a bad idea.'

'The rain's coming down hard again?'

'Not really. In fact, I can see the moon. But there sure is a lot of water out—'

A rumble beneath us sent my face crashing against the glass.

TWENTY-SIX

'Are you all right, Maggy?'

'I think so.' Trying to sit up, I groaned. Apparently when the train shifted, I'd slammed my head and then shunted onto the floor beneath our table.

Pavlik, crouched in the aisle, extended his hand toward wending me out. Once emerged, I saw that the dining car was cockeyed, the side where we had been sitting noticeably about six inches lower than the other.

Engineer Hertel came lurching up, much like his train. 'Sorry, folks. Seems like all that rain we've gotten has undercut even these tracks we've just been sitting on. The ballast might be washing away and I'm starting to fear we're on the ground. Or will be soon.'

He fears we're on the ground? Ballast? I rubbed my temple where I could feel an unsightly egg already forming. I'd been thinking about airplanes before the crash, but...

I looked around. Nope, definitely a train, not a plane. Nor a submarine. 'I hate to ask this, but do we need to get to higher ground?'

Hertel scratched his nose. 'Well now, that wouldn't be a bad idea. If we had some, I mean. Not much in the way of elevation in these parts, although you might want to stay away from the lowest parts of the train so combined weight don't go flipping us over.'

My sheriff's head was swiveling. 'The club car behind us looks like it's at more of an angle than even this one. Any idea if the locomotive we're towing beyond is still on solid ground?'

'Well, sir,' Hertel said, hitching his fingers behind his overall straps. 'You gotta be careful when you're talking with a railroad man. Being "on the ground" is our way of saying derailment.'

'Derail...?' I echoed. 'Why—'

'Because a train's place is on the tracks, you see. Our wheels touch the ground and we're in real trouble.'

Ahh, now his earlier statement made sense.

'You said you feared we might be "on the ground." So you do think the train's derailed?'

'Not a clue, pardon my pun around you folks. Like I said, the ballast – that's the rocks in the train bed – might not be laid down proper. If that's so, there could be more problems coming.'

More problems?

Pavlik seemed to think about that. 'Is there anything we can do to head them off? I'm just thinking that if something as heavy as our rear locomotive tipped, it might be putting extra strain on the rest of the cars.'

I thought I saw what he was getting at. 'You mean like a Slinky, with the locomotive being the first coil starting down the stairs and the rest of us following?'

'Well, now.' Hertel pulled on his left earlobe as he considered that. 'I'd say it depends on how much of the track is washed away. I hate to speculate, you understand, but I'm startin' to wonder if, when they were running out of money, a few corners mightn't have been cut.'

'You mean a few *more* corners, right?' I asked. 'In addition to our not having a conductor?'

'Aw. Little lady, we don't need no conductor. All's they do is boss everybody around. Those FRA guys just want to provide work.

Not that there's anything wrong with that.'

'FRA – Federal Railroad Administration?' Pavlik looked at me. 'I assume you spoke to Zoe or Missy about the train staffing?'

'Missy,' I confirmed. 'Somehow she managed to slide by the authorities – whatever they are for an "off-the-grid" operation like this – with a fictional conductor-backslash-bartender.'

'Well, now, that's not fair,' Hertel protested. 'Everything is fiction, when you think about it.'

I wasn't sure if he was talking about the mystery train or whether we were about to take a detour into Hertel's vision of metaphysics and the meaning of life.

I was inclined to pursue the subject, but Pavlik retook control of the conversation. Probably a good thing, since my mother always said if you're afraid of the answers, then you shouldn't be asking the questions.

'Assuming some of the cars are still ... stable,' Pavlik said, 'would it make sense for us to uncouple any that might do us damage?'

'If you was Superman, maybe,' the engineer said.

'I take it that's a no?' Pavlik kept his tone even.

'You ever seen two train cars being coupled, Sheriff? They bang 'em one right into the other, like two big ol' Indian elephants doing the dirty. Sorry, ma'am.' A wink at me. 'These huge C-clamps, they hook together. Knuckle, we call it. You can't undo that with no screwdriver and pair of tweezers, I'm here to tell you. But aren't you getting ahead of yourselves?'

I looked at Pavlik, a little dazed by this outpouring of train lore. 'Umm...'

'Engineer Hertel's right,' Pavlik said. 'We need to know what we're dealing with and I'd like to leave Boyce here. Are you willing to be heroic again and come out with me to reconnoiter, Maggy?'

'"Nigh-on" to heroic, I believe was your term,' I said, smiling. 'But, of course, I'll go with you.'

In truth, my head was hurting where I'd bumped it, and the second last thing I wanted to do was to go outside with *any*one. The *very* last thing, though, was to let Pavlik do it alone. 'Should we check on the passenger car first?'

As I said it, the vestibule door from that direction slid open and Zoe stuck her head in. 'You OK in here?'

'We are,' Pavlik said.

'Thanks for asking,' I said, a little snippy. We could have been lying dead on the floor for all they knew, yet it was only now our comrades had thought to check on us?

'Assuming all is well in the passenger car, Zoe,' Pavlik said, 'Maggy and I are going to go out and take a look.'

'We're fine.' Zoe had one of Missy's shawls around her shoulders and, despite her words, seemed shaken. 'You go ahead.'

Pavlik was studying her. 'I should update Boyce first.'

Zoe held up her hand, palm out, and seemed to pull herself together. 'That's the least I can do, given everything you've already done for us.'

'We shouldn't be long.' Pavlik seemed reluctant to leave. 'You sure you're all right?'

'I am, Jacob.' Zoe smiled. 'But thank you.'

Enough of their lovefest. The egg on my temple was throbbing, and I wanted to get our second expedition in the books.

'I think you'll be just fine goin' out that way.' The engineer had the vestibule door between the dining and club cars open. 'She seems to be holding steady.'

Yippee. I pulled on Pavlik's sleeve. 'The sooner we go, the sooner we'll be back. You can brief everybody then.'

'She's right.' Zoe was pulling off her shawl. 'Would you like this, Maggy?'

Even I was getting suspicious. The woman was being too courteous, but, unlike Pavlik, I didn't give a shit why. 'Thanks, but I think I'll be fine.'

'You might wanna go while it's clear and you can see by the moon,' Hertel said, cocking his head toward the windows. 'Down here, storms come on as fast as they go.'

Pavlik was watching Zoe as she opened the door and stepped back through the vestibule. 'We will, but would you mind checking on the passenger car?'

Hertel looked surprised. 'Me? I thought I'd stand by right here. Make sure you get back safe?'

'That's not a bad idea,' I said to Pavlik. 'Whatever they're doing in there, we'll find out soon enough. Besides, we may need his help.'

Pavlik hesitated, then nodded. 'You're right.'

Back in the Flagler Suite, I would have asked the sheriff to repeat that, maybe teased him that he said it so seldom I wanted to hear it again.

But now, I just nudged one of our 'fingerprint' glasses out of the aisle with my toe. Another 'good idea at the time.' Too bad, but I assumed we'd each be fingerprinted officially when help finally arrived. After all, a man had been killed.

But as the three of us moved into the vestibule of the precariously tilted club car, a murderer amongst us seemed – however irrationally – to be the least of our problems.

TWENTY-SEVEN

'Careful,' Hertel called to us as I took the sheriff's hand and jumped down to join him on the railroad bed. 'That water's gotten mighty close in.'

The engineer was right. The good news was that the cant of the club car meant the distance from the exit door to the tracks was reduced. And the moon was bright enough for us to see, at least a ways. The bad news was that it allowed us to see that the tracks were nearly submerged.

'Hope those are old shoes,' Pavlik said, looking at my kitten-heel sandals.

'They are now, or at least they have been since our last foray out here.' I held up one foot. 'I think the cork platforms are coming unglued.'

'They're not the only thing here coming unglued.' The sheriff started to slosh east alongside the tracks. 'Did you notice Zoe was acting oddly?'

'Must be the stress,' I said, following him. Or maybe I'd scared her half to death with my talk of murderers everywhere. But it was true. Someone had killed Potter and right now it could be almost anybody, including Zoe herself.

Maybe that was why she was coming unhinged.

Pavlik was squinting up the line. 'Looks like the passenger and sleeping cars are still high and dry.'

'Well, that's good, at least.' I rubbed the bump on my head. The pounding was starting to lessen as we reached the front locomotive, still in place, nose down facing the flooded tracks.

'This seems pretty much the way it was earlier,' Pavlik said.

Earlier, as in the fight to reclaim Potter's body. Pavlik and I might have won the battle, but the python had certainly won the war. At least until the thing had explo— 'It's gone.'

'What's gone?' The sheriff had stepped up into the locomotive to look around and now stuck his head out.

'Our python.' A chill ran up my back as I pointed across the gulley to where the remains of the pregnant python had been strewn on the railbed. 'And its eggs.'

'Maybe it's the tide, if there is one. Or I suppose an alligator could have claimed it,' Pavlik said, jumping down from the cab. 'Poetic justice, given what we've heard about the balance of nature out here.'

'Too bad there aren't enough Bambis and Thumpers left in the Glades to rise up, unite, and exact revenge on the lot of them.'

'By Bambis, I assume you mean deer, though I suppose it could just as easily be a hot woman from a personal ad. But what are Thumpers?'

Poor boy. Yet another classic I'd force him to watch with me.

'Thumper is a bunny.' Then, fearing he'd think I was referring to the Playboy kind, 'You know, like Bugs?'

'Bugs?' Pavlik still seemed confused. 'Even in the Everglades, I don't think they have insects big enough to consume a snake's body in just a few hours.'

'No, no. Bugs! As in Bunny—' I interrupted myself as the sheriff waded into the water at an angle away from the train bed. 'Where are you going?'

'I'm just trying to get a better view of the trailing locomotive.'

'Oh.' Now that the rain had stopped, the nocturnal creatures seemed to be out in force. And in good voice. On a Wisconsin night you'd hear crickets and toads, maybe the occasional owl.

But the sounds of the Everglades were far more exotic. Rising from everywhere and nowhere – at least nowhere I could pinpoint.

They seemed to have a physical presence and, of course, they did. We just couldn't see it.

'Hey, Pavlik, what is that?' I was looking at a mound rising from the water. Amazing I hadn't noticed it earlier, since it had to be a city block in width, or so it seemed in the low light. Directly opposite the sleeping car, the berm had a tangle of trees on it. 'Is it one of those mangrove islands you were talking about?'

'Maybe.' But he was gazing the other way.

I took a step closer to the water to get a better look. Away from civilization and its ambient light, the sky was hazy with stars. 'I think I see fireflies. But they're ... I think they're red.'

'Fireflies aren't red.' Pavlik still wasn't paying attention.

'True. At least I've never seen any this color.' I waded in a cautious foot or two and squinted. 'I think there are two of them, but they're not flitting around like you usually see. Maybe sitting on something.'

'Two? How far apart?'

'Six or seven inches?' Another step. 'It's hard to judge from here.'

'Probably an alligator.'

I turned, though, in retrospect, that might not have been the smartest move of my life. 'Alligator?'

'Its eyes, to be precise. According to the pilot of the airboat ride we took the last time I was down here, their retinas reflect red in the dark.'

We took? Who was the 'we'? But something more immediate – and considerably less catty – also struck me as I splashed hastily back to dry land. 'Did you say airboat?'

'Airboat or fan boat, so-called because the flat-bottomed vessel has a giant fan up top that propels it over marshes and shallow water.'

Like the Everglades. 'I don't suppose the transit powers-that-be thought to equip the train with one.'

'An airboat that we'd stow and deploy like a life raft? Somehow I doubt it.' Pavlik returned to the track. 'Are you staying to explore, Marco Polo, or coming with me?'

I snuck a glance across the way to where I'd seen the red 'fireflies,' but they'd disappeared. Or, more likely from what Pavlik had said, crawled away on its belly like a reptile. 'With you. Definitely with you.'

As I trailed after him, the night animals shifted into high gear.

Chk, chk, chk, OWoo, Wwaahk, Wwaak ... Quock! Quock, quock!

'That last was a night heron, I think,' Pavlik said as we retraced our steps west along the railbed toward the exit door.

'We're probably disturbing them.' Happily, we'd be out of their hair – and feathers or scales or jaws – soon. As in, safe in the train.

'Most likely.' Pavlik passed the dining car and the entrance where Hertel waited and kept right on going.

'Aren't we going back onto the train?' I asked, hanging back.

'I have to check something out first. I'm hoping my eyes deceived me.'

I hesitated before following. Whither he goest, I will go.

Whither I wanted to or not.

Hurrying to catch up, I nearly ran up the sheriff's back when he reached the rear of the club car and stopped.

'What is it?' I asked, pulling up short.

Pavlik pointed.

Our now trailing locomotive, the one that had earlier led us west, was illuminated by moonlight reflecting on the water.

The water on all *four* sides of the tipped locomotive.

'I guess there's no point worrying about uncoupling anything,' I said.

TWENTY-EIGHT

'Well, I'll say I'm not surprised,' our engineer, Theodore B. Hertel, Jr, said after we filled him in.

'You *expected* us to get stuck out here?' I asked sourly. We were inspecting the club car, walking sideways in the aisle so we could grab hold of the counters and tables along the way to keep our balance. Boyce's espresso machine had bitten the dust again. I hefted the thing onto the bar and it slid right back off. This time I left it.

'No, ma'am. Not that. It's just that once the track started to wash out, what with the rain continuing and all, like I said, the ballast...' Hertel shrugged his shoulders, the denim straps of his overalls almost touching his earlobes.

I stopped short, causing Pavlik to run into me this time. 'Are you saying we could lose these cars, too?'

'I sure am hoping not,' the engineer said, opening the vestibule door to go into the dining car. 'The rain's stopped, which is always a good sign.'

This from the man who just an hour ago told us storms roared up quickly here.

Pavlik picked up his cell phone from the table we'd been sitting at when the car tipped. 'It's nearly four a.m.'

I said, 'What are we going to do?'

'I'm not sure there's anything we can do until the sun comes up.' Pavlik was pushing buttons on his smart phone. 'When it gets light, we'll decide our next move.'

'Do you have a signal?' I asked, my futile triumph of hope over experience.

'Afraid not.' Pavlik looked up from his miniature screen. 'I tried to send a text message last night, knowing they require less bandwidth than a call, but it wasn't delivered. I was checking now to see if we might have had intermittent service and the thing sent itself. No soap.'

The thought of soap made me feel my head where the bump was, to see if it needed cleaning.

'Still hurting?' Pavlik asked as we followed the engineer to the next car.

'A little, but I was just checking to see if the skin was broken. It's not, though.'

'I could have told you that.'

'You checked?' I asked, pleased he'd been concerned.

'Of course. If you'd been dripping blood out there, we would have been alligator bait.

Or at least python nuggets.'

'Or both.' I punched him in the shoulder and then turned the other cheek, literally. 'Truly, can you take a peek? How do I look?'

Pavlik grinned and pulled me against him as we waited for Hertel to slide open the door. 'Lovely, as always.'

'Lie, Pinocchio, lie,' I chanted, parroting the old joke.

Entering the passenger car, I was surprised to see that people seemed unconcerned. In fact, they seemed to be having a fine time.

'Everything all right out there?' Prudence asked, pearls askew and her voice a little more airy than I'd previously heard it.

'Just ducky.' Pavlik put his hand on the back of the first seat and surveyed the scene. Then nearly under his breath, 'Jesus, Maggy. I think they're all drunk.'

The passenger car was, indeed, as high as it was barely dry. Zoe Scarlett was making her way to an empty seat, but instead of simply sitting down in it, she scarfed a bottle of what appeared to be Kahlua before moving on.

Pavlik shook his head. 'Well, that explains it. I'm going to check with Boyce.'

I followed the sheriff, stopping at the row Zoe had. There had to be fifteen bottles there, some on the seat, some in a box on the floor. Pete the bartender was snoring next to them, head tilted against the window.

'How'd you get the entire contents of the bar in here?' I asked Markus, who was slouching across the aisle.

'The bartender helped Audra and that kid Danny bring it to us.' He nodded about halfway back in the car, to where Audra Edmonds sat beside Rosemary Darlington.

Now *there* were curious seatmates. The widow and the woman she suspected her husband had been cheating with?

'And good thing, too.' Zoe was a few rows farther down with the Kahlua bottle. 'Since I'm not sure we'd want to go up there now.' She took a swig. 'Should have gotten glasses, though. This is unsanitary, even given the alcohol content as anti*slep*tic.'

She giggled, then stopped. Then resumed and couldn't stop.

Given the situation, it might not be the worst thing in the world if they all got drunk and fell asleep – or passed out – until help arrived, even if by boat.

Assuming it ever did.

Trying to remain positive, I continued on past Harvey/Hardman, who had his plaid jacket reversed and tucked under his chin. He probably meant it as a blanket but the effect was a really gaudy bib. Then again, you'd never see the food stains on it.

Pavlik was at the back of the car, talking to

Boyce.

'You wouldn't have seen the three of them,' Boyce was saying. 'They bypassed the dining car where you were, coming back in this exit.' He pointed to the vestibule.

No wonder we'd heard opening and closing with no one actually entering the dining car itself. The threesome had risked going out into the Everglades to smuggle the booze without our noticing.

We should have asked *them* to be the scouting party.

I put my hand on the bathroom door handle, intending to check out the bump on my head, when it slid open and Missy appeared.

'Oh, I'm sorry, Maggy,' she said, stepping out. 'Go ahead, but be warned. It's pretty disgusting with all of us using just this one.'

I looked at Pavlik, thinking of all the toilets and sinks in the sleeping roomettes. 'Do you think we—'

He shook his head. 'Sorry, but we've already made things difficult enough for the crime-scene people. The least I can do is keep that car reasonably untainted.'

I sensed his frustration and put my hand out. 'Hey, you've done a great job of keeping everybody calm during a horrible situation.'

Harvey let out a snort and began to snore.

'Not, apparently, as effectively as the booze

256

did,' Pavlik said. 'You want to take a break, Boyce? I can take over.'

'I don't mind if I do,' the other man said. 'This is one of those times I wish I still smoked, but maybe I'll just go answer the call of nature.'

I stepped aside to let him go into the bathroom, but he shook his head. 'Given the sheriff saying the rain has stopped, I think I'll venture out.'

Boyce continued on to the exit.

'Guys are so lucky,' I said. 'You can go anywhere.'

'One of our many charms,' Pavlik said. 'Why don't you get some sleep? Once the sun comes up, a couple of us will probably have to hike out of here and get help. I'd like you to be fresh.'

I sniffed my armpit. 'I'm not sure that's possible, but I'll do my best.'

Pavlik laughed.

But I put my hand on his forearm. 'Are you sure we should venture off our little ... island instead of just waiting for help?'

'I'm not sure we have a choice, but we'll talk about it before I decide. For now, though, sleep. OK?'

As if I'd sleep. So I did the next best thing – found two open seats right behind Audra Edmonds and Rosemary Darlington.

'Hello, ladies,' I said, slipping into the

window seat behind Audra. 'Don't let me bother you, I'm just taking a nap.'

'No bother,' Rosemary said, getting up. 'I'm grateful for the reprieve.'

'Bitch,' Audra said to her back as the author retreated.

'I take it Ms Darlington and you have some sort of ... history?' I asked innocently, using Missy's word.

'No,' Audra said pointedly, 'but Rosemary and my husband did, much as she denies it.'

'I know that Mr Potter mentored her,' I was using last names to create distance from the participants, 'but are you saying they had something more?'

'That's exactly what I'm saying.' Audra turned and put her back against the wall of the train, stretching her legs out across the seats before smoothing the handkerchief hem of her vintage dress. 'The man is – was – the most calculating of cheaters.'

Edmonds managed to look bored. Amazing, given the subject and the fact that her philandering husband had rather recently also become her dead one. 'You know that book of hers? That fount of smut?'

Breaking and Entering? I read Mr Potter's review of it on PotShots.'

Audra laughed. 'Review, my ass. The man was just covering his.'

'His ass, you mean?' I was confused. Again.

'Of course. You know all those things the couple does in her book? Those are the very same things Larry had been suggesting we do.'

'You mean in bed.'

'No, in the grocery store.'

And Pavlik thought *I* was sarcastic. 'You think he learned these ... techniques from her?'

'Where else? Let me tell you, a husband suddenly comes home with new ideas to spice up the spousal love life, you better believe he's probably learned it through recent extramarital experience. Larry, in particular, wasn't the type to read and follow self-help books. More the help-yourself category.'

I wasn't sure I could argue with Audra's logic, and I had to give her credit for a nice turn-of-phrase. 'But weren't you and Mr Potter working on a book of your own?'

She snorted. 'Larry's idea. Both Rosemary and he must have had so much fun, they couldn't wait to write about it afterward. He was just ticked that she dumped him and then got to it first.'

'Hence the horrible review?'

'What do you think?'

I wasn't sure what I thought. 'Yet you and he were still intending to go ahead with your own ... romantic novel?'

'The only reason he wanted my name on

the book was for the hook. It would be sort of a he-said, she-said. Or *did*, in this case.'

I suppressed a smile. 'And did *you*?'

'Do those things?' Audra exploded. 'Of course not. Which is how I know the old dog learned those new tricks from a different bitch. And probably by going to that horrible club, as well.'

'Titanium?'

She blinked. 'Yes. But how did you know?'

'The matches your husband was using.'

'So you saw them, too?'

I didn't tell her I'd also found the empty matchbook on the floor near the door where he might have made his final exit. 'I did. What kind of club is it?'

'Leather. S&M. Swingers. All of the above, and mostly mixed together.'

'You've been—?' I started to ask, but the look on her face was a conversation-stopper. 'On another subject, I know Mr Potter seemed to be having some sort of dispute with that young man, Danny. Has he been bothering you, as well?'

'You mean earlier tonight? Or I guess it would be last night, now.'

I nodded.

'Honestly? Yes. He wanted to know when Larry came up with the concept for the book.'

I didn't want to mention Carson, so I said,

'I heard Danny ask Mr Potter about the manuscript he sent him. Does he think your husband somehow stole his idea?'

'Of course. As if "boy meets girl, boy does girl and then both do everybody else in sight" is a ground-breaking development in human sexuality.'

'So you saw his manuscript?'

'Whose?'

'Danny's.'

'No, of course not. How would I do that?'

'I thought your husband might have showed it to you.'

'Larry and I share very little these days, including a bed. And by my choice, before you ask.'

Interesting. Yet the woman had taken the trouble to 'surprise' her guest-of-honor husband and seemed to have a considerable number of jealous bones in her body. A case of 'if I can't have him, nobody will'?

I said, 'You mentioned "boy meets girl," et cetera as the idea Danny thought your husband stole. How did you know what his manuscript was about if you didn't see it?'

'The naive boy told me about it, of course. In return for this stunning revelation, I assured him his ground-breaking concept was safe.' Audra Edmonds shrugged and closed her eyes, seeming to lose steam. 'Believe me, Larry's book died with him.'

TWENTY-NINE

When Boyce returned from outside, he insisted on re-taking the watch from Pavlik. The sheriff slipped into the aisle seat and put his arm around me.

I laid my head on his shoulder. 'Did Boyce see anything out there when he drained the lizard?'

'How you talk.' The sheriff nuzzled the side of my neck.

'So, I've been thinking.' I pushed myself up to see over the back of Audra Edmonds' seat. The woman was snoring softly, mouth open. 'Audra seems to be the most likely suspect in her husband's death, either alone or allied with Danny or even Carson.'

'Danny I can wrap my head round, but Carson? What would his motive be?'

I'd thought about that. 'He's in love with Audra and wanted Potter out of the way? Maybe there's a financial incentive for Audra to do away with Potter, rather than divorce him.'

'There's always a financial incentive.

Believe me, no one comes away from a divorce in better shape than they went into it.'

I could sure attest to that. Happily, other considerations – things like human decency and the law – kept us from knocking off our spouses. For the most part.

'Audra just informed me that she's scrapping what she called "Larry's book,"' I told Pavlik. 'But who knows? Maybe she's lying and fully intends to finish and publish it. Plus, Potter's dramatic "exit" will mean lots of publicity, with only the grieving widow and Carson left to rake in the profits.'

The sheriff opened his mouth to comment, but I was on a roll. 'Audra and personal motives aside, maybe Carson had a pure business reason to knock off Potter – something to do with Danny's manuscript. Carson says Danny emailed him accusing Potter of stealing it, but perhaps he already knew what was going on. Larry could even have let him see the manuscript.'

'So Carson killed Potter, his client and perhaps co-conspirator? Why? Better that they take Danny off the board.'

'We know Potter turned to Rosemary to write for him once. Perhaps he wasn't a very good writer, but Carson got him the publishing deal thanks to his notoriety and profile. Then Carson read Danny's work and saw a promising young talent that could boost a literary agent's reputation and make him more money over time than Potter ever would have.'

'Why not just represent both?'

'I don't know enough about the book business to speculate.' Not that it stopped me, of course. 'Some kind of conflict of interest? Threat of lawsuits because of . . . creative jealousy? Writers rage?'

Pavlik ignored that. 'I honestly don't see Carson stabbing somebody to death, no matter which somebody. The man doesn't like to get his hands dirty, remember.'

'Maybe that's just a front. I mean, he refused to touch the water glass so we couldn't get his fingerprints and we thought nothing of it. Convenient, don't you think?'

'And he's nurtured this faux phobia all these years just for this moment?'

Suddenly exhausted, I scooched myself back against the sheriff and snuggled in, wrapping his arms around me like a blanket. 'You have a good point, not to mention a nifty way with words. The writers must be rubbing off on you.'

'They aren't the only ones rubbing on me.' Pavlik's breath tickled my ear. 'You'd better behave or I'm going to have to do you right here and now.'

'Threat or promise?'

Pavlik's arms tightened. 'Listen, Maggy. Boyce and I have been talking. Unless cell service improves now that the storm has stopped, we may have to hike out of here.'

I couldn't imagine convincing the other passengers to step into the water just to cross the flooded track, much less hike along the tracks once they reached the other side. Unless, of course, a booze bar or a giant bottle of aspirin was at the end of the rainbow, in which case all bets were off.

I turned to face him. 'It could be fifty miles back to Fort Lauderdale. And that's assuming, given the flooding, that there's a railway bed to walk on.'

'We'd take cell phones and call for help as soon as we reached an area where there was service.'

'That makes some sense. But you're not thinking everyone would go with us, are you? Plus, what about the alligators, snakes and all?' I fought the shiver that threatened to climb down my spine.

'Actually,' Pavlik said, seeming to tread carefully. 'I was thinking Boyce would come with me, given we don't know what we may find. Not only does he have some training, but he's an outsider to this group.'

I should have been relieved but, in truth, I was a little hurt. I might not be Linda Hamilton in *Terminator 2*, but hadn't Pavlik just complimented me on how well I'd accounted for myself under dire circumstances? 'So you trust *him*.'

'Yes. And I trust you, too.'

I brightened. 'So I *am* coming with you.'

'Honestly, I was hoping you'd take over Boyce's post and keep everyone else out of the sleeping car.'

I saw the reasoning, though I didn't like it much. But then how logical was it for me to be disappointed that I couldn't again become one with the denizens of the Everglades?

'Sure you want a sociopath minding the store?'

Pavlik smiled. 'Struck a nerve, did I?'

I shifted uncomfortably. 'My roommate in college called me a sociopath once. I guess ever since I've wondered if she was right.'

'What was her reasoning?'

'You mean besides her being a psych major? I found the apartment, so I took the bigger bedroom.' I shrugged. 'It seemed only fair to me.'

'Well, cheer up.' Pavlik gave me a squeeze. 'You're probably just self-centered.'

'Thank you. Coming from you, that means a lot.'

Pavlik looked past me out the window. 'There's a glow on the horizon. The sun is starting to come up.'

So it was. I could actually see the water and scrubby grasses across from us.

'And still not raining.' I sighed. 'When will you go?'

'Soon. But not until I've kissed you properly.'

And he did.

'But the dispatchers must have missed us by now,' Markus was saying. 'We haven't knocked the next signal down. They'll know exactly what block to find us in.'

'His family is in railroad,' I told Pavlik. I knew it sounded like 'my uncle sells insurance,' but even at this short acquaintance, I trusted Markus and his information.

Despite the 148 errors in his books.

Pavlik had briefed the passengers – now sober in more ways than the obvious – on our current situation, as well as his plan.

'What do you mean by knocking the signals down?' he asked Markus.

'There are electrical circuits on the track,' Markus explained. 'When a train passes through it breaks a connection – a signal – giving the train's location. That's what causes the gates to go down at railroad crossings and stop automobile traffic. A knocked-down signal also informs dispatchers that a train has crossed into another section or "block." Or not, in our case. It may take a while, but eventually someone will come looking for us.'

'We're saved!' Grace said, clapping her hands. Everyone was sitting up a little straighter, hangovers be damned.

Pavlik turned to Engineer Hertel. 'You couldn't have told me about this?'

'I would've if they'd been working,' the old man said, pulling at an ear. 'Same with the radios, which somebody neglected to equip with batteries before we left.'

Somebody. I wondered who. Or whom.

I was starting to wonder if the engineer was, in reality, an evil genius who'd hatched a plan to not only murder Potter and feed him to a giant python, but strand us here in the Everglades 'purely in-communicado' so he could make his escape.

If only he *would* make his escape.

The whole car had slumped again.

Pavlik just shook his head. 'Since I don't know how far we'll have to walk to find cell service and call for help, it may be a while before we get back. Hopefully not too long.'

'Are we talking hours or days here?' Harvey asked.

'Hours, I hope.' Pavlik turned back to the engineer. 'I assume we're most likely to find civilization by heading east.'

'You are. Besides the track not being finished all the way west anyway.'

'Good point,' Pavlik said lightly. 'Though I'm hoping we wouldn't have had to walk all the way to Naples anyway.'

'If you're not back by, say, tomorrow morning, what should we do?' Prudence asked. 'Send out a search party?'

Pavlik and Boyce were standing at the door by the dining car – the exit The Raiders of the Last Car had used to sneak back the booze. I was on the opposite end of the passenger car, keeping an eye on the door the coffee man had been guarding earlier.

'What do you think?' Pavlik said to his new sidekick. 'Noon tomorrow?'

Boyce nodded. 'Don't send anybody out alone, though. At least two people.'

A hand went up. 'But what about snakes? And alligators?' Missy asked in a shaky voice.

'We'll take my knife and Ms Edmonds' pistol.' Pavlik held it up, index finger carefully outside the trigger guard. 'If anyone else happens to have a—'

With that, a dozen handguns appeared from holsters and handbags, fanny packs and pockets.

Pavlik shrugged. 'How could I forget we're in South Florida?'

'Don't leave home without 'em,' Harvey said. 'I think you'll like my Glock Forty.'

'I have a forty-five Colt,' Prudence said.

'Great stopping power...'

Vaguely relieved that none of The (unofficial) Untouchables had sub-machine guns, I left the group to debate the relative pros and cons of our available weapons and sat down on the stool by the door, feeling adrift. Pavlik was the only one of these people I'd known for more than twenty-four hours, and now he was leaving me here alone with them.

And one of 'them' was a murderer.

Yes, it was for a good reason. And, of course, he was taking far more risk than—

'You OK?' Missy asked quietly. I hadn't noticed her come back.

I gave her a smile. 'Yeah, just a little—'

'Scared?' She sat down on the edge of the seat nearest me, legs swiveled into the aisle so we could talk. 'Me, too. This was all my idea and it's my fault that we're stranded here. And, and...' She gestured toward the door leading to Larry Potter's body and a sob escaped from her throat.

I tried to reassure the girl. 'You had no way of knowing a severe storm was going to hit or that the track bed would become unstable.'

'But that's the point,' she said. 'The mystery train which I wanted us to take wasn't up and running yet, so I, I ... kind of cobbled things together.'

Hence, Theodore B. Hertel, Jr, the aged-out engineer, Pete the 'pretend' conductor/

bartender and the incomplete and perhaps improperly built track. All to save face – and her event.

But no good would be served by reminding Missy of that now.

'Fine mess you got us into here,' a different voice snapped. Zoe Scarlett was standing over Missy. 'Stuck here without any food and now we're even running out of things to drink.'

I was thinking cause and effect. Zoe looked like she had one howler of a hangover.

'I'm so sorry,' the girl said tearfully. 'If you want, I'll go with the sheriff and Mr Boyce.'

'You'll do no such thing,' I said. 'We may need you here.'

Pavlik came up behind Zoe's right shoulder. 'You two ladies mind if I have a word alone with Maggy?'

Missy sniffled and shook her head, disappearing into the stinky bathroom. Zoe pivoted and went a few seats back and collapsed, palm to her forehead.

Pavlik held out a smallish gun to me, and I took it from him carefully. It was a semi-automatic, but that's about all I could tell you. Nor, believe me, did I know or care whether the diameter of the ammunition was measured by caliber or in millimeters. 'Loaded?'

'It is. Plus the safety is off and I've cham-

bered the first round, so if you pull the trigger, a slug flies out of the muzzle and toward
whatever you're aiming at.'

'How many bullets in this?'

'Seven. Just level on bad guy-or-girl's belt
buckle and fire 'til they fall. Oh, and here's
some extra ammunition.' He handed me
something the size and shape – if ten times
the heft – of an old kitchen matchbox.

If I couldn't stop the killer with seven, I
somehow didn't envision having the time, or
even know-how, to reload, but I accepted the
extra rounds from him. Their 'box' reminded
me of the match*book* I'd found. 'I know this
doesn't have any bearing on our most
immediate problem, but Audra Edmonds
says Titanium is a sex club her husband
spent time at. Pointedly without her.'

'A woman scorned?' Pavlik suggested.

'A woman cheated upon,' I said. 'Believe
me, we're capable of anything.'

'Thanks for the warning.' He put his hand
on my shoulder. 'You going to be all right
here?'

I wanted to say, 'No. Take me with you.
Leave a bigger, stronger, actually *trained*
Boyce here with these strangers, one of
whom is a killer.'

Instead, I stood up. Setting the gun and
ammunition carefully on the stool, I wrapped my arms around Pavlik and rested my

head on his chest. 'I'll be fine.'

He caressed my hair. 'Take the stool and sit on the sleeping-car side of the door. Don't worry about touching things, the police can always take and then exclude your prints. If anybody tries to come through this door, warn them you'll shoot. They keep coming, blow them away.'

'Gotcha.'

Pavlik tilted my face up toward his. 'I'm serious.'

'I know you are. I won't let anybody in.'

'It's not protecting the crime scene I'm worried about. It's your being hurt.' Pavlik's eyes were about as dark as I'd ever seen them.

I pulled his head down to my lips and kissed him. 'Please come back soon. And safe. I'll be OK, but just ... please come back.'

'You got it.' He was smiling. 'Believe me, the last thing I want to tour is the inside of a python's gut.'

'Which *would* be the last thing you ever toured. Promise me if you come across any predators, you'll shoot first and worry about environmental protection later.'

'Promise.' He crossed his heart with his fingertips and then touched them to my lips.

I smiled and stepped back. 'Got your cell phone? And is it all charged?'

'Yup, and Boyce is AT&T and I'm Verizon,

273

so we've got at least those two carriers covered.'

'Would you like to take mine, too, just in
case?' I dug it out of my pocket. 'It's not
doing me any good here.'

'I could, but then how would you count
the minutes until my return?'

'Huh. That's very true.' I slipped the phone
back into my pocket. 'Now get the hell out of
here and save us.'

THIRTY

When Pavlik and Boyce left the train at 8
a.m., I waved goodbye through the window.

Happily, the day had dawned bright and
sunny. Locals said that sunset would be
around 6:30 p.m. this time of year, so that
would give the two men more than ten hours
of daylight. I hoped that was enough.

In fact, I was kind of hoping they'd walk
about 100 feet, raise the cell phones over
their heads like I always did when I was
looking for service and, bingo, there it would
be.

Once they'd been gone a half hour, though,
I decided to do as Pavlik suggested.

'I'm going to move into the next car,' I told Missy. 'Would you make sure people know it's still off limits? Pavlik told me I should shoot to kill.'

Missy's eyes grew wide. 'You know how to fire a gun?'

'Pavlik taught me,' I said. 'But what about you? I keep hearing how everybody here has a permit to carry.'

'Oh, I do, too,' Missy said, 'but I barely know which end of my gun to hold. They only have you fire three bullets to qualify at the gun range.'

South Florida sure did seem to make it easy, but given the wildlife, I wasn't sure I blamed the authorities. If an alligator or python walked or slithered into my backyard, I might want some way to protect myself and any kids or pets.

Leaving Missy behind, I went through the door into the vestibule, where I'd found the matchbook, and then on to the sleeping car. The interior of it was very quiet.

Setting down the gun and the box of extra bullets by the door to the roomette where Potter's body lay, I returned to the passenger car to retrieve the stool.

'Am I in your way?'

I turned to see Danny sitting across the last two seats on the right, back against the window, feet poking into the aisle.

'No, you're fine,' I said, folding up the stool. 'I just need to take this back. If you're going to be sitting here, could you let people know the sleeping car is still off limits?'

'Sure.' He swung his legs off the seat and leaned forward. 'Missy already told me that, though. I think she went to get cardboard and markers to tape something up on the door.'

The girl was a natural event-planner. When in doubt, make a sign.

'Missy's great,' I said, figuring it couldn't hurt to build her up in his eyes. Maybe something good could come of this trip. 'She's very ... efficient.'

Way to go Maggy. Every guy is looking for a woman who's ... 'efficient.'

'Yeah, and kind of sexy, too.' I brightened momentarily, but he finished with, 'Too bad she's not my style.'

I wondered who was. Audra Edmonds, perhaps?

I perched on the edge of the seat across from him, thinking that with Pavlik off on his mission to find help and get us out of here, this might be my last opportunity to grill Danny. Or at least I hoped it would be. 'Bet you didn't expect all this when you signed up for the conference.'

'You've got that right. I really lucked into it.'

'There's a dead man in the next car and we're stranded in the Everglades. You call that "luck"?'

'But look who the dead man is. And who I'm stranded with. I hear people bond for life over experiences like this. You can ask them for favors years later and they'll come through.'

'You remind me of my son,' I said, lying through my teeth. Eric was five years younger and an actual human being.

'Oh, yeah?' Danny said. 'Does he write?'

'No, but he texts regularly.' I smiled. 'Now tell me about your book – or is it called a manuscript at this stage?'

'Getting closer to becoming a book with every minute we're here.' He lowered his voice confidingly. 'I've snagged an agent.'

'Congratulatons!' I said. 'Who is it?'

'Carson – that guy who doesn't shake hands. Audra introduced us.'

How accommodating of the widow. And the agent. Maybe my speculation about Carson wasn't as farfetched as Pavlik seemed to think. 'But isn't that a little awkward?'

'Awkward? Why?'

'I understand your book is very much like Mr Potter and Ms Edmonds' projected novel.'

'Projected, maybe. But it's not going to happen.' The kid might be sitting down, but there was a definite swagger in his voice.

'Really?' I asked innocently. 'Have you and Ms Edmonds decided to collaborate on *your* book, instead?'

'My book?' He seemed genuinely shocked.

'Yes, of course. Since Audra introduced you to her agent, I thought she might have a new partnership in mind. Assuming,' a thought had struck me, 'this all happened after her husband was dead.'

The young man's eyes narrowed. 'What do you mean by that?'

I shrugged. 'Seems clear to me. Did Audra introduce you to Carson before or after the sheriff and I returned to the train with Potter's body?'

I could see the wheels turning in the young man's head. 'After, definitely after. I remember because I figured Audra agreed to introduce me because she was grateful for my help.'

'Your help?'

'Sure. We bonded when I took her to the club car after she nearly shot that guy.'

Boyce, standing guard over Potter's already cold body.

On the other hand, sweat was beading on Danny's upper lip. 'Shit. I hope she didn't get that idea. I mean, Audra's awfully old and this is a sex book.'

I opened my mouth to inform the little

278

twerp that even a woman of Audra's advanc-
ed age, which I judged to be early forties,
still had sex.

And then I remembered she apparently
didn't. At least, not with her husband.

Back in the sleeping car, I unfolded the stool
and situated it across from the door of the
roomette where Potter's body lay. Sitting
down, I tried to figure out what to do with
the pistol. On the floor, it was too far away
from me to easily reach. Maybe I'd just sit on
the floor next to it.

Though I'd wasted ten minutes of my life
going back to get the stool, at least my conversation with Danny had been enlightening.
If the kid was to be believed, he'd achieved
everything he'd wanted when he'd set foot
on the bus: not only was there no book
forthcoming from Potter and Edmonds, but
he'd secured a literary agent.

According to Danny, the initial contact
with Carson had been via email – almost
certainly the accusatory message Carson
had mentioned. Then, in gratitude for Danny's aid during this so-called bonding opportunity he had 'lucked into,' Audra had
introduced aspiring writer to agent.

Carson hadn't yet been approached by
Danny when Pavlik and I met with the
literary agent in the dining car but, given his

279

suspicions of the kid, wouldn't it have made sense to inform us of this new development?

Maybe the germaphobe's hands *weren't* quite as clean as he'd like people to believe.

I shivered, suddenly very glad Pavlik had suggested I camp out in the sleeping car, even if its only other occupant was a corpse. Or maybe because of that.

Moving the stool out of the way, I decided the best place to sit was with my back against the wall of the roomette across the narrow corridor from Potter's – this despite the nasty smells not quite contained inside. But this way, at least, I could comfortably keep a peripheral eye on that door as well as the outside exit and the doors leading to the passenger car.

But first...

Gun ready in my hand, I slid open the door across from Potter's, clearing that roomette as Pavlik and Boyce had.

The space was empty, of course. Once I checked that one, though, I felt like I had to do the others, just to be sure. I went down one side of the car and into both shower rooms, my still-damp sandals echoing on the tiles. Then I worked my way back up to the space where Potter's body lay.

I slid open the door and, holding my breath, stepped over the two frosting smudges and into the room. Potter was on the bunk, of course, faced away from me like he was still just napping.

I tiptoed nearer, still trying not to breathe, and—

'Maggy?'

I jumped back and turned, raising the gun, which was now moving in sync with my shaking hand. 'Holy shit, Missy! You scared me to death. What are you doing in here?'

Missy looked hurt. 'Well, I knocked on the door to give you this, but I didn't hear any answer.'

She was holding out an e-reader. 'I've got a ton of books loaded on it and I figured it would help you pass the time. Oh, and I also put a "Keep Out" sign on the other side of the door.'

My heart-rate descended toward quasi-normality. 'Thanks, Missy – that's very nice of you.' I took the reader. 'And I'm sorry I yelled. And, well, almost shot you. I must have been at the other end of the car checking the showers when you knocked.'

'No, I'm the one who should be sorry,' Missy said, her eyes welling up. 'But when you didn't answer, I was worried.'

'I appreciate that. I was just making sure everything was secure.'

She glanced over at the bunk, her nose wrinkling and her next words a little strangled. 'Can we get out of here?'

'With pleasure.' I let her precede me out the door. 'And thank you again.' I held up the e-reader.

Missy smiled. 'You're welcome. Come to the door and call out if you need anything.'

'I will. Thanks.' As she turned away, I couldn't resist saying, 'I noticed you talking with Pete. He seems like a nice guy.' Unlike Danny. 'And really good-looking.'

'I suppose, but too young. And a waiter.'

My, my, but the younger generation was picky. 'Everyone has to start somewhere.'

Missy sniffed. 'His real name is Brandon. I saw him at the restaurant last week and asked if he'd like to earn some extra money.'

'That was smart.'

'You're telling me. You know how much it costs to hire a professional bartender? And I bought all the liquor at Costco.'

You had to give the woman credit. She knew how to stretch a dollar. I hoped it wouldn't come back to bite her in the form of lawsuits by the passengers on the train and even the train company itself.

Which was another reason I'd wanted out of event planning: the liability if something went awry. At least I'd been bonded and had a corporation standing behind me. If I were Missy, I wouldn't expect a whole lot of support from Zoe.

After the young woman left, I settled onto

the floor. Propping the gun against my right thigh, I picked up her e-reader.

She wasn't kidding about the books. A ton of them and, in the mix, some of Rosemary Darlington's.

Including ... I scrolled down. Yes, *Breaking and Entering*.

Leaning my back against the wall, I punched up the book cover. Steamy, in itself. A woman in red leather, a dog collar around her neck and a whip in her hand. A man's naked body was half-hidden in shadows, the glass of a broken window on the floor nearby.

I looked around guiltily, like I was twelve and reading the early scene in Mario Puzo's *The Godfather*, where Sonny and the bridesmaid ... well, you know. I clicked to the next page. These e-readers were great – convenience, discretion, *and* they couldn't accidentally fall open to the spicy pages you've read. And reread.

The first chapter was a lot of set-up. I yawned, resisting the urge to peek ahead.

Kat opened the door, knowing what she wanted but not if she had the nerve to take it. He was lying on the bed facing the window, his skin glistening in the moonlight. The edge of the white sheet revealed his firm, naked glutes. Kat wanted – she desperately needed – to run her fingers along the curve of them.

As Kat reached out, the man roused. Stepping back, she watched from the shadows as he rolled onto his back, sending the sheet to the floor.

Kat nearly gasped aloud. She moved forward, waiting for him to settle before she let her nails barely touch, tracing his mustache and lips. The curve of the neck cords to his throat.

Thud-thud, thud-thud, thud...

The pulse suddenly stopped under her fingertips.

Panicked, Kat laid her hand flat against his chest. She was praying now, to feel something, anything inside.

A flutter. Not quite a beat, more a ... twitch? Once, twice, three times. It grew stronger and then stronger again, settling into a rhythm before seeming to coil back on itself, regrouping to race faster, heading toward a seemingly inevitable crescendo.

Then, just as Kat thought her own chest would burst, his did. Bits of tissue and cartilage splattered onto the window pane, seeming to mingle with the rain streaking down the outside of the glass.

Kat held her hand up in front of her, trying to understand what had just happened. Blood and something thick and white covered her fingers.

A movement caught Kat's eye. She looked down into the man's open chest and ... it looked back at her.

A python. Where Larry Potter's heart should be.

THIRTY-ONE

'Stay away from the pointy end!' I yelled, my head falling back against the wall, waking me.

Looking around, I waited for my own heart to settle back into my chest. Sunshine poured in from the windows by the vestibule door and I could hear voices – if not cheerful, at least reassuringly alive – in the passenger car beyond.

Apparently, I'd nodded off and managed to combine our current situation and Rosemary's book into one hell of a dream. Getting to my feet, I retrieved the pistol and, holding my breath, crossed the aisle to Potter's roomette and opened the sliding door. Still there, chest intact, no snakes in sight. Check, check, check.

My cell phone told me it was 10:20 a.m.

I slid Potter's door closed. Some guard I was. Not only had I fallen asleep for two hours, but I'd awakened with a full-blown case of the heebie-jeebies.

As I turned from the corpse I was responsible for guarding, my stomach growled. I wasn't sure what that said about me, but I feared it wasn't good.

I also needed to use the bathroom, preferably not the one in what I'd come to think of as Potter's room. I also didn't want to return to the passenger car or dirty an unused roomette's facilities.

That left the compartment Rosemary had napped in. It was at the end of the hall, but I could leave the door open so I'd hear anyone coming through from the passenger car, as Missy had.

As I flipped open the toilet, I thought about the one in Potter's room. I'd touched it when we'd found the cigarette butt and I hoped that wouldn't cause problems with the police. Potter obviously hadn't been stabbed in there anyway, because there was no blood.

In fact, come to think of it, I hadn't seen blood anywhere when I'd inspected earlier.

How could that be?

After washing my hands, I sat down on Rosemary's bed to think. Had Laurence Potter been killed when the train stopped because of the flooding? It had seemed an outside chance when Pavlik and I first talked about it, but if the victim had been stabbed outside, it would explain why there was no blood found on the floors inside the train.

But stabbed by whom? And where had Potter been up to that point? We knew he'd visited the sleeping car, as evidenced by the cigarette butt in the toilet. The possibility he'd been tucked away with Rosemary in this roomette had certainly occurred to me, as it had to Audra, Potter's wife.

Could Rosemary have faked the motion sickness to have an excuse to lie down? Perhaps she'd invited Potter to steal away for a little early evening delight and, when he'd arrived, killed him. Perfect timing and apparent alibi. The female guest of honor was drunk and sleeping it off.

Then there was Audra. She'd said she wasn't sleeping with Potter and that it was by her own choice. Was that the truth? Or the words of a woman determined to save face with people who might know more about her husband's peccadillos than she did? If I'd gotten wind of Ted's extra-curricular activities would I have shown up at one of his conferences, as Audra had?

I thought so. The only thing worse than *knowing* is suspecting. Always wondering if you're being made the fool. That suspicion, in and of itself, could make you act foolishly.

Could it also make you a killer?

Audra had been with us in the dining car when her husband had disappeared, but she certainly could have slipped out later and killed him. Ditto pretty much anyone else on the train, given the one-hour window of opportunity from nine to ten p.m. that Pavlik and I had settled on. Even Zoe Scarlett, once she'd finished her welcome speech. Much as I'd love to pin the murder on the woman, though, I couldn't see why Zoe would kill her guest of honor. Sure, she might have had the unrequited hots for Potter, but the same was true for Pavlik and he was still alive, right?

Please, God.

I twisted to look out the window, blinking back unexpected tears. But there was no Pavlik to the rescue, no anybody. A train full of people and I'd never felt more alone.

Wah-wah-wah. I wasn't the one tramping about in the Everglades with snakes and alligators.

Ignoring the inner voice that said, *No, you're the one sitting on a train with a corpse and a killer*, I stood up. Time to man my post. And man up, period. Tucking the bunk's pillow and blanket under my arm, I returned to the corridor outside Potter's room and settled onto the floor.

Pillow stuffed comfortably behind my back, I tried to think. Specifically, *not* about Pavlik.

So how about Danny? Without Audra as co-conspirator, I didn't see what he would gain by killing Potter rather than suing him for stealing his work. In fact, it suddenly occurred to me, wouldn't the kid be best off waiting until Potter's book was published, so he could jump on the bandwagon (if there was one) and really benefit from its success?

I supposed it could have been in the heat of the moment – Potter being his supercilious self and the kid just having enough – or a bit too much – of it.

When you thought it through, though, anybody who killed Potter must have done it without premeditation, since we assumed it was Potter who had carried both the hunk of cake and the knife – the eventual murder weapon – back here.

Kind of blew my original theory that Audra had been working in tandem with Carson or Danny. So where did that leave me?

In a word? Nowhere, just like Hercule Poirot in the original *Murder on the Orient Express*. And since Potter had but a single knife wound, I couldn't even fall back on Agatha Christie's multiple killer solution for my 'aha' moment.

I eyed the two frosting smudges on the floor. One marked where I'd stepped on the cake. Could the other have been where the knife lay before the killer picked it up and plunged it into Potter?

But, again then: where was the victim's blood?

I got up and scanned the walls and the carpet. Nothing was exactly clean, but I was fairly certain I'd be able to spot a blotch of blood. No, the only blood in this car was what I'd felt on the exit door handle and gotten on my hand like the fictional Kat in my dream.

Blood, in that case, and thick white ... what?

I jumped up and went to the exit. Because the sun was shining in from the window across the way, I could get a better look than I had the night before. There was certainly something dark there, but what I'd felt had been sticky, meaning the blood hadn't completely dried yet, I supposed. How long would that take, given the natural humidity of the Everglades and the artificial air conditioning on the train?

Trusting Pavlik that my prints could be excluded – and figuring I'd already touched the thing anyway, so whatever potential damage was really damage done – I gingerly touched the door handle. No longer sticky, but dry and crusty. Crouching down, I saw something else – something glistening. I touched it with my finger and this time it did come away sticky. And red, almost gelatinous.

Wait a second. First warily sniffing it and then touching it to my tongue, I realized it was cake decorating gel. The stuff that had been used to represent blood on the cake.

Returning to Rosemary's bathroom, I washed my hands in the pull-down sink, taking a paper towel out of the wall dispenser to dry them as I walked back.

The piece of cake Potter had taken – the foot – hadn't had any of the fake blood on it. That decorative touch was concentrated around the knife 'wounds.' That meant whoever had touched the door handle had also held the knife.

Potter? And ... his killer?

I settled back down onto the floor of the sleeping car and picked up Missy's e-reader. I didn't expect to get any more reading done, even if the story had intrigued me. Of course, what I'd actually read and what I'd dreamed might be two entirely different things.

I pushed the toggle on the reader and the John Steinbeck screensaver morphed into words. Curious to see what the last paragraph I'd read was, I saw:

Kat opened the door, knowing what she wanted but not if she had the nerve to take it. He was lying on the bed facing the window, his skin glistening in the moonlight. The edge of the white sheet revealing his firm, naked glutes. Kat wanted – she desperately needed – to run her fingers along the curves of them.

As Kat reached out, the man roused. Stepping back, she watched from the shadows as he turned onto his back, sending the sheet slipping to the floor.

'Oh, dear,' Kat nearly gasped aloud.

I laughed, recognizing Missy's pet expression. I'd forgotten that Missy had worked with Rosemary on the book, though apparently my subconscious hadn't. It had even inserted snakes, though that vignette might have had to do more with our current situation than my conversation with Missy about researching them for *Breaking and Entering*.

Regardless of Rosemary's writing and my imagination, though, it was very nice of her to insert a piece of Missy in the book. I'd bet the girl was thrilled.

Then I shifted, intending to do a search for 'snake' in the text and see if Rosemary had been more imaginative in its use than I had. I had a feeling my dream had been much tamer than the real thing – or the real *fictional* thing, to be precise.

I slid over the pistol to get comfortable, in the process accidentally setting it on the damp paper towel I'd brought back.

'Better not do that,' I said to myself, a little punchy despite my nap. 'Guns are metal and some metals rust.'

Pulling the towel out from under the fire-arm, I leaned forward, intending to dab at the frosting on the carpet in front of me.

At the last moment, I pulled back. If I was right about the cake and the knife lying there, I'd be an idiot to mess with the evidence. Not that it would be the first time.

The paper towel and the cake reminded me of something, though. What was it?

The towel wasn't unusual. From what I'd seen, the same ones were used in the bathrooms throughout the train. In fact, Missy had left one on the table in the dining car when she'd thought Zoe was going to introduce her as Mrs Hubbard.

Instead the woman had introduced Audra Edmonds, Larry Potter's wife.

But why would that be significant? By then Potter was already missing. Whether he was dead, we didn't know. Missy had gone out even earlier, taking Rosemary Darlington to the sleeping car. Could our event planner have seen Potter on her way back?

Had – and I couldn't even believe I was thinking this – had the two of them quarrel-led and Missy stabbed him, then stopped to wash the blood off her hands, brush her hair, apply lipstick and return to the table?

Ridiculous. And even if it were possible, why? What possible connection could there be between the slightly awkward young woman and the great Laurence Potter?

The e-reader was still in my lap. I toggled the switch and the page came up, the words 'Oh, dear,' leaping out at me.

Missy was a researcher and worked for Rosemary Darlington on this book.

Missy, the seeming innocent, knew what 'Titanium' was when I showed her the matchbook.

Breaking and Entering was a complete departure from anything Rosemary had ever written.

Potter had said the woman he'd known 'could never have written this current pile of excrement.' Were the words an overstatement, made for effect, or did the reviewer actually believe Rosemary Darlington didn't write *Breaking and Entering*? And if so, how would Potter be in a position to know that?

'Position,' I said out loud. Audra thought her husband had 'learned things' from Rosemary. What if, instead, both of them had learned them from Missy. Rosemary Darlington, literarily, to use in her book and Potter ... literally?

Could Potter and *Missy* have been involved in an affair? She certainly wouldn't be the first insecure young woman to fall victim to an older man who's more interested in punching her ticket than validating it.

Missy would see Potter as a famous,

interesting, and therefore powerful figure in the industry. Very different than Danny and Pete, who were too young and unsuccessful for her taste. But if Laurence Potter wanted her, that was different. It would mean *she* was different.

So what had happened? Had Potter been angry after reading Rosemary's book? Had he recognized Missy as the true writer and threatened to expose Rosemary?

If so, both Rosemary and Missy might have a reason to kill him. Could they have teamed up on the guy? Only if all three of them – the two women and Potter – were here in the sleeping car together.

I got up and went back to the vestibule and the exit, taking the paper towel with me. First, I examined the surface of the door as well as the walls to its sides. I didn't see any signs of blood or even frosting, but the lab would know for sure. Since I'd already done enough preservation-of-crime-scene damage, I used the towel to carefully open the door.

It slid without difficulty. Certainly easily enough for even a small woman to yank it open and let somebody with a knife in his back 'exit the train' with no one the wiser.

I jumped down onto the railway bed.

The water seemed to be receding. At least three feet of gravel stretched from each side of the track before the bed sloped away into the wetland. A big improvement over what Pavlik and I had dealt with during our trips outside.

Across the way, I saw that the 'island' I'd spotted on our last excursion was, indeed, a rise of land supporting the growth of saw-grass, tangled shrubs and even some scrubby-looking trees. I wished Pavlik was here to tell me if they were mangroves or not.

The sun was nearly straight-up noon. The sheriff and Boyce had been gone for four hours, and it could be many more before they returned. In fact, they'd told us to wait a full twenty-four before even sending out another scouting party. I wasn't sure I could stand by and do nothing for that long.

Turning back to the train, I stood on my tiptoes to reach the top of the vertical grab bar next to the door. Running my hand along the bar, I knew I was searching for some kind of confirmation.

If Potter had been stabbed outside the train after we'd stopped, his assailant would have gotten gunk on the railing or outside door handle as he – or, more and more likely, she – had swung back in. And then again on the inside door handle, where I'd already found it, when the killer closed the door.

But ... nothing. No stickiness on the grab bar or on the outside door handle, which I checked next. I supposed the driving rain could have—

A shadow shifted on the opposite bank, just twenty feet away.

'Alligator,' I said out loud, if in a slightly ragged tone.

'Oh, dear.'

THIRTY-TWO

Missy's voice had come from behind me.

I turned. The girl must have circled the end of the sleeping car and was standing about as far away from my position as the shadow had been across the water in the other direction.

'You scared me,' I said for the second time that day.

'Sorry, Maggy. We're all going stir crazy in there, so I thought I'd come out for a stroll in what passes for fresh air this time of day.'

Missy was right about the 'passes' part. You could nearly see the steam rising off the plants in the midday sun.

'Is it safe to be wandering?' I glanced toward the alligator. Or the void where it had been. Suddenly an alligator you couldn't see was worse than one you could.

'Don't worry.' Missy lifted up a revolver with a short but stout barrel, her hand holding the 'right' end. 'I have a gun.'

Oh, I was worried, all right. Mostly because I did *not* have one. I'd left the semi-automatic Pavlik had given me on the floor of the train when I'd jumped down, thinking I'd quickly finish what I needed to do and be back inside. Like they say, though – the first step was a doozy.

And so here I was.

Missy raised the muzzle of her gun on a line with my belly button, then stepped toward me. 'What were you doing?'

'What do you mean?' I was trying to keep my voice casual.

'You were polishing that railing or whatever it is. Did you find something wrong?'

'Nope,' I said. 'I'm just a little ditzy. I fell asleep reading a passage on the device you so kindly loaned to me, and I had a dream about snakes. I came out here to reassure myself that none were poking around the train and, umm ... dried off the rail so I wouldn't slip getting back in.'

It was a little weak, but then so was I at the moment.

'Oh, were you reading *Breaking and Entering*? I'm surprised you got to the snake part so fast. Were you skipping ahead?' Missy looked so proud I decided to go with it.

'Couldn't resist. I also noticed the use of your catchphrase. That was so nice.'

Her face darkened. 'What do you mean?'

'The "oh, dear." You say it all the time. I thought it was a great compliment to you that Rosemary had Kat using it.'

'Oh, yes,' Missy said, lowering the gun's muzzle. 'That *was* nice. Sort of a ... a—'

'Tribute,' I finished for her. It was apparent to me that Missy hadn't even realized until this moment that, as a writer, she'd given her main character her own subliminal signature. 'In gratitude for all the hard work you did, researching and all.'

'Yes.' Missy tried to smile. 'That was ... nice.'

Allrighty then. 'Well, I'd better get to my post. Good talking to you.'

'You, too.'

As I grabbed the bar to pull myself up, I heard the sounds of Missy starting to move away, the staccato of the glittery heels on the gravel, the swish of the evening gown in the abominable humidity. Then stillness.

'You know.'

I debated whether I should continue my swing up onto the train and slam the door closed.

In that second of deliberation, I lost that option.

When I looked back, Missy was still there, gun levelled at my waist. 'I said *you know*, don't you?'

I let go of the bar and dropped back down to the railroad bed. 'I don't know anything, Missy.'

She smiled, but unhappily. 'No, I'm the one who doesn't know anything. Not even what I put in my own book. Or Rosemary's, I should say.'

'So you ghost-wrote the novel. That's perfectly legitimate. And you did a good job. Rosemary must be very pleased.'

'She is,' Missy said. 'Or at least she was, until Laurence wrote his review. I couldn't understand why he would rip it apart like that.'

'Did he know you wrote *Breaking and Entering*?'

Missy gnawed on her lower lip. 'I think he guessed. There were scenes he,' she flushed, 'might have recognized.'

'He was planning on writing a book of his own, using those kind of ... "scenes."'

Had I actually read the book instead of falling asleep for two hours, I might have known exactly what we were referring to. I believed, however, that Missy's manner gave me the gist of it.

As my allusion to Potter's projected novel seemed to sink in, Missy looked genuinely astonished. 'But Laurence hated *Breaking and Entering*. He called it smut. And he honestly wasn't very good at...' she blushed again, 'most of the scenes anyway. He didn't even like going to Titanium.'

'So, you went to Titanium?'

Missy must have heard the surprise in my voice. 'Why shouldn't I?' she said defensively. 'It's the perfect place to meet people.'

Yikes. 'Is that where you and Potter met?'

'Of course not.' She seemed shocked at the very idea. 'We met at Mystery 101. I knew it was ... kismet. Laurence was so different than any man I'd met before.'

Might have something to do with 'meeting' them at a sex club.

'He wasn't a user, like the others,' Missy continued. 'I did everything they wanted and more and it still wasn't good enough. Laurence thought I was special. He called me "Melissa," and taught me things. I taught him other things in return.'

'That was very ... reciprocal of you,' I said lamely.

Missy's brow furrowed. 'But like I said, Laurence just wasn't very good at sex. Why would he want to write a book about it?'

'To make money, I suppose. All I know is that it was supposed to be a he-said, she-said, authored by Audra and him.'

'Audra? But he didn't *love* her.'

301

'That's what they all—' I stopped myself.

But not in time. Missy waggled the gun toward me the way a kindergarten teacher might her index finger at a misbehaving child. 'You were going to say, "That's what they all say." But Laurence wasn't like that.'

This time I had the smarts not to even open my mouth.

'He told me he loved me.' Missy's eyes welled up and overflowed. 'And now he's gone.'

She started to sob. I moved close enough that I could have put my arm around her. But first, I needed a little clarity. 'I'm sure you're right, Missy. But what did you mean before when you said that I – Maggy – "know"? Know what?'

Missy lifted her head. 'About Laurence and me. I felt you look right into my soul when you said what happens in Fort Lauderdale, stays in Fort Lauderdale because that's where we first met. In fact, it was at this very conference last year.'

Ohhh. 'To be honest, I believe I was talking about Potter and Rosemary. I really wasn't thinking about you.'

'Oh, I'm glad.' Missy shuddered, but now was nearly glowing again. 'We worked very hard to be circumspect. Laurence would even be ... well, nasty and condescending to me in public. We would laugh about it later.'

Ha-ha-ha. Me? I would have smacked him. 'Well, you two had me fooled. In fact, I was sure we'd find him with Rosemary when you and I first went back into the sleeping car.'

'Laurence was incapable of doing something like that.' The gun in one hand, Missy swiped across her eyes with the back of the other.

'Of course he was,' I said hastily. 'At the time, though, I didn't know about your relationship.'

'Relationship?' Missy scrunched up more than wrinkled her nose. 'That's not why it was impossible, Maggy.'

'Then...?'

'Why? Because Laurence wasn't on the train anymore.'

THIRTY-THREE

Maybe Theodore B. Hertel, Jr was right. Maybe, in the end, everything *is* fiction.

Because this sure felt like make-believe.

The sun was shining brightly, the alligators and snakes off on frolics of their own. I was wearing a flowered sundress and kitten-heel sandals, albeit a little worse for wear. Missy, the leading lady, was in a silver evening gown and spike heels. The revolver that completed her ensemble could have been a prop.

I cleared my throat, trying to choose my words carefully. If I played it straight – treated Missy like a co-investigator rather than the killer I feared she was – maybe she'd let her guard down. 'So Potter wasn't on the train when you and I went to check on Rosemary. Can you be sure of that?'

'Yes, but it's a long story,' Missy said, waggling the gun toward the door of the train. 'Would you mind if I sat down? These heels are killing me.'

I felt myself relax a bit, thinking my half-baked plan might be working. Or maybe, even, that I was wrong in my suspicions. 'Be my guest.'

Missy, casual as could be, handed me her gun, grabbed the rail and pulled herself up, settling on the floor of the doorway through which Boyce had carried Laurence Potter's body.

'I hate to get this dress dirty,' Potter's lover said, tugging it down, 'but I'll have it thoroughly cleaned before I donate it back to the Salvation Army.'

'Good idea.' I was looking at the gun in my hand, trying to put together what the hell was going on.

'So, shall I continue?' Missy was swinging

her legs like a first-grader on a jungle gym.

'Please.'

'As you know, I took Rosemary to the sleeping car and settled her in. As I started back, do you know what I saw?'

'No.'

'The piece of cake you stepped on, along with my staghorn knife. Both on the floor. Can you believe that?'

'No.' I figured the shorter my responses, the less likely I'd screw up.

'I was so angry somebody had not only *cut* a piece of cake without asking, but then dropped it right there and didn't even bother to pick it up. How would that look when Sheriff Pav— I mean, Jake, was pretending to be Ratchett?' Missy looked like she was going to cry again. 'And that's not even counting that the knife was supposed to be the murder weapon!'

'Inexcusable.'

'Exactly what I thought. I picked up the knife so nobody would step on it and opened the door to check on the room. Imagine my surprise to find Laurence there. Not only had he filched the cake – unsuccessfully, I might add – but he was smoking.'

'Smoking?'

'Yes, and we all know that's not allowed on the train. We could even be fined for it.'

'Gosh.' Even if I had wanted to say something stronger I wasn't sure what it would be.

'The window was open and the air conditioning was woofing right out into the Everglades. Cake in the hallway, and Laurence just sitting there. Do you know why?'

'Uh, no.'

'He said he was having a smoke.'

'And ... he wasn't?'

Missy looked at me like I was the one who was nuts. 'Of course he was. I just told you that.'

'Right, sorry. So what happened next?'

'I asked about his wife showing up. I wasn't mad, Maggy. I just thought it was a good opportunity for us to confront her together.'

'About...?'

Another Maggy-you-stupid-idiot look. 'About *us*, of course.'

'Do you mean he was leaving his wife?' At least this time I didn't add, 'That's what they all say.' Just my luck, I'd been married to the only cheater who'd actually meant it.

'As it turns out, no. But apparently Laurence was nothing but a hypocrite anyway. Writing scathing reviews of our book when you say he intended to publish one just like it. Assuring me he was leaving Audra when he clearly had no intention of doing so. Laurence said,' Missy elongated her neck like a chicken in an imitation of Potter, '"your ardent desires aside, Melissa, I have no desire to make an honest woman of you."'

Melissa. I'd corrected Potter when he'd called her that, but it hadn't been a mistake – probably more a signal between them. Potter had made his young mistress feel special. Maybe he was the only one who ever had, despite the fact that she tried so very hard. 'I'm sorry, Missy.'

'Oh, Laurence didn't stop there.' Missy's feet were still dangling and she was kicking her heels against the train's side as she talked. 'He told me I was pathetic and should just grow up. That he thought "Murder on the Orient Espresso" was a juvenile idea, and he wouldn't be part of it.'

A five-minute conversation, and the man had managed to undercut the woman in every area of her life. 'What did you say?'

'I didn't get the chance. Laurence just scooped up his cigarettes and matches, turned his back on me and stalked off.'

One of the shoes flew off with enough force that I flinched and nearly had to duck.

'I couldn't believe it.' Missy was sobbing outright now. 'He stomped right past that cake he'd dropped, with me following. I said he had no right to treat me like this.'

I held the gun ready.

'Laurence wouldn't even turn around!' Missy looked past me, as if she were watching the scene unfold. 'Just opened the door into that vestibule, intending to go right on into the passenger car. He was shoving his stupid cigarettes into his pocket and dropped his matches by the exit door. I called to him, but he didn't hear me. Maybe because of the noise of the train or maybe because he just didn't want to.'

The second shoe went flying, also barely missing me. 'What did you do then?'

Missy seemed surprised at the question. 'I picked the matchbook up, of course. But when I tried to hand it to Laurence, he knocked it right back out of my hand. Said the thing was empty and nothing but trash. That he had no further use for it.'

She braced a hand on each side of the doorway and leaned forward. 'He wasn't just talking about those matches, you know, Maggy.'

'No?'

'No.' Her eyes were staring at something I couldn't see. 'The cake knife was in my hand and when he made to leave again, I ... I stopped him.'

'With the knife?' I asked in a hoarse whisper.

Missy nodded up and down, up and down, like she was in a marching band and had to perfectly synchronize with its other members. 'He fell against the door, bleeding.

I had it on my hand already, but before it got all over I just . . . just slid the door open.' The last words were barely a whisper.

'It' being her lover's blood. Missy took 'tidy' to new heights.

I was trying to understand, or at least appear like I understood. 'Listen, I know you didn't mean to—'

But before I could finish my sentence, Missy Hudson launched herself from the doorway where she was sitting, toppling us both into the shallow water of the Everglades.

THIRTY-FOUR

I held the revolver high, thinking Missy was going to fight me for it. Instead, though, she put her hands on my chest and shoved me under the eight inches or so of swamp water and kept right on going, as if we were playing a soggy game of reverse leapfrog.

Scrambling back up, I coughed and gave chase.

Missy was already slogging toward the berm/island on the other side. I followed, trying to keep the gun from getting wet.

I didn't call for help, which was probably dumb, but I was the one waving the firearm and chasing someone. Who would the citizens' militia behind me choose to shoot?

Missy had made it across to the other bank, the one with the mangroves growing on it. She'd taken about three feet into the sawgrass when she froze and said, 'Don't move.'

'Me?' I looked at the revolver in my hand. 'I have the gun. *You* don't move.'

Over her shoulder she whispered, 'It's a python.'

'Good,' I said, much more calmly than I felt. 'How about you and me retreat slowly back to the train and leave the monster alone.'

'I don't think she'll let us.'

I crept up behind her and peered over a shoulder. A mottled nest of white eggs was not four feet in front of Missy's bare feet. The nest had a head. A pointy head.

'Is this the kind that's pretty protective?' I asked, backing up. I was remembering the old joke about not having to outrun the bear, just the person with you.

'*Really* protective,' Missy said, grabbing my arm so I couldn't move without startling the snake. 'Don't leave me here.'

'I won't.' I was feeling ashamed of myself. Murderer or not, Missy didn't deserve to end up as snake food, despite the fact she'd turned her lover into it. 'Don't worry.'

'I won't.' And with that, she gave a brutal yank on my arm, sending the gun flying and me staggering into the snake's nest.

THIRTY-FIVE

The female python and I were eye-to-eye.

I tried to get back up, reminding myself that they didn't bite so much as squeeze you to death.

And then eat you.

The thing started to uncoil almost casually, like a cross-armed street punk, breaking away from his gang with a, 'Wait here, dudes. This won't take me long.'

Only this reptilian thug intended not only to put the squeeze on me, but have me for dinner. And not in a Welcome Wagon kind of way.

I managed to get to my feet and take a step, only to be tripped. While I was busy watching the head, the coils had snuck up on me from behind, launching me back nose first into the sawgrass.

Frozen in fear, I felt something thick glide

over and then around my leg. The monster would envelope me like the banyan tree did its 'host,' first strangling the life out and then enveloping me as if I'd never been there at all.

I pushed up on my elbows hoping to scrabble away, but the coils had continued to climb, reaching my waist. I wanted to scream, but couldn't seem to get my breath, whether from fear or the creature's evolving death hug.

Yanked back, I fell off my elbows, my face grinding into the ground. When I turned my head, the python's head slid into view. A split-tongue lashed out, nearly touching my nose. I tried to evade it, but the rows of backward-pointing teeth drew—

An explosion. And then nothing.

No sound. No light. Nor could I feel the painful, suffocating clamp of the python any longer.

Was this how it felt to die?

If so ... hey, not so bad.

Sure, I could use a little music or maybe a pearly gate or two. But I'd settle for a simple dazzling light to move toward. It was awfully da—

'Maggy?'

I opened my eyes.

Missy was standing straddled over the python. The creature's head had been blown apart.

Before I could open my mouth to thank her, the girl turned the gun in my direction. 'I'm so sorry, Maggy.' She seemed dazed.

'It's all right, Missy.' I was holding up both hands as best I could. 'I know you didn't want to hurt anyone.'

But she was shaking her head, back-and-forth, back-and-forth. 'That's just it. I think in a way I did. After—' She swiped at a string of snot hanging from her nose. 'Afterwards I was glad Laurence was gone. Dropped into the Everglades to be dealt with by animals like him. It seemed ... right.'

No muss, no fuss. I hoped I wasn't her next recycling project.

'But you—' She gestured toward me with the gun. 'You don't deserve to die.'

I didn't know what else to say but, 'Thank you.'

'You've been nothing but nice to me, Maggy. And I almost killed you. Or, at least, let the snake kill you.'

'But you *didn't*,' I insisted, hoping it was a self-fulfilling prophesy.

'Thing is, with you gone no one would ever need to know. They might not even find your body. It would be so ... neat, so orderly. Life *should* be orderly.' The gun was shaking.

'Hello?' Markus's voice called from the direction of the train. 'Who's out there?'

Pushing myself up on my hands and knees, I lunged upward just as Melissa 'Missy' Hudson put the muzzle of the gun in her mouth and pulled the trigger.

THIRTY-SIX

The shots brought people running from the train at a gallop, Markus in the lead. 'Oh, my God. What happened?'

I was sitting next to Missy's body on the ground. She still held the gun in her hand, the back of her head horribly ... just not there.

'Missy killed herself and,' I hesitated, 'Potter.'

'Are you sure?' Zoe Scarlett had arrived, quickly followed by Prudence and Theodore B. Hertel, Jr. 'I mean, you're the one who's alive and she's not.'

'The girl still has the gun in her hand,' Markus pointed out before I could answer.

'And why would Maggy kill Potter?' Prudence demanded. 'She didn't even know him.'

'Why would *Missy* kill him?'

A new voice. 'Because she loved him and

he was an asshole.' The crowd parted, revealing Audra Edmonds. 'I don't know why I didn't do it myself, years ago.'

'Well, will you look at that snake in the grass.' Engineer Hertel didn't seem to take any notice of Audra or even Missy or me. He was ogling the python. 'This here's gotta be another of those rock pythons – look at how broad she is. And them eggs! They're about to pop and I hear tell they come out striking.'

I got up and took two steps back. 'We need to get Missy out of here,' I said. 'Markus, maybe you and,' I saw the literary agent coming toward us, 'Carson can carry her back to the train?'

The germaphobe in his white suit looked down at Missy, covered in swamp water and snake remnants, the back of her skull gone, but he nodded. 'Of course.'

The two men picked up the pathetic little rag doll, all dressed up with literally no place to go. I followed after them as they conveyed Missy across the shallow water to the train. As I went, I stopped to retrieve first one glittery shoe and then the other.

When we got to the door, Markus climbed into the train. Carson handed the girl up to him and then the rest of us hoisted ourselves in.

'Wait,' I said, awkwardly retrieving the

semi-automatic and Missy's e-reader which I'd left on the floor. I kicked my pillow aside and opened the door of the roomette across from Potter's. 'Put her in there.'

When they'd placed Missy on the bunk, I covered her with a blanket and put the e-reader next to a hand. Then I picked up her shoes from the floor and we left, softly closing the door as if we didn't want to awaken her.

The rest of the group continued on to the passenger car, but Carson was standing in the corridor, staring at his filthy hands.

'Why didn't you tell Pavlik or me you were representing Danny?' It didn't matter now, but I still wanted to know.

'Danny?' Carson was holding up both hands like a surgeon who'd scrubbed for an operation, and was impatiently awaiting sterile gloves.

'Your new client? The one whose sexy book will now take the place of the novel Potter was writing?'

Carson had the grace to look embarrassed. 'I told him to send me the manuscript. I was intrigued. I didn't say I'd represent him.'

Given the agent's personality and, more importantly, Danny's, that made sense. The kid had gotten carried away – just assumed the agent would take him on.

'If you want to wash your hands...' I

opened the door of the roomette next to where we'd just left Missy and flipped down the sink. 'And thank you for helping out there. I know it couldn't have been easy for you.'

'You're welcome,' Carson said, trying to operate the faucet with his elbow. 'I've found I can do these things if necessary. Or ... appropriate.'

'Me, too.' I leaned in, turned on the water and left him.

Since there was nothing left to guard or anybody to guard it from, I returned to the passenger car, sinking wearily down into a window seat.

'Here, drink this.' Zoe Scarlett gave me a plastic cup with about an inch of brown liquid in it.

I sniffed. 'Kahlua?'

She nodded. 'I hoarded it for later if I needed a drink. But you've earned it more than I have.'

Greater love hath no woman than to share her coffee-flavored liqueur with a sister. 'Thanks. This is very nice of you.'

'Not really. In fact, I haven't been very nice at all.'

I shrugged and tossed back the Kahlua. It was so thick it didn't toss well. 'In fairness, you were drunk quite a bit of the time.

Besides, you wanted Pavlik and I had him. Correction: I *have* him.'

I glanced out the window, wanting nothing more than to see my sheriff riding in to save the day, or what was left of it.

Zoe sat down next to me. 'You can't blame me. Jaco— Jake's a good guy.'

'He is that.' I was sticking my tongue into the glass to dredge up the remains. 'I hope he and Boyce are OK.'

'Me, too. It'll be getting dark again in a few hours. I really don't want to spend another night out here. If Missy wasn't already dead, I'd kill her for getting me into this.' Zoe tried to laugh, but it didn't come off.

'Missy saved my life,' I said woodenly. 'Instead of running – and maybe escaping – she stayed there and killed the snake that would have killed me.'

'Run to where?' Zoe demanded. 'We're in the middle of the Everglades. Besides, you knew she killed Larry Potter. Missy would have been hunted down and tried for murder.'

'If the snake had finished me, no one would have known,' I said stubbornly. 'Missy knew that.'

'Apparently I have more faith in the sheriff's ability than you do,' Zoe said, sounding a bit more like her obnoxious self.

'I have plenty of faith in him, but we'd ...

well, I guess if I was dead, *he'd* be leaving for Wisconsin.' And in mourning, I hoped. 'Not staying here to investigate.'

Zoe's head dropped back on her shoulders and she seemed to study the ceiling of the train. 'I just don't know.'

'Know what?'

When Zoe met my eyes, there were tears in hers. 'I don't know if Missy could have lived with what she'd done. She was such a persnickety girl – that's what made her so good. What made her valuable to someone like me, of the more scattered type. In Missy's world, everything had to be just so and, given what had happened...'

'Nothing could be right again. Ever.'

Zoe nodded.

I couldn't argue with that. In fact, everything I'd witnessed today, everything Missy had told me, bore that out. The girl had tried her best to please, but it hadn't been enough. At least, not enough for her.

I looked down at the glittery shoes, clutched so tightly my knuckles were white.

Poor, lost little murderer.

It was nearly four in the afternoon when we heard the whistle of a train.

Piling out, we raced around our locomotive to see another engine chugging up the track toward us. Pulling a single car, it

319

stopped on the opposite side of the water-filled breach.

I pushed my way to the front of our little group of castaways just as Pavlik hopped out. He was followed by Boyce and about a dozen men and women in all kinds of uniforms.

Forgetting the dangers of the Everglades – or maybe feeling I'd already faced the worst of them – I splashed through the shallow water to the sheriff and threw my arms around him.

Pavlik kissed me hard. 'Told you I'd be back. Is everything OK here?'

I looked down at the two glittery shoes I'd carried with me.

'You'd best sit down,' I said, pointing toward the doorway of our rescue train. And then I quoted the killer who'd saved my life: 'It's a long story.'